Haven

Other Five Star Titles by Irene Bennett Brown:

Reap the South Wind
Blue Horizons
Long Road Turning
No Other Place
The Plainswoman

Irene Bennett Brown

HAVEN

Five Star • Waterville, Maine

First Edition
First Printing: December 2003

Set in 11 pt. Plantin by Al Chase.

Printed in the United States on permanent paper.

Library of Congress Cataloging-in-Publication Data

Brown, Irene Bennett.
Haven / Irene Bennett Brown.—1st ed.
p. cm.
"Five Star first edition titles"—T.p. verso.
ISBN 1-59414-088-X (hc : alk. paper)
1. Women pioneers—Fiction. 2. Inheritance and succession—Fiction. 3. Architects—Fiction. 4. Oregon —Fiction. I. Title.
PS3552.R68559H38 2003
813′.54—dc22 2003049422

Dedication

To my artist daughter, Shana
for the wonderful covers you give my books.
Thanking you with pies is no longer enough.
This book is for you!

Chapter One

Laila Mitchell stood on the boardwalk before a shabby Boise hotel. A light rain misted her face and blurred in her hazel eyes below the tan toque drooping wetly atop her dark pompadour. Her cold fingers gripped her satchel that seemed to grow heavier the further she traveled from St. Louis. The street was a muck of mud. Shops and saloons lining it were shadowy in the drizzle.

Shivering and tired to the bone, she wondered if management of this hotel would give her a room for a short period? Wages for work—cooking in the kitchen, waiting tables, or working as a chambermaid? Her stake for her journey west was disappearing far too fast. She now doubted the wisdom of buying her traveling wardrobe: the simple, velvet-trimmed Eton suit of emerald broadcloth and matching cape that she wore, the tiny pendant watch pinned to the lapel. Inside her valise, a collapsible parasol the color of eggshell, thin and intended to hold off the sun, was useless in this weather.

She licked the rain from her lips. There was terrific noise all around her, rattle of wagons and buggies, the creak of leather, shouted voices, laughter. The noise and a very empty stomach dizzied her.

Despite the dismal April weather and the depression of 1893 that left so many out of work, people had evidently gathered for some kind of celebration. Townspeople, miners, ranchers, and drifters, filled the muddy streets. At the hitchrails, horses stood in cesspools of yellow-brown ooze. She drew her cape closer, gripped the handle of her valise tighter, focused on the necessity of food, a place to stay, a way to earn a few dollars.

"If you're as near the end of your rope as you look, Miss," a woman's hearty voice spoke nearby, "maybe I can help. I'd be glad to share my room, be glad for the company."

Laila turned to look down into the twinkling gray eyes of a woman she'd spoken with casually when the Union Pacific train made a stop in Denver. Short and square as a box in a shiny gray taffeta dress and cape, she stood settled back on her heels, a smile on her broad face. The damp breeze stirred the tall green plume on her hat.

"Oh, no, that isn't necessary. I'm fine. But thank you." She wished her needy state didn't show so much. She wanted more than anything to be independent, to take care of herself properly and well. She smiled, then gazed at the muddy toes of her boots so the woman wouldn't guess her next thought: What if her money did run out and no one gave her work?

"Sometimes it don't do to be too proud," the lady warned. "I'd say this is one of those times for you, Miss." When Laila looked up from her feet to meet her gaze, the woman stuck out her gloved hand. "Name's Kate Boston. I've been to trouble and back myself a few times." She laughed softly. "I'd say you've been there, too, maybe."

She nodded, "I have, and I do appreciate your kind offer. My name is Laila Mitchell. I'm trying to get to Oregon, but—" The sudden blare of brass horns, the thump of parade drums down the street took her by surprise and she fell silent. The town was celebrating the arrival of spring, perhaps. Marching children in gaily-colored flower costumes approached in the mist and passed, decorated wagons filled with waving, fancy-dressed passengers rolled along the muddy thoroughfare. Riders on horseback followed. A handsome cowboy tipped his hat and smiled at Laila and she returned a tentative smile.

Laila tried again to explain to Kate Boston that she wanted

to work, didn't want charity, but the blare of the brass band bringing up the rear of the parade rose to an ear-splitting level, drowning her out. From the corner of her eye she watched as a four-horse team of Belgians, hitched to a huge empty dray a short distance down the muddy, rutted street, suddenly spooked at the booming racket. The band marched on, seeming unaware of the trouble they left in their trail. The Belgians, eyes rolling white, reared, whinnied, and bolted free from the hitch-rail. With the wagon careening behind them, they came straight at the two women, clots of mud flying.

She dropped her things and grabbed for Kate, but Kate, confused and heavy of foot, moved further into the path of danger instead of out of it. At the same time someone tossed Laila aside to safety like a rag-doll. Barely landing on her feet, she got her bearings and screamed a warning, "Ma'am! Kate!"

Above the sounds the horses made, the clatter of the huge dray, the shouts of people on the street, she heard Kate's rending scream.

The crowd blocked her path when she tried to hurry to where Kate lay. She prayed that Kate had been only knocked aside, not run over and trampled. She hadn't been able to see just what happened.

As she elbowed her way, men shouted; a few of them were racing to stop the team. Others were yelling bets on how far the runaways would go. Other than herself, few people seemed concerned about the woman who lay in a crumpled gray taffeta heap on the street. Or maybe they didn't see her.

"Beg pardon! Let me by, please!" Laila cried over and over. She forced her way forward through the resistant pack. She struck with her fists and kicked out when she had to, and finally reached Kate Boston.

She was stirring, was trying to sit up. Laila knelt beside her, gently caught her shoulder, asked in a stricken voice, "Are you all right? How badly are you hurt?"

With a deep groan, Kate answered, "I'm alive, I reckon. My head feels like I got a good konk there. Don't know about the rest of me. Was that a team and wagon run me down, or the Union Pacific?" She moaned again, and rubbed a hand down her face.

Laila sighed her relief. At least Kate was of a piece, and she retained her sense of humor. "Can you move, can you stand?" The crowd, the parade, had moved on down the street and they were alone in the cold drizzle.

"I hope I can move. I'm not partial to staying here in the street and allowing another rig to run me down. Help me up, dear, please. Don't think anything is true broken, just battered a bit."

A while later, Laila moved slowly up the hotel's mud-clotted wood stairs, valise in one hand and braced to support the sagging weight of Kate Boston carrying her own case.

The desk clerk Laila had spoken to below hadn't bothered to hear her out before declaring they had no work for her. But they had gotten a room for Kate, and the clerk agreed to send up a pitcher of hot water. They entered the dark room, and Laila helped her toward the shadowy bed. She removed Kate's muddy hat and tossed it aside, then eased her back onto the pillow. "There now."

Kate groaned and waved a hand toward the single window. "Let some light in so we can see the damage."

As Laila's eyes grew used to the gloom, she saw they were in a small room, shabbily furnished from a past era. Garish floral wallpaper was stained and peeling. She went to the window and drew the flimsy curtains aside, let the blind up, returned hurriedly to where Kate lay on the bed rubbing her muddy hands.

To start, she examined Kate's head. There was a minor cut, she was going to have a magnificent bump there, but mostly the wound needed cleaning and a little tincture. When the hot water arrived she filled the basin on the bedside table and went to work.

Gray eyes looked up at her from a face spattered with blood and mud. "I reckon I'm lucky to be alive. Never saw or heard that team and wagon comin', with the noise and all. Then there it was, bigger than a courthouse comin' at me. You coulda' been killed, too."

Laila managed a smile at the 'courthouse' exaggeration. "We're both lucky, but I'm sorry you were hurt." She finished washing Kate's scalp, and then her face, with gentle swipes. Taffeta rustled as she unbuttoned the long sleeves of Kate's frock, then the bodice.

"Let's get you out of that muddy dress so I can treat your cuts and bruises." Kate's left arm, Laila saw as she pulled the dress free, was badly withered, half the size of the other one, which was plump and pink. Laila rushed on with her work.

Kate laughed, her large bosom rising and falling under her white petticoat. "Lord knows I didn't get such a pitiful arm from the wagon knocking me off my feet out there in the street. Happened back on the farm in Missoura when I was ten years old. I got caught in a tussle with a mule while I was driving a cutting sickle. That arm dried up on me, useless old thing. You can see I wear rings on them fingers, trying to pretty the awful thing up some." She held the thin, stiff appendage in the air. "Causes me pain, dull like a toothache, when the weather changes."

"Maybe I can help. I have medicines." She lifted her satchel to the bed and undid the snaps. She retrieved the small medicine kit she'd put together before leaving the Saugrain mansion, right after Old Ben Saugrain's funeral. Out in the big world, she'd thought then, anything could happen. She might need the medicines for herself, or possibly she could use the tonics and bandages in a nursing job of some sort. Starting at age fifteen, she had had years of practical nursing experience caring for Old Ben. His doctor believed she was too young for the work but at Old Ben's insistence, the doctor had tutored her in medical aid. In another moment, she sat on the edge of the bed and daubed lotion of arnica on Kate's scrapes and bruises with a square of cloth.

With an occasional flinch, Kate observed the young woman working over her. She took note of her gentle, yet competent touch. Below dark brows, her warm hazel eyes held remnants of sadness, more than a little worry.

Pretty, though. Tall and slender. A nice nose, slightly tilted at the tip. Mouth a little wide. Light, rosy-olive skin. Her square face ended in a soft, vulnerable looking chin. An innocent if Kate ever saw one, but spunky. This one was a top-shelfer, wherever she came from, wherever she was going, alone.

"Are you comfortable, Kate?" Laila plumped the pillows behind her rounded back and shoulders, drew the worn quilt higher. "Is there anything else I can do? Perhaps get you some tea, or a sandwich from the kitchen?" Her own stomach felt ravaged from hunger. Her final pay from the Saugrain fortune, given to her by Old Ben's stingy son, Rolph and his high-toned wife, Yvonne, had been anything but generous. A close watch on her funds as she journeyed west had kept her from ordering regular meals and it seemed she was hungry all of the time.

"No need of that. I got some cheese and crackers over

there in my things, and a little spirit lamp we can use to make our own tea." She pointed, "In the little canvas bag looks like a bucket, the blue, embroidered one, yeah, right there. We'll just have us a bite, and a chat."

Laila got out the food for them, prepared the tea, brought the room's only chair closer to the bed. She sat down with a glad sigh. It was hard not to gulp her food, but good manners taught long ago by Mama held sway. She ate slowly, listened politely.

"Feel like I ain't had any good chats since I left my friends back home to come west on my big adventure," Kate was saying. She laughed heartily, then gasped at a pain. "You been good to me, dear," she added a few seconds later. "Don't know how I would have gotten out of that mud-hole in the street if you hadn't helped me."

"Glad I was there," Laila answered. "But I wish I'd been able to warn you in time and prevent the accident." Kate had caught Laila's interest, talking about her own trip west. "You said something about adventure? That's why you left Missouri and came to Idaho, you wanted adventure?" She fixed a second cracker with cheese. She had no objection to a good chat, herself.

She had been kept so busy at Saugrain's back in St. Louis, there were few opportunities to make friends. The person she spoke with most often was Ben's doctor when he came to discuss his care. She was also acquainted with the apothecary from whom she bought his medicines, and with a few other merchants. She was supposed to have Sundays off to do as she pleased but that almost never happened.

Kate was answering, "Adventure, yes'm, and to get me a man if I can. Them's the reasons I came west, right enough."

Her honesty made Laila smile and she nodded for Kate to go on.

"Wanted me a fresh start, a little excitement maybe. Mean to have something in life, yet." She chewed for a moment, took a sip of tea. "I was sixteen and silly, Joe Boston twenty years older, when we got married. No adventure in that, I tell you, though my Joe was kind to me. He always called me Katie Rose." Her expression grew tender, a bit of cracker stuck in the corner of her mouth. "Never did call me Kate."

"He was a farmer?" Laila sipped her tea, and waited for Kate to continue.

Kate's head went back and forth on the pillow propped behind her. "Nah, Joe wasn't no farmer. Him and me operated a grocery and dry-goods store in the town of Buffalo, Dallas County, Missouri. Then, in the twentieth year of our marriage, Joe was shot up by renegades tryin' to rob our business. They made 'im an invalid. He died three years later, an' I took it hard, I tell ya. Never quite knew 'til he was gone how much my Joe meant to me. He was no house-afire but he loved me and I loved him." She sighed as she wiped away a tear.

Laila reached to touch her shoulder. "Oh, Kate, I'm sorry. Are you all right? Have you had enough to eat? Maybe you'd like some hot soup?"

"Now do I look like I need more food?" Kate patted the mound of her stomach. "Good thing next to eating, I enjoy talkin', an' if your pretty little ears ain't tired of hearin' me . . . ?"

"Goodness, no, I don't mind." She needed to find work and a place to stay but this brief while with Kate was comforting to them both, she suspected. She got up to put their food things away, said over her shoulder, "Did you stay on at the store after Joe died?"

Kate rubbed her withered arm. "Nope. I joined up with one of my sisters—I come from a family of ten children. Sister and me set out to run a boarding house in Springfield. Worked out fine for a few years. Then, sister up and deserted me, married one of our boarders and run off with him to live in Virginia. Even for a workhorse like I am, it takes more'n one good arm to do all the hard work runnin' a boardin' house, and I couldn't afford help."

"That's when you decided to come west?" Laila took her chair again. She felt relaxed, her hunger for now appeased.

"I'd had enough of central Missouri. Like they say, 'enough is enough and any more is a dog mess'. Wanted to see more of the world. I bought me one really good dress—" her eyes were bright as she boasted, "—black, high-collared, trimmed with lace and beaded braid. Bought a fancy hat and satchel. I repaired the rest of my wardrobe and set off."

"I'll help you clean the dress you had on," Laila offered.

"Wonder it wasn't my good dress, but I'm savin' that for the day I meet my gentleman." She looked over at Laila and rolled her eyes, laughing heartily, then with a grimace she sucked in a ragged breath, and took several slow, deep breaths.

Laila's smile faded and she leaned forward, concerned. "Maybe I should get you a doctor?"

She had determined from examination that Kate had no serious wounds and, though badly bruised, would mend. She wasn't a professional medical person, however. As a young child she'd gone with Mama when she went to help neighbors in time of medical need, had helped her tend wounded and sick animals on their Kansas farm. Later, wandering the streets of St. Louis, alone and half-starved, she had witnessed Old Ben, a stranger then, being attacked by a ferocious dog. Fearing that the dog was mad with hydrophobia, no other passerby would go to the old man's aid. Laila, seeing only that another human being was in desperate need, had chased the dog away with a stick, and then quickly cauterized the ragged and bloody bite on Old Ben's hand with his own burning cigar. He cursed her for the pain, but she'd helped him to the hospital where a nurse told them admiringly that Laila had done the right thing in the emergency, burning away the animal's saliva. Laila couldn't explain where she remembered the treatment from, it had seemed to come automatically. Possibly she'd heard of it in a story her father or mother told. The dog was not rabid, as it turned out, but Old Ben had been impressed with Laila. He felt she had saved his life when others would have let him be torn to pieces by the dog and he hired her to nurse him through the ills of old age. Days before, he'd fired a professional nurse for being too costly, so his miserly nature had much to do with his taking her on, as well. The doctor had to visit him anyway, and could teach young Laila what to do.

"Now, Laila, dear, didn't we decide I got no broken bones?" Kate Boston broke into Laila's thoughts. "A doctor wouldn't do no more for me than you did, except he'd charge an arm and leg to do it. I just got my paddin' bunged up a little is all." She laughed. "Now, you want to hear my plans for this gentleman I started to tell you about?"

"Yes, definitely." It would be wonderful to be happy and carefree, with one's thoughts chiefly on love. But for Laila that was impossible. She must concentrate on finding her grandparents, and getting settled. Love and marriage were a ways off for her, if they were in her future at all. But it would be a delight to hear about someone else's romantic plans, enjoy them vicariously.

"When I was still back to home I ordered me batches of newspapers from out west," Kate told her. "An' I read advertisements in them papers like they was dime novels. I decided Idaho was maybe far enough west, no use to chase across

Oregon to the ocean. I answered an ad printed in the *Idaho Statesman* paper." The corners of her eyes crinkled, and she glowed with excitement. "This gold-mine owner, his name is Mr. Austin Corbett, wants a housekeeper to come work for him at his place in the Snake River Canyon on the Oregon side of the river. Now, I know that sounds like the end of the world, a spot off from civilization the way it must be. But think about it, Laila, the man owns a *gold mine*."

After looking off into space a moment, Kate went on, "The way I see him, he's middle-aged, like me." She turned an intent expression on Laila. "He's plumb tired of his own cooking, way I figure it. He wishes his house wasn't such a mess, or," she shrugged, "maybe he lives in a cabin. Anyhow, he's powerful lonely, and he wants a wife! Mr. Corbett didn't say so in his ad, but I'm sure he's waitin' to size up the woman he hires, then he'll pop the question. Now, what d'ya think, will I do for him?"

"Of course. You'll do fine."

"Good. I think so, too. I tell you the truth, no matter how old or ugly Mr. Corbett turns out to be, I intend to marry him and his gold mine and we'll live happily into our golden years." She shook her head, her lips puckered, "My age and his, we ain't got time for a lot of honey-fussin' aforehand. Young folks, like you, can waste time courtin'."

"I suppose," Laila mumbled, privately amused that Kate had pictured to the last detail how she would speedily marry a man she had never met. Still, stranger things had happened.

"I should be going now," Laila said in a while, reaching for her cape and rising slowly. "You need a chance to rest." She looked toward the window where the sky was graying with dusk. She controlled a shiver and tried not to show her reluctance at leaving good company and the warm safety of the room.

"Laila, honey," Kate said softly, "sit on back down. Whatever ideas you got for yourself, I'll wager mine are better, so listen to me. 'Cause of the accident down there on the street, I might not be able to get around too good for a while. I'd like for you to stay with me, help me, then go on to the canyon with me, too. If it turns out I'm down in the back or somethin' from that runnin' over I took, you could work for Mr. Corbett in my place 'til I'm solid on my feet again."

Laila hesitated, started to shake her head but Kate persisted, "Think on this: You got money to throw around on a room of your own, when I'm plumb glad to share this one with you? Why don't we stay together at least for the time bein'? It's a whole lot safer than a woman travelin' alone; you 'member that seedy feller stalkin' you back in the Denver station? You don't need that sorta thing. Turns out later you don't like my company, then you go on and do as you please. I'd want you to."

Kate's offer was generous, a godsend, and she'd be helping Kate, as she said. Laila nodded, smiling her relief. "Thank you. I'd like to stay at least tonight. But if I go on with you, as much as I can I intend to pay my own way."

"Sure, dear, but we don't have to talk about that now. I'm just happy you'll be here with me. I'd be as lost as a kitten in a rain pipe, otherwise. Now, Laila, tell me about you. Where ya from? You got family in Oregon, or a sweetheart you're meetin' there, maybe?" Her eyes twinkled.

Laila hesitated, smiled tentatively, "No sweetheart waiting for me. There's not a lot to tell," she said on a sigh. "I was born on a farm in Kansas, near Emporia. I loved it there, so much: gathering eggs from the henhouse with Mama when I was little, and helping her in the garden. Riding in front of Papa, his arms around me, on his big horse, Blackie, on the way to bring cows in from the pasture at twilight. Picnics at

Soden's Mill in the summer, and on a frosty winter morning, the smell of Mama's pancakes, coffee, and frying bacon, drifting up to my room."

Kate beamed, "Them's nice memories!"

Laila nodded. "Yes." Her voice lowered and she frowned, "But—after a few years Papa lost the farm. He died of liver ailment when I was thirteen; Mama died of pneumonia when I was fifteen."

She hesitated a moment. Her mind went back with dread to the two years between her parents' deaths when she and Mama had to take care of themselves however they might. They drudged in a laundry for a time, later they toiled in a factory canning pickled pig's feet. When Mama got sick with pneumonia and Laila stayed home in their small room to care for her, they were fired from the pickle factory. They were evicted from their room when there was no money coming in to pay the rent. As a last resort, they moved with other homeless to a tent slum on the banks of the Mississippi, where, in the chill and mud, Mama got sicker. Laila was reduced to begging scraps of food from grocery vendors and restaurants in the city, to keep them alive. And stealing an apple here, a loaf of bread there, when there was nothing else she could do. Mama died of pneumonia there in her arms in that awful place, and she could do nothing to save her, a memory that would haunt her forever. It broke her heart to see Mama buried in Potter's field. Stumbling along a St. Louis street a few days later, she saw Ben Saugrain being attacked by a vicious dog and with scarcely a thought went to help him.

Laila drew a breath and continued, "For the past five years I provided nursing care to an elderly man who owned a cigar manufactory in St. Louis. He died two weeks ago and suddenly I was free to—make a new life."

"How come you set your mind on Oregon?"

"I hope to find my grandparents, they're the only family I have—if they're alive. Grandmother and Grandfather Chapin are my mother's parents. They left Kansas when I was a little girl, but as I remember it they homesteaded in Oregon near a town called La Grande. Kate, isn't that a pretty name for a town, *La Grande?*"

"Sure is! And you're the prettiest thing just sayin' them words."

"Well, Oregon will be a new beginning, in any event, but I thank you."

Next morning, Kate's battered body was tender and sore and exhibited several enormous bruises. It was difficult for her to move. Laila helped her through her toiletry, then massaged her sore back and limbs with liniment.

When that was done, Kate showed her the letter from Mr. Corbett and chortled over the words *Ruby Gold* engraved in large scroll at the top, "The name of his mine!"

He wanted Kate to come to the canyon as soon as she could. He hoped she would like the country. He had had a hard time finding help. Few ladies were interested in making a home in the rugged Snake River Canyon of Oregon which was mostly mining country and no fancy settlements, but he would do his best to make her welcome and comfortable.

Reading his brief letter gave Laila serious doubts about what Kate was getting into, and all she was planning for. Kate, though, had such confidence, was so excited to meet her future "Mister," that Laila couldn't bring herself to say anything negative.

Regardless of what Mr. Corbett or his desolate canyon might really be like, she supposed it wouldn't hurt to go ahead and have a look. Kate could always change her mind, her plans, that was a woman's privilege. If Kate wasn't satisfied with what they found in the Snake River canyon, they could go on together to La Grande. To wherever else they might make a place for themselves. Laila was just glad she'd found a friend to share a future with, be it only for a brief time.

Chapter Two

The fast-moving Snake River whipped the small wood rowboat along as though it were but a tossing leaf in the churning current.

Following instructions from Corbett's letter, Laila and Kate had hired the vessel and boatman after arrival by train at Huntington, which lay south of their destination. Laila had sold her pendant watch to a jeweler in Huntington for enough money to pay for her share of the boat trip and a little extra.

Their earlier overland train journey from Boise, through some sixty miles or so of lovely farmlands, had passed largely uneventfully. And now their gaunt boatman and guide assured them, sweat dripping from his brow, they could reach the Conner Creek area more quickly by these rough waters than by land. Deep draws through the mountains that bounded the river made land travel not only slower but at times more treacherous.

Laila held on to the rough plank seat, her trim booted feet planted flat on the rowboat's wet floor, while opposite her, Kate sat like a brown bear deep in her coat. Kate's face hardly showed, was white more from fright than from the weather, which was actually mild.

She was frightened, too, Laila admitted to herself as she looked around. At the same time she didn't want to miss a single bit of this brand new experience, so different from being nurse-servant to Mr. Saugrain back in St. Louis. Her father had taught her to love the outdoors when she was a tot, and, in spite of feeling edgy, she could appreciate this unique, awe-inspiring scenery all about her.

Periods of "Oregon dreaming" in years past had led her to expect dense emerald forests everywhere, but big trees were all but absent here on the eastern edge of the state. On either side of the Snake River, barren mountains crouched like great beasts bathed green-gold by the sun. Rounded buttes loomed up into the high dry air and were only pocked here and there by a bit of sagebrush. Following Laila's glance, their boatman told her, "Nothin' up there, Miss. Save cheat grass, nettles, an' rattlesnakes in the rock slides."

She shivered, returned her gaze to the blue depths of the water. Their boat, if turned into kindling, would hardly be enough for a decent bonfire. Her glance skipped to the water's edge, to *land,* where a spindly-legged bird raced along the shoreline as though late for an appointment. Or possibly the bird was fleeing an enemy, as she was running from an unhappy past.

The boat suddenly made a swift full turn and Laila, heart in her throat, was facing the other way, the bird to her back. She gripped the plank seat as the boat continued to toss and rock in a treacherous eddy. Water dipped into their boat. Their boatman, who resembled a tough cadaver of unguessable age, stood and battled with the oars to swing them about in the right direction. They again headed downriver in a wild dance over diamond and sapphire riffles and rapids. Laila's lips parted to take in a long draught of air to settle her leaping stomach. Her emerald suit was splattered with wet spots the size of silver dollars. Her jaws ached from clenching her teeth.

She lifted her face to the sun, welcomed its warmth as she made further effort to relax. The sky was a match for the river, breathtakingly blue. Up there, three large birds wheeled, seemed to part puffy clouds with their beautifully spread wings. They might have been marking a wedding ring quilt pattern in the heavens as they circled.

They had traveled the twisting river some distance when she took note of an enormous stack of twigs on top of a granite cliff. "Could that be an eagle's nest?" She felt a small thrill when their boatman assured her, "Yes'm, 'tis."

"Kate, look!" she pointed excitedly at the *eyrie,* but her traveling companion barely lifted her chin, her eyes looked glazed.

Laila made a soft sound of sympathy, and smiled. She was no more used to the boat's endless bucking on the sun-gilded surface of the water than Kate was. The Snake River was aptly named, coiling, mad, plunging on to get where it was going. And yet, despite the river's hurry, they seemed to make small progress—the trip without end.

The nearly toothless boatman seemed to read her mind as they bobbed up and down in sickening motion. "Just hang on, ladies, I be gettin' you there directly." He grinned, brown tobacco juice dribbled down his chin.

"Thank you." She felt some relief. He'd claimed he could take them all the way by river, to Corbett's place near the foot of Sugarloaf Mountain, a distance of fifteen or sixteen nautical miles from Huntington. Have them there by suppertime. He'd made no mention the river might feel endlessly threatening to greenhorn ladies.

As they moved deeper into the canyon, the gargantuan hills showed a faint green broken by stark plateaus and granite rimrock. On coming nearer, a seeming cloud shadow on a lofty rock wall above them turned out to be a cave. The brief ledge in front of the cave was worn as smooth as a country porch.

Excited by the discovery, Laila at the same time felt akin to the creature, human or animal, who'd found shelter up there—in this wild, beautiful country.

As afternoon waned, purple shadows crept from the river's edge up lower canyon walls, while the mountaintops remained gold in the sun. She thought the canyon walls were higher on the Oregon side of Snake River than on Idaho's side, high and breathtakingly primeval in any event. The rugged canyon *was* beautiful. A breeze carried a pleasing fragrance of grass and shrub. She thought Kate might have fallen asleep, but when she looked, Kate's eyes were open.

They rounded a bend, and the scene ahead changed drastically. Both women gasped.

"My goodness, what is that?" Laila stared at the dreamlike oasis. A sandbar stretched, seemingly for miles, along a wide bend in the river. Acres deep, remote from the rest of the world, the orchards were laid out in rows and rows of fruit trees on the sandbar, leaves glossy green in the spring sunshine. Pinkish white blossoms were just popping out on the trees.

The boatman laughed at Kate's wide-mouthed expression of shock. "That's where I'm takin' you, Missus, like you asked. That's Ash Corbett's peach ranch."

"Well, that's not the right place. I was hired by a Mr. Austin Corbett who owns a gold mine." Kate sat stiff, staring.

"Ash and Austin is one and the same man, Missus. Goes by either handle. But he don't own no gold mine that I heard of. Hereabouts he owns the Ruby Gold peach ranch you see there." He spat over the side of the boat. A fish leaped from the water a few feet away, spangled high, returned to the depths.

"Ruby Gold is—*peaches?* Well, I declare!" Kate looked at Laila. "I declare. The man said plain in his ad that his place was in mining country. Gold mining country. Never said a word about peach orchards."

Laila collapsed her parasol and sat with it across her lap as they turned in toward shore, the boatman paddling furiously as they rocked along. "This is the last place I'd expect to see peach trees growing," she admitted. "But won't it be nice to set foot on solid ground again?"

"Best place in the world for peaches," the boatman said, as he pulled hard at the oars. "Fruit grows like weeds along these river sandbars. The high mountains on either side keep the canyon down here warm and protected, hot in summer. Ash's Pa knew what he was doin' when he planted them trees years 'afore now. Ain't no shortage of water. Ol' Snake is right there. Corbett's peaches is the best eatin' in the country."

"But how does Mr. Corbett get them out of this remote canyon to market?" Laila asked. "I can see it's a perfect place to grow them, but isn't shipping a problem? We're miles from anywhere!"

"They be taken by team and wagon to the train at Huntington, shipped to Idaho," the boatman explained. "And by wagon sixty-five miles t'other way to Baker City. Long, hard trip, either one. We be talkin' to get a railroad down Snake River from Huntington, or a railroad from Baker City. Then, by gar' them Ruby Gold peaches could be sent anywheres on God's earth."

"I suppose," Kate mumbled. She seemed still to be grappling with the idea her employer tended peach trees instead of a gold mine.

A final thrust of their boat parted the water like an arrow and the prow *thunked* solidly against the dirt bank. The boatman rested his oars, leaped to shore, and they swayed in the water as he wound the boat's rope to a post planted in the ground.

Laila looked around, fascinated. This oasis in the wild was like nothing she'd ever seen. Beyond the orchards and backed by a brace of poplars, she could see a large stone ranchhouse. "What are those other buildings?" she asked, pointing, as she climbed unassisted from the boat.

"Packin' sheds and a boardin' house for hired help. Mr. Corbett is a go-gettin' fella in these parts. I hear tell he owns a big hotel in Portland, but he stays here in the canyon for now because his old Pap wouldn't be happy in the city. Long as the old man's alive, Ash'll be nursemaidin' them peaches right along with his Pa."

She turned to help Kate from the boat. The boatman hustled off, saying he "hadn't et or whetted his thirst since mornin'." He would be going to the Corbett cookhouse, where they could find him if they needed him.

Kate was still shaking her head. "I reckon keepin' house for a peach rancher can't be all that different than for a miner and maybe someways better?" She looked to her for confirmation.

She nodded, suppressing a smile at her friend's confusion.

Kate looked further disappointed, on the verge of stubborn anger, when they spotted the man coming down to the dock where they were picking up their things. If this was Austin *Ash* Corbett, he was neither middle-aged nor ugly, but a rugged individual in his late twenties or early thirties. Laila guessed from Kate's expression the older woman was seeing her marriage plans crumble on the spot, unless Corbett's father was a prospect.

The younger Corbett was a tall, broad-shouldered man with an easy walk. She saw as he came closer he could have gotten his nickname from the ashy-tan color of his hair that showed below his wide-brimmed gray felt hat. A thick moustache, a shade darker than his hair, defined a face the color of warm bronze. He chewed a blade of grass. For a supposedly well-to-do hotel owner, he looked naturally at home in the rough but clean garb of a working man.

"Hello." He flipped the piece of grass aside and sized up Kate and Laila with blue eyes charged and shining in the shadow below his hatbrim. "Thought I hired one lady. You've turned into two." He didn't sound upset, just surprised.

That the man was nowhere near her expectations seemed to have robbed Kate's tongue, so Laila spoke for her. "This is your housekeeper, Kate Boston, Mr. Corbett." She laid her hand on Kate's arm, held out her other hand. "I am Miss Laila Mitchell, Kate's friend. I'm only traveling with her this far, then I'm going on shortly." She motioned downriver.

The deep canyon looked forbidding in charcoal and purple shadow, but their river guide had explained that's where the mines were. And where there were working men, there ought to be work for her: as a cook, a laundress, or as a nurse to their ills and accidents. But she'd see Kate settled in and all right, first, providing she wanted to stay. For herself, she welcomed the chance to earn some money for the rest of her journey to La Grande.

Corbett was looking in the direction she pointed, then back at her. "A woman? Going on the hell *where?*" His head reared back to examine her face, his expression indicating he felt he spoke to an unknowing idiot.

Laila stiffened at the insult, her face turned hot. "I beg your pardon?"

"I'm sorry." The man's voice was edged with grudging sincerity. He removed his hat, and a soft breeze tousled his thick sandy hair. "I'm used to talking to men of late, not ladies. I meant to say that this part of the northwest hasn't been tamed. It's frontier that quite possibly won't ever be civilized much. It's rough country, Miss. Hard, dangerous. Where you stand isn't much of a place for a woman, and the gorge downriver sure as hell—sure isn't."

"But the boatman said—" She looked around for confirmation, then remembered their escort had gone ahead to the cookhouse. "He said there are a few small settlements for miners farther on." Remote, practically inaccessible, was how the boatman described places deeper in the canyon but she was willing to put up with that for a while.

Corbett yanked his hat back on with long, tan fingers. "I don't know what the damned fool said." His glance leveled at her, and he didn't apologize this time for his slip in language. "There's hardly anybody down in that country but a few prospectors panning the creeks. Oh, yeah, a few outlaws hide in the draws 'til they can cross the river to Idaho, away from the law. Up on the rims you might find a lone sheepherder, a couple of cattle ranchers and their wives, neighbors living so far apart they maybe see one another once a year. We're talking raw *wilderness*, Miss—?"

"Mitchell," Laila told him. "Laila Mitchell. From St. Louis." *And once upon a time from Emporia, Kansas.* More than that about her would be none of this fellow's business—not that he'd asked.

"There are no fancy stores down in there, no hotels, no streetcars," he continued in a voice like rough-edged velvet. "Nothing like the life any fool can see you're used to."

He took in the fine cut and fabric of the young woman's emerald traveling suit, the beribboned toque perched on her dark head, the silly parasol held by long fingers in ecru kid gloves, the delicate skin of her face with its square jaw and defenseless chin. A young lady of refinement, surely. "You'd hate the country. You wouldn't last a month."

Did he think she saw the Snake River Canyon the same as downtown St. Louis? She wasn't that big of a fool. She knew she would still see hard times, but she also knew she wasn't the lily-flower he assumed her to be. They'd only barely met, for goodness' sake. He knew nothing about her.

She could manage what came, as long as she was her own boss, making her own choices. Whatever brought him to his swift calculations about *her kind,* he was overstepping, telling her what she could and couldn't do. She'd had enough of that working for Mr. Saugrain, bowing to his orders and Yvonne's and Rolph's. "I'll see Kate settled comfortably in your house." She spoke in a soft, reasonable tone that only seemed to irritate him. "And then, as soon as possible, I will be traveling on downriver."

His glance held hers another intense moment, and a blush grew beneath the hickory tan of his skin. Finally, his strong jaw set, he grabbed Kate's satchel in one hand, her bag in the other. In that last second before he turned to lead the way to the house, she saw something else in his mesmeric eyes. Arguing with a woman wasn't something Ash Corbett was used to, or liked to do, because he held women, probably all women, in high regard. If not for that, she might have been more put out with him than she was.

Chapter Three

A short while later, Laila decided Mr. Corbett's rudeness at the riverbank could be excused. He was really a kindly, well-intentioned man who took his time showing them his home. They visited the large efficient kitchen, a lovely dining room and parlor, and had a brief peek into his study where Laila noted a cream-colored envelope lying on his desk. The letter was addressed to Mr. Corbett in fine, feminine-looking hand-writing. Was the letter from a friend, a relative, or a sweetheart? Laila wondered, before mentally scolding herself for her nosy curiosity.

Mr. Corbett said to Kate, as he led them into the large, well-furnished upstairs bedroom that would be hers, "I'm sorry to hear about your accident in Boise, Mrs. Boston. Please don't feel rushed. Your employment starts whenever you feel up to it. In the meantime, you and Miss Mitchell are my guests."

He grinned at Laila, his earlier animosity absent. "Choose either of the bedrooms you like, across the hall from Mrs. Boston. And don't feel in a hurry to leave, wherever it is you intend to go." He motioned at the rooms from where his lanky form leaned against the doorframe.

She nodded her thanks and returned his smile, hiding the fear he'd set in her heart about what she'd find deeper in the canyon. She'd have to do what she'd have to do.

He turned to go. "I'll leave you ladies alone now. You must want to freshen up and rest a while. Come downstairs whenever you're ready. Supper's on the stove."

He started to close the door, then stuck his head back in.

"Beefsteak, mashed potatoes and cream gravy, string beans, biscuits with peach butter, and peach pie for dessert. Cooked it myself." He shut the door.

The women looked at one another with raised eyebrows, then laughed.

The door opened again. Corbett's wide thick brows bunched in a frown. "You'll meet my father, Tom, then." He scratched his jutted chin. "If the old cuss didn't drown and gets back from fishing." There was a hint of exasperation behind his otherwise good-natured grin.

A few moments later, Kate all but chirruped like a plump little bird as she sat on the bed and looked about the room. "I've never lived in a place as fine as this." With her good arm, she waved at the rosewood bedroom set, the tall, intricately carved armoire; at the lace curtains and silky rose drapery that framed the two windows. "Did you see? Oriental carpets in nearly every room but that big pine kitchen with the stone floor. And Mr. Corbett, he ain't so bad."

Laila smiled, nodded slowly, holding at bay her envy of such a nice place to live and work, be safe. Who knew what she would find for herself in the future? She sat down on the vanity bench, her back to the ornately framed mirror, and removed her hat. "You'll love it here, Kate, I'm sure. Mr. Corbett seems very kind."

"Indeedy, and he's a handsome devil, too." Kate giggled behind her hand. "I sure fooled myself in my thinkin' about him, didn't I? He's more suited as a husband for the likes of you than me."

Laila's heart gave an unexpected little lurch. She waved off the remark, at the same time admitting silently she'd never met a more appealing man in her life. Not that she'd met many men. There just weren't the occasions for it during her time with the Saugrains.

As a young girl, she had dreamed of meeting someone very special someday. And she had prayed for the hope and joy, the love, such a meeting would bring into her life. Then gradually, as the years passed at Saugrains' she had let the fanciful dreams of romance slip away. It was less painful, and easier, she had decided, to simply accept what life granted her, and be thankful. Now, what she wanted most was to be an independent woman. She drew her attention back to Kate, who had grown equally serious.

"Do I got any chance of convincin' you to stay here with me, Laila? Not just a day or two, but for good?"

"I couldn't do that! I wasn't the one hired—nor am I family to Mr. Corbett. I can't just make myself at home here."

"I know. I know. But you heard what Mr. Corbett said about it being no place for a woman downriver, didn't you?" A deep frown creased Kate's usually placid face.

"Of course I heard what he said, he was very clear." That didn't mean she was ready to become a charity case in his house because of her new friendship with Kate. She told her, "I doubt very much that he needs both of us to work for him. When you're strong on your feet again you'll be able to take care of this place. And I want to make my own way. Whatever I decide to do, you mustn't worry about me, because I'll be fine."

"We'll always be good friends, though?"

"Absolutely!" She smiled. "Now, shall we go down to supper?" Kate's expression brightened at the mention of food. Laila, as well, meant to enjoy this meal, which might be her last in civilized company if what Corbett said was true. She took Kate's arm and helped her down the stairs.

The dining room just barely accommodated the large, oil-rubbed mahogany table and chairs. It was a tranquil, almost summery room with walls of light gray, trimmed in blue wainscotting. Gilt-framed paintings added dimension, ferns on stands on either side of the fireplace added greenery. Hanging on the wall above and between twin doors at one end of the room was an enormous rack of elk antlers.

Ash's father, Old Tom, was late hobbling to the table. He brought with him the distinct aura of fish. He shakily pulled out the chair next to Laila and dropped into it. "What're all these people doing here?" he asked his son as he grabbed a slice of bread from a platter without waiting for it to be passed.

"These two ladies are our guests, Pa." Although Ash's eyes glinted, his voice was mild. "I expect you to be nice to them. Mrs. Boston," he nodded at Kate, "is going to keep house for us. Miss Mitchell—"

"I'm only here for a short time." Laila turned to the old man with a smile. "I'm not staying."

"Good!" he growled. His knotty hand shook as he slathered his bread with butter.

Ash threw his father a look. "Christ, Dad, what'm I going to do with you?"

Tom met his son's glance with fire. It was like two versions of the same man, one old and crotchety, the other young and trying to be patient; both handsome.

"You could take me outta here to where there ain't so damned many people. Place's gettin' so crowded a man can't breathe."

"Dad, the Snake River canyon is about as remote as country gets. You planted them damn peach trees out there, and you're going to stay right here and enjoy 'em! No more movin' on to yet another wilderness. That's that. Eat your supper." He looked at the women, clearly trying to bring his ire under control. "I'm sorry."

Laila gave him a smile to indicate she didn't mind.

Kate complimented Ash on the meal, which was delicious.

Several minutes passed in silence while they ate. Then Tom discovered a lump in his cream gravy. He separated it out on a silver spoon and held it wordlessly toward his son.

"Damn it, Pop! Pretend it's one of those infernal sourdough biscuits you made me eat when I was a kid."

The old man didn't reply, though he scowled. He spooned the lump into his mouth, chewed with great exaggeration, as though masticating a gob of glue.

Laila fought not to smile. A child wouldn't have gotten away with such misbehavior, but the man was Ash Corbett's father. He ate noisily. The other three pretended not to notice, carrying on polite conversation about the weather and the food.

Tom finished his meal first. With a final, "Humph!" he shoved away from the table with a loud scraping of his chair. He glared one last time at the women, and tottered from the room as slowly as molasses poured uphill.

Ash shook his head after his father departed. "I'm sorry. Pop was a strong, wild man in his time. Old age isn't setting well with him, to put it mildly. He can be an ornery, rude son-of-a-gun, no matter what I say to him. I'm afraid at this late date he's not going to change his stripes."

Over their peach pie, Ash made up for his father's lack of manners. He entertained the women with stories of the canyon's history and some of the more colorful characters living in the area.

When Laila asked about the orchards, he told them that since he had to be there for his father's sake, he was doing what he could to get a railroad into the canyon, a better means to ship the products he was developing—peach extracts and candies, dried fruit and of course fresh peaches—

to any part of the world.

Laila found herself fascinated by his nearly every word, and for her the evening sped by. Later, with much pleasure, she cuddled deep into the lovely bed assigned her. She fell asleep almost immediately.

Ash sat back in his chair in his study, long legs crossed on top of the desk next to the lamp, his face in shadow. For several minutes he held Claudine's letter in his hand. The letter was postmarked from Portland and had taken a week and a half to reach him in the canyon. By now she was on board a steamship, on her way to Europe. He started to reread the letter, but he knew well enough its contents.

When Claudine returned in the fall from her summer tour of Europe, she expected Ash to have moved his father to Portland. She and Ash had a lot to do there and he must be on hand to plan their wedding and begin construction of their new home. She had been patient as long as possible. Ash must not spend so much time away from the city and besides, his father would be better off "in civilization".

With a grunt of frustration, Ash tossed the letter onto the desk. He didn't care for ultimatums and Claudine's letter sure had the ring of one: he could move his father or forget marriage to her. He rested his head on the back of the chair, closed his eyes, and rubbed his hand down his face. Invariably, in the past, given an ultimatum, he chose the opposite of what the ultimatum-giver wanted. But this was different, Claudine was his intended bride and she was right that he needed to be on hand for their wedding preparations, and planning their home. Pa ought to be willing to move, but he'd never go willingly to a place like Portland.

Ash had the summer to figure out what he could do. He didn't want to force Pa, and yet, Ash didn't want to lose

Claudine, either. Claudine Galen was every man's ideal. She was breathtakingly beautiful, a sensual blond with a knock-out hour-glass figure. She was fun, educated, well-traveled, socially-sure, and the first woman—after courting dozens—he thought he could settle down happily with. Not that he needed their contacts, but the Galens were socially prominent, their wealth made from shipping, commerce, and real estate. Ash had met Claudine initially through her father, when he bought land from Galen on which to build his hotel, The Portland Grand.

With a heavy yawn, Ash pushed back his chair and stood up. His mind drifted to the young woman upstairs, Laila Mitchell. *So pretty. So proud.* If she was high-borne St. Louis society, as she appeared to be, then she'd likely fallen on hard times due to the economic depression or she wouldn't be here in the canyon. Too bad what the depression had done to a lot of people like her. They found themselves in unbelievable straits, impossible situations. Or it could be that her family had disowned her, had thrown her out on her own for something she'd done or was thought to have done, an act dark and terrible—although that was hard to imagine.

She was so damned determined to go on downriver! If he couldn't talk her out of it, he'd have to allow her to find out for herself that he was right and hope she didn't get hurt, or worse, before he rode down to check on her and bring her back. She could decide at that time what she wanted to do, where she wanted to go that was better, and safer.

Down at the boat dock in a silvery dawn a few mornings later, Laila gave tearful Kate a final hug, and extended Ash Corbett her hand. His lean fingers wrapped around hers in a quick warm grasp. He explained that Tom was exhausted from a rough day fishing yesterday and was grumpily staying in his bed that morning. She said she understood, insisting she'd enjoyed her brief stay very much, which was the truth.

"I wish I could talk you out of this, Miss Mitchell," Ash said, waving toward the boat. "You really don't realize—"

"Thank you, but I'm sure I'll be fine," she cut him off with a smile, trying to hide the reluctance that assailed her as she climbed into the boat. She must take care of herself, and that was that. She gave her cadaverous guide a nod and in another moment he rowed them out into the river's surly current. She waved back at Kate, at a frowning Ash Corbett, then watched over her shoulder until the Ruby Gold peach ranch faded around the bend.

Ash's description of the river and the canyon was true enough. If desolation was what his father wanted, the old man had no cause for complaint. The wilderness, austere in an other-worldly way, sang quietly by as they traveled toward a downriver community of miners, a place the boatman had only briefly described, but where she was sure she could find work.

Again and again she held her breath as the silent boatman maneuvered their bobbing, swaying craft over and around the dragon's teeth of rock that formed repeated rapids. She cried out as they plummeted down foaming chutes that seemed bottomless.

They approached a particularly long stretch of foaming, turbulent water, and she resisted the urge to throw herself to the bottom of the boat. Her knuckles turned bone-white as she gripped the sides. The boatman told her, as if it would make her feel better, that there were stretches of white water on the Snake, miles ahead in the deep chasm, below Idaho's sky-reaching Seven Devils Mountains, where only a few had gone by boat and lived to tell about it.

For the next hours, he entertained her with a rambling, off

and on story he swore was true about a steamboat named Norma, a sternwheeler built in '91 at Bridgeport, Idaho, across the river from Huntington, Oregon. The Norma was intended to carry ore from the Seven Devils' mines to the railhead upriver at Huntington. "Trouble was," the boatman told Laila, "rapids was too much for the Norma to maneuver in high water, shallows too shallow for her to navigate in low water. She was laid up after the first trip or two, trapped where she was. Reckon she'll rot there, they don't figger how to get her out."

Laila remembered the broad, slow Mississippi and the beautiful, frosted-cake looking steamboats that traveled its miles. "In general then, the steamboat can't ply the Snake River?" she asked on a *whoosh* of breath as the boat dipped.

"Right enough. Mighty dangerous river, the Snake, an' she don't never give up her dead. Some call where we're at, 'Hell's Canyon'."

The story didn't make her feel any better. In fact, she now considered Ash Corbett's warning about what she was getting into not strong enough. He ought to have stopped her. *No, I have only myself to blame for what I'm doing.* She'd wanted to do things her own way.

The towering canyon walls on either side of the river were no place for human habitation, male or female, she began to think. Her apprehension grew with every watery mile, in spite of her attempt to feel stalwart and brave. She felt locked in by the sky-reaching, steely perpendicular cliffs. She felt tiny, alone, and very far from anywhere safe.

Occasionally, when she least expected to see any sign of human activity, a prospector's claim would appear at the mouth of a creek. There would be a tent under a tree, a homemade wheelbarrow made of half a barrel, a pile of equipment, a washtub on a bench. Her guide seemed to know the men by name, and the degree of their success, which was usually small. Her glance would fasten to the white flag of a tent until they were past, then she would turn and hold to the spot with her eyes until they rounded a bend into utter desolation again, with the only sound the chortling of the river.

At mid-day, to her delight and relief, they made to shore at a family homestead not far from the banks of the Snake, and a little north of where the Powder River fed into it. The homesteader, Mr. Robinette, a Frenchman, was full of talk about his planned town that would boom as soon as the Oregon Shortline Railroad reached them. After dinner, his wife, lonely for company, showed Laila about her two-story, eight-room house which was surprisingly comfortable for its remote location.

The children followed as the women went outside to see Mrs. Robinette's large garden. They paced the leafy rows of carrots, potatoes, onions, and beets. Small lumps of green fruit were formed on Mr. Robinette's peach, apricot, and apple trees. When Laila commented about the isolation, Mrs. Robinette told her that sometimes they lived at Sturgill Bar, five miles away on the Idaho side, where her husband mined. Sometimes they moved inland west to Richland, some ten miles away on the Oregon side, so the children could go to school. Mrs. Robinette insisted they would never leave the homestead at all, if it weren't necessary. She loved it there.

Laila gave the matter some study as her fear subsided, and she thought that could be possible. The homestead was in the most beautiful spot she'd ever seen, a marvel, really, for its distance from the outside world.

Her courage, her determination to make her own new life, returned. She would, at the very least, enjoy the scenic beauty of the area for as long as she worked for the miners. Depending on her future, such an opportunity might never come again. There were poverty-stricken folks in St. Louis, cramped, overworked, who would think she had landed in heaven. But others, citified and spoiled, would likely think she'd found hell. She could be grateful she was not one of the latter.

The boat trip continued. Laila became soaked to the skin from splashings as they rocked and rolled their way over repeated rapids. She ached with tension, expecting to be tumbled into the river any second. Near dusk a small huddle of buildings once more came into view, on a bar that looked carved into the steep canyon wall like a pocket.

As they neared, she stared at the rough, unpainted shacks and a scattering of tents among the pine trees. She clenched her teeth to keep them from chattering. She asked the boatman, "Shouldn't we stop here for the night?" She crossed her fingers tightly in the folds of her damp skirt.

"Yup." Oars flashed as he fought the current that wanted to hurtle them on downstream. "This is as far as I go, anyhow, Miss," he shouted as he struggled to aim them to shore. In another minute, away from the current, the water flattened out and the going was easier.

"You mean this is as far as you go *today?*"

"Nah," he shook his head, "I mean this is where me and my boat turn back from, tomorrow. As it is I'll be days gettin' back, fightin' the current upstream. Like I told you, Miss, from here on downriver it's puredee hell."

This then, was her stopping place? She looked more sharply at the crude hamlet, only half listening to the boatman explain that the community, called 'Venture,' was some five years old, and growing. There was mining up in the side canyons, searches for copper, silver, and gold. Miners lived in the shacks and tents.

The Ironstake Mine, the largest such in the district, was situated a little over a mile above the community. From up there, Laila could hear the muted growl and thump of steam-powered machinery, could see the movement of men around the dark face of a tunnel and the nearby crude mill. She reminded herself again that she needed work, and where there were men working, there must be jobs for a woman.

But right then, she wanted to feel solid ground under her feet more than anything else. She scrambled from the boat as they reached shore. Her legs felt rubbery from sitting so long, and for a moment she was afraid to take a step. She fought a strong urge to inform her boatman that she would be returning upriver with him to the Corbett peach ranch. Back to the comfort, kindness, and good company there. She was no beggar, though, no weakling. Not really. She had announced her plan to one and all to find work in this place and to that aim she would do her best.

With a resolute sigh, she paid the boatman from her meager funds. He thanked her, bit off a chew of tobacco and worked it in his jaws, then started off up the riverbank. She gripped her satchel and, listing sideways, ran to catch up.

"Just a moment, please! Which of the buildings houses the hotel, a boarding house? I see no hotel sign."

"There ain't no sign," he told her patiently as he scratched his dirty-flanneled ribcage, " 'cause there ain't no hotel, yet. No boardin' house that takes women, neither."

A chill settled over her. "But where will I stay? You brought me here, you must have known—why didn't you say something about there not being a place I could put up?"

He shrugged sweat-stained shoulders. "You said you'd pay me to bring you into the canyon to where there was a bunch of folks livin' and I brung you. I thought you was meanin' here," he pointed at the ground at his feet, "and it's as far as I go."

Ash Corbett had warned her, hadn't wanted her to make this trip. Laila was angry at herself for going ahead so blindly into *this*. But she'd thought at least to have a place to stay, decent shelter. She fought weariness and a threat of tears as she struggled her way up to the settlement.

Rough trails that she supposed passed for streets dissected the community into irregular blocks, or lots, for the nine or ten clapboard shacks, drab frame houses, and tents, among the pine trees. Garments fluttered from a clothesline behind one of the bungalows; from behind another a dog barked. It wasn't St. Louis.

With a heavy sigh, she turned toward what appeared to be a blacksmith shop, one of the newest-looking, larger buildings. A figure moved in the deep shadows within, raising the clang of hammer on iron. The man might know of someone who would take her in, give her bed-space for long enough to get her bearings.

Chapter Four

The sign, crude black letters painted on raw yellow wood, said: WAGONWORKS, Hutton B. Ginther, Wheelwright.

In the shadows beyond the wide open door, a stooped older man worked at pounding an iron rim onto a wheel, his back to Laila as she approached. The shop smelled of wood-smoke, fresh cut pine, linseed oil, varnish, and axle grease. Wheels, wagons, and stacks of lumber filled the corners. Unaware of her presence, the man looked the wheel over speculatively, wiped his brow on his sleeve and again struck hard steady blows with a clanging that set her ears ringing.

The next time he stopped pounding to examine the wheel Laila cleared her throat. Again, the wheelwright didn't respond. She went to his side and tapped his shoulder. He whirled, raising an arm as if he expected to be struck. Behind his rough, steel gray moustache, his time-creased face took on a look of total amazement, his blue eyes stared. He put down his tools and rubbed his hands on his tan leather apron. He hadn't expected a woman, if anyone. Laila smothered her amusement. "I'm sorry—" she apologized for startling him. "Mr. Ginther?"

"How do you know me?" he asked in a shy, husky, accented voice. Was he British, maybe? Australian? He looked behind her and with a puzzled frown took in her lone womanly shadow on his floor. "Where'd ya' come from, then, Miss?"

She smiled. "Your name is on your sign . . ."

He looked embarrassed. "Aye, I only put the sign up a few

days ago," he explained, "an' my mind be slippin' about it. But you, how—?"

She told him she'd come by boat and needed a place to stay. "I believe there's no regular hotel?" She hadn't expected fancy accommodations, but she had thought there would be *something*.

"There ain't no place you can stay here in Venture, Miss. Nobody but men livin' here just now," he told her in a thick brogue.

She nodded that she had guessed as much, but she couldn't help the shadow of worry, the frown that replaced her smile.

He went on, "It's mostly miners here, and the rest of us who provide services to the mines and to the men workin' 'em. Sam Hutchinson, he was married, but he lost his wife to pneumonia last winter. Desper Thornhall is married, too, but his wife, Opal, is away the summer visitin' her sister over in the Willamette Valley."

"But she—she'll be back, won't she? And—and there must be *someplace* I can stay—right now—today?" She was tired, hungry, ready to climb under a bush and call it home, if need be. "Can't you think of anything, Mr. Ginther? Maybe one of the houses is empty?" She fought feelings of fear at being the only female around as her desperation grew. She'd gotten herself into this mess, she'd make the best of it, somehow.

He shook his grizzled head. "No, Miss." He hesitated, and she saw in his eyes a reluctance to tell her whatever had come to his mind.

"What is it?"

He walked out past the corner of his shop and stood looking northward. She followed. He pointed. "You follow the river about three miles." She listened carefully, because, as he continued, it sounded like he was saying, "sty on the trial an' it'll tyke you to a plyce called Linding." When he saw her puzzlement, he repeated more clearly, "Stay on the trail an' it'll take you to a place called Landing." He explained with a smile that he was an Aussie, originally from "down under."

He waved his hand up toward an area of broken rimrock and steep slopes with a smattering of pine. "About another mile or two up the side canyon, there's a cabin. By a creek. Other wayfarers have taken shelter there in the past. Some for a season, others for just a night or two. Cabin belongs to a rancher who lives over in Pine Valley. He sometimes keeps cattle in the basin where the cabin is. Don't think he's ever objected to the cabin being used when he has no need for it. Nobody's livin' in it, right now."

Laila heaved a sigh, her smile broadened. "Then that's it! Thank you very much, Mr. Ginther." She offered him her hand. His work-gnarled paw took her fingers gingerly, as though he was afraid he'd break them.

Kindly eyes looked down at her. "The cabin's rough, no place for a pretty young woman like you. Not to stay in for any time. You better go on back, tomorrow, to where you came from. Aye."

Going back to St. Louis was something she'd never do, and it had been so long since she had left Emporia that that time seemed like a dream. "I'll be fine, Mr. Ginther." She could see he hated not to be able to offer her something better. He would be a friend if she stayed, and for now she must. "Can you tell me, Mr. Ginther, where I might buy supper fixings? A few supplies?"

Minutes later Laila thanked him and told him good-bye. She took a dusty path that had been churned face-powder fine, toward a gray, false-fronted building. From the faded, amateurishly lettered sign above the door and pair of windows, she made out the words: THORNHALL'S GENERAL MERCHANDISE. There was a rough-hewn bench under one of the store's windows, a row of barrels under the other. There was an open-sided shed and small house in back of the store.

Venture's general store was run, Mr. Ginther had said, by a man named Desper Thornhall. Thornhall was also a community official of some sort, like a mayor. The hamlet itself seemed nearly empty of other humanity. The only sounds breaking the late afternoon quiet were the clanging from the wheelwright's shop, and muted noise from the mine up the canyon, the rhythmic *thump thump* of sledge hammers against rock and the constant *chuffing* of steam-driven equipment.

She stepped into a circling clump of bushes to relieve herself, unable to believe her life had turned so crude, but it had been a long journey on the boat. Moving out of the clearing moments later, a movement caught her eye. Laila stopped short, and drew a sharp breath. Her heart almost stopped its beat and her satchel slipped from her fingers to the ground.

A barefooted wisp of a little girl in a faded, tattered brown dress dodged behind a cluster of dirty white tents several yards ahead to Laila's right. The child had looked so much like Laila at that age, it was as though Laila saw a ghost of herself. She clutched both hands to her chest until her breathing returned to normal. Her knees felt weak as she took up her satchel and moved on, unsure now that she had actually seen a small girl with long tangled brown hair and a tiny, snub-nosed face. Was her mind playing tricks? There might not be another woman in the community, but she was not the only female, if the little girl was fact and not an apparition.

Inside the store, Desper Thornhall, a reedy oldster with watery gray eyes, stared at Laila with surprise equal to Ginther's. She asked for credit until she could find work and pay for the supplies she needed.

"Credit?" he mumbled, continuing to stare at the lovely young woman who had appeared out of nowhere.

"Please, I'm desperate. Perhaps I can clean your store to pay for food?"

"I clean it, all it needs."

If she only had something to offer as collateral. She said reluctantly, "I have a small medical kit I could allow you to hold. Of course I'd need to borrow it, if I was called on for a nursing case. I don't really have much to give you to hold until I can pay. My hat, my gloves, my parasol—?"

He looked suddenly embarrassed. "That's not necessary. You don't have to clean, and you can keep your kit. Gorry sakes! If I can't trust a woman as honest as you look to be, I can't trust nobody." He waved her to help herself. "Could be you'll find more work than you can handle, in this place that's got so few women. You pick out what you need." He trailed after Laila, curious at this lovely rarity, as she moved about inside the small building selecting carefully from his stock of goods.

Besides food staples—flour, sugar, salt, beans, potatoes, tea, crackers, a few tinned foods, and syrup—Laila chose matches, a pair of boots, two blankets, a can of coal oil and a lamp. A bolt-lock in case the cabin didn't have one, a pocket knife, bucket, a handful of nails, and rope.

The Venture store was out of writing paper—Mr. Thornhall said he'd get some his next buying trip to Baker City. "Please," Laila said earnestly. She would write a letter to her grandparents in La Grande and pray that it would reach them. She would tell them she was coming soon. She was sure they would be glad to see her.

There was only one way to get her purchases to the cabin and her final selection was one of the half-barrel wheelbarrows.

As Laila took up the storekeeper's pen to sign the bill, he asked in a thin, raspy voice, "Where is your man, your husband? Ain't he with you?"

"I don't have a husband, Mr. Thornhall," she smiled. "I make my own way. I promise to pay my bill as soon as possible." She'd waste no time seeking work. With women so few in the area, and no others at all at present, she'd likely have more paid tasks—sewing, cooking, laundry, nursing—than she could manage.

Thank goodness for her small stock of medicines. She hoped, though, to dole them out *not* by the bottle, but by spoonful and by rub, and to be paid for the treatment, and for nursing. The pills and tonics would last longer that way. Also in her kit was her little red book, "First Help In Accidents," to guide her. Not by any means could she be considered a professional, but as Mr. Thornhall wrote her purchases on a tab, she told him where she would be staying, that she would come if he heard of someone needing a nurse.

Afraid of sounding the fool if the little girl she'd seen was a trick of her mind, Laila hesitated at the door of the store to ask, "Do you have a little girl, Mr. Thornhall, or does one of the miners have a child? I thought I saw a girl of about six dashing behind a tent, but I saw her for only a second. I was told there were no women here, except for your wife who is away for the summer. Are there children?"

Desper Thornhall chuckled, "That would be little Tansy Sellers that you saw. She doesn't belong to me, or to anybody else lives here at Venture. Not surprised you only got a glimpse of her, she's wild as a little feral kitten."

"What do you mean? Where does she live? Who takes care of her? Where are her parents?" Laila stepped back inside the store, wide-eyed with shock.

"Tansy doesn't trust hardly anybody, trusts me only a

little. I give her candy now and then, and a meal when she's hungry. She sleeps in a pallet in my storage shed. Child won't hardly let anybody come near her. My wife, Opal, planned to take Tansy with her to the valley this spring, turn the child over to an orphanage in Salem. She'd be clean, then, with a real roof over her head, and somebody to look out for her all the time. But come time for Opal to leave, Tansy vanished and my wife had to leave without her." He laughed, "She's smart, that Tansy."

"What about her parents?"

He sobered. "Well, that's a sorry tale to tell, for certain. Tansy's Ma and Pa, Minnie and Wally Sellers, came here to Venture about two years ago. Nobody knew where they came from, but rumor had it Wally was running from the law. Minnie was a lazy young gal, 'though not hard to look at: black hair, yellowish brown eyes, nice figure. She was—pretty friendly to the miners, if you know what I mean. About six months ago, Wally was killed in an accident up at the mine. Right afterward, Minnie took off with one of the miners leaving this part of the country. He was not much more than a boy, named Moony Joe, I think. Nobody knows where they went."

"Minnie just walked off without her little girl, without Tansy? She abandoned her after the child had just lost her father?"

"That's the size of it. But Minnie never took good care of Tansy, anyhow, when she was here. Don't know that Tansy's much the worse off for being left behind."

Laila departed Thornhall's store shaking her head, finding it near impossible to believe that a mother would abandon her child to live like an animal in a camp of miners.

Grunting occasionally in rhythm with her steps, the handles of the barrow pulling at her shoulders, Laila trundled her way a good three miles along the river's edge. Her satchel sat atop her newly purchased load. Wild ducks paddled at the water's edge on her right. A smaller bird, tan and white, raced on long legs in front of her. There were slithering sounds coming from the grass to her left that she did her best to ignore.

At sound of a soft cough behind her she stopped and whirled around. Several feet behind on the trail, Tansy crouched like a brown bunny that thought by being very still it wouldn't be seen. Laila took a deep breath, and called softly, "Tansy? Tansy, come talk to me." Tansy sprang to life, bare feet flying as she sped back the way she'd come. Laila sighed, her heart going out to the child who had no one to truly care for her. Given time, she'd somehow make friends with Tansy, help her if she could. She knew what it was like to be alone.

'Landing', as Mr. Ginther called it, was hardly more than that, Laila saw when she finally reached the place. Tied up at the riverbank was a plank ferry for crossing to the Idaho side. On land a few yards west of the river was a shanty built on a second raft, that, if dusty muslin curtains blowing from an open window were a sign, was somebody's home. There were a few young apricot and walnut trees. No one seemed to be about when she called out, "Anyone home?" She abandoned hope of resting a while or being treated to a neighborly cup of coffee.

From Landing, she turned up the deep gulch, shoving her load up a rocky, barely discernable path almost straight up. Concerned about the gathering dark, she tried to hurry, but that was next to impossible. Panting, stopping now and then to rest, she moved her wheelbarrow up the grassy, rock-strewn slope in spurts.

Finally, she came upon the rough little cabin squatting in a rather good-sized basin. The building was framed by tangled brush trying to be trees on either side. The plank door hanging from leather hinges creaked open at her push. It was useless to compare but the place reminded her of the playhouse Papa built for her when she was little back in Kansas. It was that small. She sighed and returned outside to carry in her supplies from the wheelbarrow.

Chapter Five

She filled and lit her new kerosene lamp, felt buoyed by the friendly beacon on the crude little table centering the room. She had shelter, for the present, anyhow. There were a few chunks of wood near a small rusty iron stove at the back wall. After a few wasted matches—she was out of practice and would have to regain her old skills at roughing it—she managed a feeble fire.

Finding a kettle on a shelf behind the stove, she went outside, making her way in dim light to the noisy creek, where she scooped up water to boil for tea. Back inside, she encouraged the fire by opening the stove door and blowing on the flames. Later, while the water heated, she spread her blankets on the narrow bunk built onto the west wall of the tiny cabin.

Supper was crackers, cold salmon from a tin, and wonderful hot tea. Laila reflected as she ate that except for the most basic cooking skills, like baking bread, making soup and such, she was embarrassingly wanting, but she'd learn. After hiring on as Ben Saugrain's nurse, caring for him was her total role. His housekeeper, Miranda, a quiet woman and all business, did the cleaning and cooking.

Looking about the small crude room from her rickety chair, she decided that the nest she'd made for herself in the past hour—teakettle bubbling on the stove, quilts on the bed, was quite cozy. Then, with the sound of her movements stilled, the quiet set in, filling the room with a suffocating, lonely feeling. She shivered. To cover the sound of her own breathing, which seemed to her as loud as fireplace bellows, she began to hum softly, then to sing in a whispery voice:

I had a piece of pie and I had a piece of puddin'
I give it all away to see my Sally Goodin
I looked down the road and I saw her comin'
I thought to my soul that I'd kill myself a runnin'
Hey dey diddle, the cat and the fiddle
The cow jumped over the moon, moon, moon,
The little dog laughed to see such sport
That the dish ran away with the spoon, spoon, spoon . . .

Heavens! Surely it was a lifetime ago that Papa had taught her that ditty. It was her favorite to sing when she was about five and spent so many happy afternoons, swinging in the elm tree on the farm, trying to touch her toes to the wide Kansas sky.

Laila woke groggily next morning. Sunlight filtered through the cabin's one small window. The night had been filled with unfamiliar sounds and she had slept little, and her head ached. She lay quietly for a moment. Wistful embarrassment crept over her as she recalled now that when she did fall asleep she had—she reached both hands to cover her warm cheeks, remembering—she had dreamed about Ash Corbett. Of all things. She had dreamed of them as a pair! Insane, foolish dreaming—fantasy touching, fevered kisses, delectable feelings of being loved and cared for. A whole lot of things she knew nothing about, except by instinct. Nonsense, really.

She had *not* come to Oregon for anything other than to be independent. A relationship between her and a man like him was impossible, anyway. They were as different as night and day; and for all she knew, Ash was romantically involved with someone else. A man that handsome, that kind . . .

She sat up suddenly. The dream, silly short visit to paradise though it was, was certainly nothing to get herself in a stew about. She threw aside her quilt.

A short while later, bent from the waist and brushing her long wavy hair, Laila decided that after fortifying herself with hot, strong tea and breakfast, she would waste no time getting on with her plan to find paid work. She straightened up and shook her head, letting her hair fall to the back of her waist. With flashing fingers, she made a rope of the heavy silken waves and fastened it with hairpins into her usual loose pompadour.

She had unpacked the night before and this morning she dressed in one of her plainer dresses, a soft lavender print.

The Ironstake Mine was located almost directly above the town of Venture in a saddle between draws. Laila breathed hard from the steep climb, stopping twice to rest, and checking to see if Tansy were in sight. She wasn't. As Laila moved on, she noted an odd but not unpleasing mixture of fragrances in the morning air: tangy sage, dust, the perfume of wild yellow and white flowers she had no names for, yet. Below her at the foot of the slopes the Snake River was a curving, sapphire ribbon.

Running through her mind was the information she'd gotten about the mine from the wheelwright, Mr. Ginther, whom she'd stopped to visit this morning on the way. Although worked by locals, a group of Pennsylvanians held title to the mine. Mainly copper, but some gold, was being taken from the wormhole-like tunnels eating into the mountain; production was not yet what was hoped for; a stamp mill would be added to the operation soon.

Before she argued him down, Ginther, in his Aussie brogue, had been persistent in his offer to accompany her up to the mine. In another situation she might have agreed with him that a young woman going to the mine unchaperoned was hardly proper. But she believed a different way of life required different rules, very different, sometimes. Anyway, already as a working class girl in St. Louis, she had had more freedom—although she rarely had time to make use of it—than that allowed a young woman of propriety and class. She expected even more freedom here. If regulations were needed to order her life, she would make them herself.

Puffing, lost in thought, she reached the mine site. Several men, their work-clothes rough and dust-coated, ceased work to stare at her; a few grimy faces grinned lewdly in her direction. Men made comments to one another she could only guess about. Her face heated, but she held her ground, asked, and was directed to, the manager of the mine.

Hob Riley, the boss, a massive, dish-faced man, added to her humiliation by his attitude that he considered her an annoyance. Ignoring his rudeness, as well as the stares of the rest of the men, Laila inquired after work as cook and laundress. She was brusquely informed she wasn't needed. The mine operation had adequate cooks, a man and his boy helper, who also took care of laundry chores.

The mine manager pointed to where—some distance away from the activity around the largest gaping mine tunnel—a makeshift kitchen was arranged under a long roof of peeled logs. At one of the several tables, a fat bald man and a stringy boy of maybe fourteen—dingy white aprons tied about their middles—peeled vegetables for what was likely the noon meal coming up. Laila was surprised to see the girl, Tansy, standing near the table. The cook looked in Hob Riley's direction, then quickly slipped the girl a raw carrot. She snatched it and went flying down the hill, dirty bare feet carrying her in a blur.

"Hey, you, girl!" Hob shouted, fury blazing in his face and

waving his fist after Tansy, "You stay away from here! Dammit, Cook, I ain't paying you to feed some little left-off stray who ain't our concern. You do it again, you're finished here."

"He only gave her a carrot," Laila said in defense of Tansy and the cook. "What harm is there in that?"

"You feed an alley cat," Riley growled at Laila, "and you can't never get rid of it. That kid is a damn nuisance and she's got no business up here at the mine."

Laila agreed that the mine site wasn't a proper place for Tansy, but Riley's lack of compassion was beyond her understanding. "Tansy is a human child, not an alley cat," she said quietly. "You have no work for me, at all? I could sew, mend as needed. And I have nursing skills."

Riley's carbon-black eyes roved brazenly over Laila from head to toe. "There's only one other job for a woman around here and my bet is you couldn't handle it, not like that little girl's mother could, before she left here." He laughed at the shocked expression on Laila's face. "Just as I thought. Get your dainty behind off this mountain while you can. Go home to Mama, darlin'. Men in this country want real women an' a lot more'n you got to offer."

Sickened by his insults, Laila gave the man a dark look before turning away. She left the mine site at a fury-driven pace, but in time calmed down. Truthfully, she'd found the few western men she'd had contact with to be just the opposite of Riley in manners. Men like Hutton Ginther, Ash Corbett, and others, were respectful and kind toward women, would be toward *any* woman, she suspected. That Ash had come to mind again in a favorable way, a standard by which Riley paled, took her by surprise and revived memories of her dream. Her face warmed and she paid closer attention to the present moment, trying to decide the way she should take to reach the cabin.

Rather than go back down to Venture and along the river, then up to her cabin, she decided to cut through the high bunchgrass northward across the hills and draws. On the main, she followed a narrow path marked with the small crescent tracks of deer, finding it hard to keep to her feet on the rough and rocky slopes. Finally, her cabin was a small rectangle below. Starting that way, she saw an animal print unlike the others, faint and crosswise in the dirt path. She stooped to examine it, mildly curious, then she drew a sharp breath.

With some trepidation, she lay her hand down next to the paw-print of a cat. The print was larger than her whole hand, was perhaps seven inches in length. Her stomach tightened. Not a house-cat, this one. Unsure how fresh the track might be, she stood up slowly and looked about her. Was the animal still in the area? Her heart pumped.

Here and there, rock ledges clung to the mountain face. Wherever there was soil, there was deep, waving grass sighing in the mountain wind. Places a tawny cat could prowl or lie in wait for someone like her, or Tansy, to pass. Deep worry gripped Laila. Slipping, sliding, she ran the rest of the way to the cabin, keeping an eye out for Tansy on the way. Evidently the child had returned to Venture and the company of Mr. Thornhall. Laila felt safe only after her cabin door was bolted behind her.

Out of need to return outside, to relieve herself and to get wood and water, came the reasoning that if she was going to live and work in the wild canyon any time at all, she'd have to find a way to exist with the creatures already residing there, both human and otherwise. But she wished she had a weapon.

Outside again, after carrying in her water and wood, she gathered and made a pile of large green and blue stones, interlaced with heavy sticks, in a kind of abstract bit of decoration by her door. Only she need know the sticks and stones were her arsenal of weapons, in case they were needed. A gun, though, would be mighty handy, considering both the wild and human animals in the canyon. Learning to fire the weapon would be only one of many things she would need to learn, in order to survive here.

The second night in the remote cabin, Laila dreamed she was falling from the high cliff of the gorge, tumbling and turning. She screamed and screamed but was alone with no one to see, or hear, or help.

Sitting bolt upright in a cold sweat on the hard little bunk, she realized after a vague, sleep-drugged minute that the screams she heard were not her own, nor were they from her dream. They were real and came from outside the cabin. The sound of a female being tortured. *Tansy?* Laila frantically shook herself awake and listened more carefully. The screams sounded too full and strong to be a child's voice.

Trembling from head to toe, Laila lit the lamp and tiptoed hurriedly with it to the door. She eased the door open a crack, then wider. She peered outside, holding the lamp high, the wick flickering as her hand shook. Illumination revealed only her woodpile, the pile of stones and heavy sticks by the doorstone, and the hill path heading down into pitch dark.

Nothing else. The sound had stopped.

Shivering, Laila drew back and slammed the door shut and bolted it. Supposedly there were no women at Venture just now. She understood that Mr. Wheeler, the ferryman homesteader at Landing, was at present a bachelor. And yet the sound she had heard was surely the scream of a woman reacting from terrible pain.

As she tried to make sense of it, from the recesses of her mind came an image of the cat's paw-print that she'd found coming home from the mine. With a jolt of certainty, she had the answer, recalled learning at some time in the past that a mountain lion's wild yowling could sound very much like a woman's scream.

Laila returned the lamp to the table with an unsteady hand. She cupped her palm above the globe, blew the light out, then hurried through the gloom to the bunk where she brought the blanket to her chin. She was satisfied she'd heard the cry of a wild animal, not a human in pain. Even so, a return to sleep was slow in coming. She felt haunted by the scream, by the nightmare of falling, alone.

In the cool of next morning, under a sky of cobalt blue, she hurried down to Desper Thornhall's store for yeast to bake bread, though equally as much to visit with another human being and inquire further about Tansy.

She cautiously brought up the matter of the wild cat, not wanting to sound too much the helpless female where she didn't belong. Desper dismissed the cat with a shrug. "Heard him myself a few times, but I'm fair used to it. A hunter will get the noisy, yellow bugger one of these days, or a rancher who is tired of losing calves to him will bring him down."

She nodded, her fear eased somewhat by his calculation. She privately hoped the cat would just go away on its own, to some other area of the canyon, or further into the mountains. "I looked for the little girl, Tansy, on my way here this morning but I didn't see her. I worry for her. Is she safe from the wild cat?"

"Tansy knows to be careful. Little as she is, she knows this canyon, these hills, as well as anyone. She was here a while ago. She was going to Ginther's wood shop to ask for scraps to build some toy or other. She'd be down there now. I 'spect Ginther will give her her noon meal. He does that, sometimes, if she hasn't already begged food from me or somebody else."

★ ★ ★ ★ ★

Off and on the next few nights, Laila woke to hear the mountain cat's bone-chilling cry. In spite of efforts to conquer her fear, sometimes at night she wished to be anywhere but in the lonely depths of the canyon. She tossed and turned and stuffed her blankets up around her ears.

Fortunately, in the bright light of day, her fears for the most part washed away. Desper was sure the cat would eventually be brought down. She had to have faith that would happen or that it would move on to somewhere else.

She had been in the canyon a little over a week when Ash Corbett appeared unexpectedly at her open cabin door, his horse, a sturdy seal-brown, stood ground-reined a few feet away. Laila recovered her surprise, but found herself happier to see Ash than she could have foretold. She hoped her leaping heart wasn't reflected in her face.

He stood spread-legged on her threshold, nearly filling the cabin doorway, hat in one hand on his hip, a large basket gripped by the handle in his other hand. His electric blue eyes were taking in with some surprise the small homey improvements she had made inside the tiny room. "Afternoon," he finally spoke. "Kate sent me. She wants me to make sure you're all right. I brought venison steaks and a peach pie. But if you've changed your mind about stayin' here, it won't be any trouble at all to take you back with me, Miss Mitchell. *Today*," he emphasized. From his confident expression he believed that Laila would admit he was right, and retreat with him.

His attitude rankled her. She was still getting used to the canyon and she was sure she was going to like it. Most especially she didn't want this man's pity, or his charity. She told him confidently, "I'm staying. I appreciate your kind offer, however, Mr. Corbett, as I surely appreciate your food gifts."

He shoved his hat back and stared at her. His tan forehead knotted in a frown. "You're a puzzle, Miss Mitchell, you surely are. I can see you don't appreciate my butting in, and I can't force you to leave with me. But I don't understand you're wanting to be here. There's not one woman in a thousand that would find this country agreeable."

"I do."

He grunted an unintelligible comment under his breath as he handed the basket over to her. There was doubt in his tone and his crooked grin as he asked, "You've found work, then, a means to keep the wolf from the door?" He stood watching as she put the pie in her pine-crate cupboard, the meat in a skillet where it could be cooked right away.

For now she was more concerned with keeping a wild cat from her door than "the wolf." She hedged at answering his question about work and declared without turning, "There are plenty of things I can do around here." She was convinced she *would* find work as soon as word got around of her presence in the canyon. It was only a matter of time until she would be needed. It was neither here nor there—not his business at all as a matter of fact—that she hadn't found actual work yet.

She decided to change the subject, and turned to smile at him. "Will you come in and have coffee? I can fix a meal, or we can just have pie and coffee." She looked forward to a long chat. She didn't want his pity, or his opinions of what was right or wrong for her, but she would like his friendship.

He shook his head. "Wish I had time. I'm here to talk business with some of the local men. If you're sure you won't come back with me, I have to get on."

"I'm staying."

He nodded and with reluctance edged back outside.

Laila followed, bleak disappointment settling over her.

The visit had been far too short, hardly more than a minute or two. Even with the unpleasant aspects of their exchange, she liked his company. She spoke quietly, "I'm sorry you have to leave, but I'm doing just fine and I'd appreciate it if you'd relay that message to Kate, too." In the yard, she watched his long fingers settle his hat tighter in place. She swallowed a dryness in her throat. "Thank you again for the food, and give my love to Kate."

A peculiar loneliness, coupled with an odd yearning, gripped her as she watched Ash ride away, his body swaying in the saddle as his horse picked its way down the hill. Her feelings were due, of course, to the brevity of their visit, she told herself, and to the fact that he clearly considered her foolish when she'd like him to think well of her and realize that she was a sensible person who knew what she was doing. On top of everything else was the very real loneliness, the quiet, of the canyon after he'd gone. She reminded herself to be grateful that Kate had sent him at all, and that he was gentleman enough to pay a neighborly call and offer her aid. Even if she didn't need it.

Chapter Six

When Hutton Ginther learned that Laila had been turned down by the miners, he said he had far more work to do in his shop than he could keep up with. He offered her a job and she quickly accepted.

The wagonshop was a pleasant-enough place to work, although sanding, puttying, and painting the wooden wagon parts was very tedious once the novelty of learning how was past. She looked forward much more to brush-stroking fine decorative stripes on spokes, took real pleasure in painting the colorful, intricate scroll and stripe designs on the wagon gears. The work was piecemeal in the days that followed. The pay was a pittance to what she really needed for her fresh start, to pay her bills, and eventually to travel on to La Grande. But she would survive.

The first time Tansy came to the shop and found Laila working there, she wouldn't come inside. She came a second time and stood at the open door, scowling. Laila took a few minutes from her work sanding the spokes of a wheel, and squatting, sawdust sweeping the hem of her dress, took scraps of wood and began building the foundation of a tiny toy cabin. Feeling Tansy's eyes on her, Laila casually asked, "Would you finish it for me, please? I need to do my work."

It was another minute or two before Tansy slipped inside, and kneeling beside the tiny structure, began adding more pieces of wood to the walls, the roof. Laila, thrilled, secretly watched. For days that pattern of activity continued, Laila beginning a toy—a corral for pretend animals, a small house and tiny tables and chairs, a train—and Tansy carefully finishing them. In a while, Tansy began to speak aloud to herself, in play dialogue with the wood toys. Hutton Ginther would look at Laila and wink.

On a trip to the store, Laila found that the stock of writing papers Desper ordered had arrived. She lost no time writing to Grandma and Grandpa Chapin, addressing her letter to the city of La Grande since she had no other address. They had lived on a farm, but surely the postmaster would know where to deliver her letter.

One morning, Laila knelt at the river's edge washing her hair. She looked up, strands of hair dripping around her face, to see Tansy watching. "Would you like to smell my soap?" Laila asked softly, holding it out. After a moment, Tansy crept close and pressed her small, dirty, turned up nose against the lilac-scented soap.

She looked at Laila shyly, "The soap smells nice."

"I could wash your hair with it, if you like. Just let me finish with mine."

Tansy looked uneasy, then nodded.

To start, Laila sat Tansy on the riverbank and gently and patiently attacked the chore of combing the nasty tangles from her matted dark hair. Thankfully, there didn't appear to be lice, but her hair was filthy. The process took a long while and it puzzled Laila that Tansy didn't shrink from the hurt that the combing and untangling surely caused. It then occurred to Laila that Tansy was absorbing the gentle care, relishing the tender touch of Laila's hands. Swallowing her emotion, Laila cradled Tansy over her arm at the river's edge and with her free hand sudsed Tansy's small head again and again with the lilac soap, then rinsed her hair thoroughly.

When they went to the store later, to show off Tansy's

shiny new braids, Thornhall swore he didn't recognize the pretty little girl. Tansy surprised them with a burst of giggles, "Now I smell like her, like Laya," and she pointed at Laila.

"Indeed you do!" Thornhall answered, "An' a mighty improvement, too."

At Conner Creek, under a brilliant blue sky, with plumes of smoke lifting from the back of the orchard, Ash, leather lines in hand, walked behind the double-harrow drawn by a team of grays between the rows of peach trees. His boot heels sank deep in the pulverized soil, his back and shoulders ached from keeping the team on course between the trees and trying to prevent them from running off to the river. It was a tedious, mind-dulling job but necessary. Earlier in the spring he'd plowed under the cover crop of crimson clover. Keeping the soil well harrowed, until he planted another cover crop in mid-summer, created a constant top layer of fine mulch which held the earth's moisture deep where it belonged, at the roots of the trees.

Ten orchard rows to his left, three straw-hatted workers washed the trunks of trees with a lime-sulphur solution to protect the orchard from peach borers. The borer insect, he'd learned from his father, caused more trouble to an orchardist than any other insect or disease. At the back of the orchard, where the trees were much older, other workers were cutting out and burning those trees that had been killed by the borer.

Ash's mouth set in a grim, dusty line. Not that *he,* Ash, was meant to be an orchardist by any means. He was a damn fish out of water, a misplaced hotel owner and architect who spent far too much time in the canyon, and not enough with his business and personal concerns in Portland. Claudine was right that his answer was to insist Pop move with Ash to Portland, either live in Ash's hotel, or in a small cottage of his own, downtown.

What Claudine couldn't know was the impossibility of the task she asked for. She saw the canyon as the god-awful end of the earth, and she'd expect anyone to leap at the chance to leave it behind for life in the city. But the habitat she understood and loved was a way of life Pop had spent his life escaping, because he hated it.

If Pop had his way, they'd move to an area even more wild and remote. Would have done so already, if old age hadn't caught up with him.

Ash wasn't sure where time had gone this last year and a half. He'd put much of his own life on hold to spend time in the canyon with his father. Had intended to continue that way until his father passed on. Then, Ash had fallen for Claudine; they saw one another as much as possible when he was in the city. One evening, in a grand mood as they strolled the city before heading to the theatre and dinner, she showed him a ring she liked in a jeweler's window. Ash bought it for her the next day, and asked her to marry him. She wanted a wedding, wanted them to begin their life together as soon as possible. She and Ash should not postpone their own plans to pamper his father, she insisted, whenever Ash tried to explain how it was with Pop.

Ash couldn't remember dreading anything as much as the chore of telling his father that they were moving to the city. But it had to be done before summer ended, before Claudine returned.

A few evenings later, after supper, Ash decided not to put off the confrontation any longer. He sat with Tom on the veranda, catching the cooling breeze off the river. Ash brought them each a fresh cup of coffee with a dribble of whiskey and a little sugar in it, the way his father liked it, and waited for the drink to soften his father's mood. "Pop," Ash finally broke the companionable silence, leaning toward his father's wicker rocking chair, "Pop, I want you to move to Portland with me." Ash made his voice firm, with no room for debate, "We're going to sell this place."

Tom sat so still, a few feet away, Ash thought at first Tom hadn't heard, or that he'd stopped breathing. Had just up and died, maybe. Then Tom turned to stare at Ash, and his voice shook, "I ain't moving nowhere, and—and since this place actually belongs to me, I—I'll say if and when it will be sold."

In the gloom, Ash could see that there was fright in his father's faded eyes, and Ash felt suddenly sick. He couldn't give up, though, and he persisted, "I want to get married, Pop! And the chances of that happening are next to zero as long as we stay in this canyon. My true work is not here, either, in the damned orchard!"

"Nobody asked you to stay on here," his father was belligerent, beginning now to shake. "You can leave any damn time you want to."

"You're not young, anymore, Pop. You can't manage this place without me. I'm wasting my life away, here, and I want us to sell out."

"No, I say, no!" His father's voice was a croak, a wail.

"And I say we sure as hell are!" Ash gripped the arms of his chair and as he turned with determination he heard his father's small cry. Tom grabbed at his chest, toppled from the chair, and lay in a crumpled ball on the floor. Horrified, Ash could only stare in shock for a second, then he scrambled to where his father lay. "Pop," his hand cupped his father's face, "are you all right? Can you hear me? What happened?" Ash could see the pulse moving in his father's wrinkled throat, and one old eye opened just a slit to see Ash's reaction. "Dammit, Pop, are you all right? Are you in pain?"

He scrutinized his father as, wordless, but seeming all right, Tom sat up. Ash sighed in relief. The old man's eyes batted and he accused in a surprisingly strong voice, "You giving me a heart attack? Is that what you're trying to do?"

"No, hell no!" Ash shook his head. He studied his father intently for another minute or two. The old man breathed normally, there was no grimace of pain. The sudden attack was a put on, but the tears flowing from his father's faded eyes and pooling in the crinkles at the corners of his mouth were real. Ash felt like he'd been stabbed in the heart. He ran his fingers through his hair and knelt by his father's side. "It's all right, Pop," he said, rubbing his father's bony shoulder, "We're not going anywhere. Forget I mentioned it. We'll figure out something else, but don't worry."

Claudine would just have to understand. The trouble was, she could be as adamant in what she wanted, as Pop was. Leaving *him,* Ash thought—a string a cusswords choking in his throat—in the middle without answers.

As the days wore on, Laila, occasionally with Tansy's help, spent hours picking up driftwood along the river's edge, and chopping out good-sized trunks of sagebrush from up on the hillsides. It was hard work that left Laila's muscles tingling and sore, her fingers blistered. She reminded herself ruefully from time to time she was only temporarily impoverished, her fortunes would change. In the meantime, she was slowly toughening up and bit by bit learning the ways of primitive life in the canyon.

One day a movement a few yards up the slope from where Laila and Tansy had come to gather wood took their attention. Laila gasped at sight of the large tawny cat as it fed on the freshly torn and bloody carcass of a tan doe. Her stomach churned. She wanted to run, but another slight movement, to her left, made her turn her head slowly. A half-grown fawn stood nearly invisible in the brush-choked gully a few feet away. Tansy had seen, too, and they both stood frozen. Not knowing what to do, Laila's fingers were wrapped tight around a piece of wood. Her heart went out to the fawn which was now motherless thanks to the cougar.

A breeze eddied around Laila and Tansy, and the large cat must have caught their scent. The tawny head rose and turned their way. Then the cougar began to slink backward, turning finally to lope out of sight behind some sagebrush. Later a flash of movement, streaking gold, brought Laila's gaze upward. "There," she whispered to Tansy, pointing. The cougar seemed to be floating away up the mountainside, into the granite rocks.

"The little fawn's gone from the gully, too," Tansy whispered.

Laila looked and nodded. She prayed the beautiful little deer wouldn't be the cougar's next meal.

The very next morning Laila had a feeling of being followed as she made her way back to the cabin from the creek with a bucket of water. Very slowly and with her heart in her throat, she turned. The fawn she'd seen the afternoon before trailed in her tracks. Laila went weak with relief; a strange, almost motherly warmth filled her chest.

When she held out her hand, the fawn stopped. When Laila moved again, smiling, the fawn scuttled away up the gulch on thin, stick-like legs. Later that day, Laila got three dried apricot halves and placed them on a log near where she'd spotted the fawn following her. Then she sat in the cabin doorway and waited for the fawn's return. Though she sat quietly while the winds rustled up the lonely canyon and evening birds sang mournful songs, she didn't see the fawn again that day. Next morning the apricots were missing, but she knew that any number of mountain creatures might have gotten off with them.

Hutton Ginther came every now and then with a request for Laila's assistance in his shop, but she thought he also came to the cabin for company, and to help her learn whatever difficult, outdoor task faced her. The perfect gentleman, he came in the daytime and stayed for only short periods, visiting with her in the cabin yard while Tansy played nearby.

While they sat opposite one another on boulders in the shade thrown by the spindly trees, he sometimes told her about his childhood in Australia, where he'd been born. Stories about animals, flowers, and people different from those found anywhere else on earth. Yellow wattle blossoms, gum trees, the kangaroo, platypus, the koala, the native people—aborigines, all had fascinating parts in his tales. "Every rice in the world lives there," he told her, and by now she knew he meant, "every race."

His parents had owned several thousand acres of land where they raised sheep; he called it a station rather than a ranch or farm. The property had gone to his older brother when their parents died. Hutton had come to America to seek adventure, a fortune of his own making, then had fallen back on the simple trade of wheelwright he'd learned in Australia as a young man from an employee of his father's.

"As a boy, I was never in a town larger than Kalgoorlie, a gold town in the southern part of western Australia," he told her one time almost proudly, stroking his long silvery moustache. "And to this day I have no use for cities, I don't." She was reminded of Ash Corbett's father, Tom, when he went on to say, "Aye, I came here to the Snake River canyon to get away from all the fuss and ruckus of the outside world. Too many people out there for me. Besides," he chuckled, "don't need the city. I've got all the business I can handle, I do. Roads in the canyon and up in the mountains break up wagons almost as fast as I can repair or build them."

"And of course the miners and ranchers must have wagons to transport what they can't carry horseback or by pack mule. You've an important business, Mr. Ginther."

"Sy, you been doing a bite-iful job for me!" he complimented her. "We work very fine together."

"We do." Laila smiled and nodded.

One day, when he suffered a nasty cut on his hand at the wagonshop, she cleaned and bound it for him.

Looking down at her, he said, "You have a gift, Miss, you do."

She laughed softly. "I only bound your hand, anyone could have done it."

"You're a very special young lady," he insisted, "I'm thinking you really don't know it, though."

She nodded thanks for the compliment and let it pass.

Over her protests that she could do for herself, *must* learn to manage on her own, he brought her fresh trout, elk roast, and venison steak. On her own she found a patch of healthy blackberry vines and a graceful elderberry bush growing near her creek. Possibly they had been planted by an earlier resident of her cabin. With visions of delectable pies, jellies, and wine in mind, she gathered the small juicy blackberries, and clusters of purple elderberries, always keeping an eye out for the cougar that roamed the mountain.

She returned the wheelwright's favors with jars of jelly. Next thing she knew, he was bringing bundles of woodscraps from his shop for her stove, although driftwood and sagebrush limbs she'd herself cut were already stacked neatly to the eaves of the cabin. With Tansy looking on, and retrieving a tool or nails as necessary, Laila made a bench, with back and arms, from part of Ginther's scrap lumber. It was crude carpentry, she'd hammered her own thumb in the process and hopped about howling with pain for a full minute, but the bench would serve and Laila was quite proud of it. Tansy and she hauled the creation inside and padded it with a blanket. The padded bench was used as a settee during the day, and as a bed for Tansy, when more and more, she began to spend the night. Laila built a second bench, this time without hurting herself, and sparing more pennies for nails from Desper's store. The bench was backless, again crude but serviceable, and intended to hold her wash-tubs outside.

Coming in most handy was knowledge remembered from the old days of scavenging, making do—or even—doing without. Every small accomplishment added to her confidence and she applauded herself with the private thought that city women without the struggles that she had had wouldn't be able to manage half as well.

The wheelwright's visits helped dispel the loneliness of living so far from civilization. Laila knew he liked her. Often she'd find his eyes on her in shy appraisal as they worked in the shop or when he visited the cabin. She hoped he wasn't getting the wrong idea about her, that they'd make some kind of "match." She cared for him only as a friend, she didn't want to encourage him toward something that could never be.

She kept their conversations friendly but casual, telling him one day as they sat in her yard about the fawn that had become a regular visitor. "He never comes closer than over there," she pointed to the far side of the cabin yard. "I have long conversations with the creature, feed it special treats I can ill afford, but Tansy and I have come to love the little thing."

"Oh, sy," he told her, setting his coffee cup on a stump, a

frown of sympathy clumping his silver brows, "I'm going to get you a cat, for a pet, in Boise, next time I go for supplies."

She told him about the cougar, then. He nodded with a worried scowl, "Aye! There's mountain cats in these parts, all right. You be careful." He studied her, his expression perplexed. "You don't fit this place at all, Miss Mitchell. Every time I come up here, I expect to find you dead, kidnaped, hurt or something. I'm sorry to paint such a scary picture for you, but really, it's bloody dangerous your being here. If you got kin, you ought to go to them, let them take care of you."

Her recent feelings of accomplishment faded that he didn't see her more capable than that. "Heavens, what about Tansy? If she can survive in the canyon, surely a grown woman can. I'm not fragile or delicate, Mr. Ginther, if that's how you see me." He was as bad as Ash, or Kate, believing she couldn't take care of herself. She told him she had no kin, except her grandparents and they might be dead, but she was happy where she was for now. When he'd gone back down the hill, she set herself to building a snare, a trap for small game animals, similar to those she and Papa used to build long ago in Kansas. It took three tries before the trap was as she wanted it, but when she was finished she had a feeling of "so there!"

There were rabbits and quail on the sagebrush hills; wild ducks and geese down at the river. She was surrounded by a veritable feast, if she could find ways to trap the birds and game. Her cabin was free, most of whatever money she earned—however she might earn it—and after repaying Desper for her charges at the store, could be saved toward the mystery of her future.

Laila was down at the river's edge one afternoon, up to her elbows in blood and fishy slime from cleaning the small salmon she'd just caught. At a noisy clatter of river rock she expected to see Tansy but instead she looked up to see an erect, broad-shouldered rider in blue denim coming toward her from the direction of Venture.

Ash Austin Corbett. He'd come back. Her heart did a crazy dance in her breast. She stood up slowly, aware how unwomanly and wild she looked, how unfit for sociability. She'd cut and sewn the simple unbleached muslin shift she wore, herself. Chose the 'Mother Hubbard' style so she might feel cooler and unencumbered in hot weather. Lack of enough fabric resulted in embarrassing exposure of her bare ankles. A tangle of dark hair blew into her eyes. She brushed the lock back with the cleanest part of her arm, and still felt a wet brush of slime on her temple. She wasn't really surprised that the peach rancher had returned. He simply hadn't been convinced she was a capable woman and she intended to stay where she was. Or had he thought some terrible tragedy had befallen her by now? And he'd come to bury her remains?

Chapter Seven

"Mr. Corbett," Laila called with a smile, "Hello." She was inordinately pleased to see him, way beyond good sense or reason. The weeks since his last visit had passed like an eternity. Her face heated as she knelt again at the water's edge to quickly splash her arms and hands. Doing her best to control her odd, runaway feelings, she shook silvered water drops into the wind and strode to meet him. She wondered as she went what he carried this time in the basket resting on his thigh, the basket handle held in the thick masculine grip of one hand while the other reined the horse to a halt.

"How is Kate?" she asked him, the only thing she could think of to say at the moment. She would argue him down, later, if he was here to try and drag her out of the canyon.

"Mrs. Boston is fit as a fiddle, well over that accident she had in Boise. Thanks in the main to you, she says."

Laila shrugged, and smiled.

"She says to tell you that she'll come along with me another time, when she's finished putting up fruit and vegetables. You two can have a nice long visit." He went on, "I couldn't ask for a better housekeeper, and the lady is a fantastic cook." He scratched his stubbled chin and finished in deep, masculine hardpan, mischief shimmering in his eyes, "When she comes around to admitting that Oregon peaches are far superior to those grown in Missouri, we can say Mrs. Boston is about perfect."

"And your father, how is he?"

"Ornery as ever."

Laila laughed. He handed down the basket to her and she

lifted the lid to see a dozen or so rosy peaches. He told her, "Early Elbertas, that's the name of them. Only a few have ripened so far." He removed his hat, his eyes crinkling as he wiped perspiration from his brow.

"My goodness, thank you!" A peachy aroma met Laila's nose from the basket and she leaned to sniff deeper. "Mmm! I do thank you."

"No thanks needed." He planted his hat back on his handsome head, and drawled, "Hot enough to fry an egg on sand today, isn't it?"

She nodded, waiting to see if he had more to say. The sound of any human voice was welcome in the desolate canyon, but she found Ash Corbett's slow, soft-spoken speech especially nice. She wished he'd keep talking. He loafed in the saddle, though, looking back at her for so long she felt a deeper flush creep into her cheeks. "What's brought you down canyon, Mr. Corbett? Surely you didn't come all this distance to deliver these peaches?"

"Since I was coming this way on *road business,*" he said with concerned disgust, "Kate asked me to visit you so I could let her know how you're making out."

The way he growled, "road business" aroused her curiosity, along with a faint, nonsensical disappointment that his main reason in coming there hadn't been to see her. "There's hardly a road here, I don't understand—?"

He nodded and explained as he dismounted, "I was elected by some other county ranchers to make a report on the Snake River road up above us, such road as was built a couple years ago. Traveling the high grades is to sign your death-warrant, almost. We're tryin' to get old Smoothbore Struthers, the county judge, to part with some of the taxpayer's money for road building and improvement. Some stretches I found impassable for a wagon, other places there is no more than six inches of leeway to going over a precipice." His lips tightened and his eyes flashed, "Homesteaders and miners coming into this country deserve better from the elected officials."

"Yes, they do." Laila nodded. She'd heard talk in the Thornhall store that the Snake River country's potential could only be developed with better roads and additional railroads. Some swore that was never going to happen. Personally, she would hate to see the canyon's rugged beauty ruined, but people did need a safe way to come and go.

"Mr. Corbett, I have a fresh salmon back there on the riverbank. If you'd like to stay for supper—?" She hoped he wouldn't turn her down this time.

The corners of his eyes crinkled under thick, neat brows. "Name's *Ash,*" he said, "and thanks for the invitation." With reins in hand, leading his horse, he followed her to where her fish lay on the wet rocks by the river. "Nice catch."

"Yes." She beamed as she leaned over the silver beauty. She slipped her fingers into the rosy cavity below the gills. With her other hand she grabbed her homemade fishing pole, a gift from Ginther, and led the way from the river.

They headed up the hill, her trail through the cheat grass and sage now worn to creamy dust. She was acutely aware of Ash, behind her. She didn't welcome these strange, giddy new feelings he caused in her—which had no future. But she was glad he had agreed to stay for a meal; she would enjoy his company.

At the cabin, she lay the fish on the bench outside by the door and, wiping her hands on her apron, turned to Corbett, who was tying his horse to one of her spindly little trees. "If you're not in a hurry, Mr. Corb—*Ash,* I'll cook the salmon out here. Roast some fillets over hot coals in the firepit."

"I'm in no hurry, and I'd like to sit a spell." He added with a grin, "After the trip I've made the past few days, I feel near jolted to pieces." He stretched, muscles rippling beneath his sweat-darkened shirt. He seemed almost as tall as her twin trees.

Laila tore her glance away and headed to the cabin to get a chair for her guest. Inside, Tansy was curled up, asleep, on the settee. She suffered from a mild summer cold, but even more doted on the special attention Laila gave her. Laila tiptoed back outside where she found Corbett squatted down on his boot-heels, arranging sticks of wood in her firepit. "Mr. Corbett, I would've built the fire. . . ."

He ignored her and went about his business as she stood over him. With hands on her hips, she watched his long tan fingers readjust the kindling, before lighting the wood from a block of matches he took from his vest pocket. The lucifer fouled the air for a full minute, then the flame caught and Ash added two more small logs. He stood up and looked at her. Both of them were silent, breathing in unison, studying one another.

Laila moved first. "Let's sit a while, 'til the fire burns down and the coals are just right." She hurried to a flat-topped boulder that Ginther helped her lug home in her wheelbarrow one day. Normally the big rock served as a table for her wash basket when doing laundry, the tubs taking up the bench. Smoothing the rough muslin of her dress, gesturing politely, she offered her guest the chair planted in her dirt yard.

Ash poked at the fire, then sat down. He leaned forward, elbows on his knees, and looked around. "My father made my mother miserable holding her to hard, wild places like this. You must hate it. Surprises me you're still here."

So that's what was behind his insistence that she wouldn't like it there, *his mother*. She hadn't liked it, so why would

Laila? She tucked her naked feet further from sight. "This is a beautiful place, I like it. Why wouldn't I want to be here, stay a long time, if I choose to?"

"Pretty country, yes," he agreed. "But the livin' is rough, sometimes downright hell." He stared into the fire, then across at her, his brow furrowed. "Kate says she doesn't know much about you, that you don't talk a lot about yourself." He picked up a stick, and with a pearl-handled pocketknife peeled the bark away to greenish-white. "Not to pry," he ground out solemnly, "but you're not living close to the bone just because you found beautiful country." His eyes met hers in a wait for her to explain.

"I'm here of my free will, and I don't know that anything else is important."

She gave him the same brief story she'd told Kate about her past: she was born in Kansas, her parents died when she was a girl; she'd been employed as a practical nurse the last few years to an elderly man in St. Louis. She came west hoping eventually to locate her grandparents. "I'll spare you rest of the boring details of my history. In any event, I'm getting along here in the canyon." And her future wasn't engraved in granite. She might not always stay here and she might not always be alone.

"Miss Mitchell—"

"Laila," she corrected.

He shook his head, skepticism in his dry chuckle as he reached over and stirred the fire with his peeled stick. "People come to remote country like this for a good many reasons. Maybe they want solitude, or they come hoping to regain their health away from the city. Some bring money with ideas for adding to their wealth through mining, or raising cattle. More are poor and destitute and looking for a new life, especially now with the depression going on.

Normally, I mind my own business. Where people come from and why isn't my affair. But you're a refined lady, however you've made your living in the past, any fool can see that." He went on to state what he saw as not only strange but impossible, "You came here alone with no one to look out for you."

"Yes, I did." She found it remarkable that he saw her as refined, too delicate for the life she'd picked, and her mind stumbled on that. He obviously believed, as did most of society, that the only way a woman, a *lady,* could be safe and happy was to have a man look after her. Which was balderdash. The trouble was, women were rarely given a fair trial, a chance to manage anything other than a home. For a woman to be her own boss and do what she wanted was unthinkable to most minds.

Ash was telling her in an earnest growl, "If you don't starve to death first, a hell of a lot worse can happen to you. I could have kicked myself for letting you leave my place at all. You could have stayed on the ranch, helped Kate if you wanted. You didn't have to come on down here. Minding my own business is one thing, standing back and allowing a woman to get hurt, maybe even lose her life, is quite another. That's something no decent man would want on his conscience."

She spirits sagged with unwelcome disappointment that he saw her in no way personal to him, other than as a probable accident he didn't want to be blamed for. And he was remembering his mother's unhappiness. Perhaps he knew other women who wouldn't like the canyon but that had nothing to do with her. She shook her head, smiled stiffly. "I appreciate your concern, I really do—Ash. But I'm capable of looking out for myself." For goodness sakes, he was worse than Mr. Ginther! Were they cut from the same cloth?

"I've been thinking about you ever since you came to my

place with Kate. I came here to tell you that I'll take you anywhere you want to go that's civilized."

She wanted to tell him that she would leave in her own good time but he wouldn't let her get a word in as he held up his hand for her silence and went on, "I'll make you a loan if you're in need of funds and if that's the only way you'll accept help." He looked at her, then back at the fire, eyes squinted as the smoke curled upward in front of his face. "Baker City is a fine town. I was just there. The population is ten thousand folks and growing. Not just a mining town, Baker City is stable and you could likely find decent employment. Twenty hotels, schools, churches, more department stores than you can count."

His offer held some appeal. But how to tell him that with each day she was getting more used to living in the canyon, that she loved the beauty of the place? She took pride in fending for herself, treasured her freedom. When the time was right she would leave. But she would not borrow—and be beholden to Ash who saw her as a helpless charity case. Again she tried to interrupt, to explain, but he went on, "All right, Huntington, then. It's a little smaller, but a good town, right on the Union Pacific railroad."

"Please, Mr. Corbett! Ash—" she protested. "I'm not going anywhere, but thank you for your offer to—to—" she waved her hand, "get me out of here. I am not leaving." At times she felt the place might hold something special for her. Some wonderful, life-affirming, *something*. Independence, self-reliance, peace of mind, her own brand of happiness, for starters. She wasn't sure he would understand, nor did she understand totally, but she felt that she followed a mysterious treasure map of life, the end of the road not clear, but a journey that certainly should not be abandoned halfway, not now.

She said only, "I'm getting along quite well, really." She stood up, her smile a bit grim. "Excuse me, Ash," her bare foot patted the dust, "I need to go inside and peel some potatoes to fry. Go ahead and thread the salmon on the spit, if you will."

He didn't like that she'd dismissed the conversation, she could tell, but he got up to do as he was asked, mumbling at her back, "You're determined to stick it out on this dirt hill, then?"

She told him over her shoulder, skirt in hand, "Yes, Ash. For now, that's what I intend to do." She hesitated before going in. "Stir the coals, please. I'll bring you a cup of coffee while you see to the salmon." She smiled at him again, watched a slow red fill his face in reaction to her assertive manner.

Ash stared at the closed cabin door. *Damnable snippity woman! Did she think he was nosing into her private affairs because he took pleasure in it? Hell, he was trying to save her pretty neck since she didn't seem to have the sense to do it herself.*

In his mind he still saw her slender figure—her exceptional beauty in spite of the crude dress and his whole body began to heat up.

"Hell's Bells!" Remembering Claudine, his intended wife, he turned his attention to the fire with a tinge of guilt. He stirred the coals until a cloud of crimson and gold sparks shot several feet into the air. Finally, he calmed, but still wondered, *what on God's green earth was this gorgeous hardheaded woman all about?* And why did he care? Given that he was already betrothed to a woman who was everything he wanted and suited him in every way, and who would be his as soon as he untangled the problem of his father?

Laila hummed under her breath as she peeled potatoes.

When the skillet was full, with bacon grease from morning added, she took it out to Corbett to put on the edge of the coals. Ignoring the oddly stormy look he gave her, she returned inside to make a salad. One day at the river she had found greens growing at the water's edge. They reminded her of watercress. Mr. Ginther said that they might be cress, or peppergrass. They both decided the green plant was safe to eat. It turned out to be quite tasty and she had the greens often with a dressing of oil and vinegar. Now she mixed them with a little wild onion and a bit of carrot. The French, who first introduced salads in their fine Paris restaurants, would be impressed, she thought.

Seeing that Tansy was awake and starting to sit up, she asked her, "Would you like to come outside and meet Mr. Corbett, my guest? He's building up the campfire and we're going to cook a salmon for supper, doesn't that sound good?"

"Can I just have soup?" Tansy asked, rubbing her eyes. "I don't want to see nobody." She lay back down, wriggling to show how comfortable she was. "I like it here, in our cabin." Tansy loved her clean bed, loved having a clean dress, perhaps had caught cold from all the hair washing and bathing in the river of late.

Laila laughed softly and went over and felt Tansy's forehead and cheeks with the back of her hand. "You don't seem to have a fever, honey. I'll warm you some leftover soup, if that's what you really want. But I think your problem is that you're just shy around strangers. If you change your mind and want to come join us, please do."

"Thank you, Laya. I'll have soup."

Laila warmed the soup and was heading out with the bowl of salad when she nearly ran into Ash at the door. He was looking past her shoulder at Tansy who was sitting up in her small bed with a bowl in her lap and taking large bites of bread in-between spoonfuls of soup. Ash's blue eyes were rounded in surprise and question.

"Ash, I'd like you to meet my little friend, Tansy Sellers, who recently came to live with me. Tansy, this is Mr. Corbett, our guest I was telling you about."

Ash was a few seconds recovering, and then he smiled, "Hello, Tansy. Want to come outside and eat with Miss Mitchell and me?" He nodded toward the outdoors.

Tansy had stopped eating and looked at Laila in a panic. "You don't have to come out, if you don't want to, honey," Laila told her and Tansy visibly relaxed. She didn't continue eating, though, until Ash returned outside.

Laila followed him, and explained about Tansy. "She's staying abed because she has a bit of a cold. She's a sweet little girl, very wild when I first came here, but slowly she's come to trust me. We're good company for one another. Next time you come—" she blushed, and continued, "if you come again, she'll be more friendly. It's just that she's shy with people, at first, and because of how she's been treated, she's not sure who to trust."

"Nice of you to take her in," Ash said, when Laila explained that Desper Thornhall's wife had wanted to deliver Tansy to an orphanage over in the valley. "She's a lucky little girl."

"I'm glad you stopped by, Ash," Laila told him as they ate salmon, fried potatoes, and salad, from plates held in their laps. "It's nice to have company now and then." In the shrub by the creek, a bird opened a mournful song to day's end, and was joined in trilling chorus by another chirper.

Using her flapjack turner, Corbett shoveled more fried potatoes from the skillet onto his plate. "I'd have come more often if I'd known I'd be eating food like this. Don't tell

Kate," he added with a grin that made her heart skip. He took in a mouthful and his intense blue eyes rolled in pleasure, the muscles of his strong jaw worked under his tan skin. If he was still angry that she'd turned down his offer to get out of the canyon, it didn't show—and he was eating like there was no tomorrow.

"Tell me about your peach orchards, Mr. Cor—Ash, they looked perfectly lovely when I stopped there with Kate. Has the ranch been in your family a long time?" She ignored the itching of a mosquito bite on her ankle, a lady didn't scratch in front of company and she hadn't turned pure heathen, yet.

He nodded, taking a moment to finish a bite. "My father planted the first trees. The ranch was the last place he settled, trying to get away from the rest of the world."

Though she would have little of account to tell him about herself, Laila felt a strong curiosity regarding Ash's background. In a strange way, he seemed to both *fit* the canyon, and stand out from it at the same time.

He took a long draught of his coffee and set the cup on the ground. "Dad was born back east in the New Hampshire mountains, a fiddle-foot who couldn't stay put for long. From the first he wanted to go west. Had to work his way across country. His and my mother's paths crossed in Indiana. He'd been employed as a carpenter, was helping to build a church. The latter certainly put him in my mother's good graces. Besides, he had a way about him back then, and he was a handsome devil—"

Not unlike his son. "He still is."

"More old devil than handsome!" Ash grunted, causing Laila to laugh. He went on when she motioned him to continue, "My mother, Phoebe, was probably much too good for my father. Her family was well off. Her father and grandfather owned the largest hotels in Terre Haute, Valparaiso, and

Gary, Indiana. She could have done better, but once she laid eyes on my father she didn't give any other man a chance." He fell silent.

Laila took a sip of coffee, waited. Crossed her ankles and slyly scratched one foot against the other.

"My grandfather, my mother's father, set the newly married couple up in the hotel business, a nice but small hotel on the outskirts of Indianapolis. My father hated every aspect of running that hotel. Disliked people coming and going all the time, the business end of it, too. I was born there. I was a tad when the hotel burned down." He looked at her, the campfire dazzling a reflection in his eyes. "Even as a youngster, I suspected my father burned that hotel on purpose." He ignored Laila's gasp, and told her, "It happened at a mighty convenient time, when almost everyone from the hotel was away at a Fourth of July celebration. The few people who hadn't gone to the celebration easily escaped."

Laila made a small sound of disbelief and shook her head. "Surely, your father didn't—?"

"I'm positive that my mother believed he did," Ash went on, "for all the evidence that showed it was an accident. Anyway, seeing how desperate my father was to get away, my mother gave in and came west with him, though it must have been hard for her to leave her home."

"She didn't like it, out west?"

"She might've, if we'd stayed in one place for any length of time. My father homesteaded here in Oregon more than once. If anyone moved within ten miles of him, he'd pull up stakes and move on, afraid somebody would ruin his deer hunting. That's how he was; she could never seem to tame him. Made his living—" He stopped suddenly, looking at something over her shoulder. "The hell—!" he said huskily.

She turned to see and laughed softly. "Shh. That's our

fawn. He comes to visit every few days. Growing up fast, he is. Go ahead, he won't mind us. Later, I'll put the rest of our salad out for him. Don't know if he'll eat the potatoes."

Ash looked aghast. "You feed 'im? You should see what those little devils do to my orchard! I spend half my time runnin' 'em off so they don't chew the trees to the ground."

She shrugged. "They can't hurt anything here, I don't have a garden. I love to watch the wild deer." The only deer she'd seen before coming to the canyon had been one time at the zoo in St. Louis's Forest Park. "You were telling me about your folks—" she urged him on with a warm smile.

"Yeh. Well, my dear Poppa made his living by improving land, when he wasn't off hunting and fishing. Soon as a place was half livable, he'd sell out to somebody else and go off to prove up another homestead, more primitive than the last."

"And your mother—?"

"As much steel as she had in her backbone, she could only tolerate so much of dad's itinerant way of life. She'd come from something much finer, easier, and it was waiting, back in Indiana. When I was about sixteen years old, she told Pop she couldn't take any more."

His face shadowed as he went on, "The two of us returned to her old home. I don't think she ever stopped loving my father, and that was the tragedy of it all. She couldn't have adjusted to his way of life if she'd stayed a hundred years. She was beautiful, cultured, proud. She saw that I got an education back east."

He looked at Laila, hard. She had the feeling he was again comparing her to his mother, and he was so wrong, she was nothing like that, refined, cultured, used to a soft life. She was nothing like *him.* He seemed desperate for her to backtrail, to return to where she'd come from before something terrible happened and he'd feel to blame. His mother's unhappiness must have bothered him all of his life, affected him still. But she and his mother were different people. There was no niche in fine society waiting for her, no other home at all.

"People want different things, have different dreams, Ash. We're not all cut from the same cloth." He had judged her from appearance only, and from the fact that she was a woman. He knew little about her, really, what she was made of or how her past formed her. Nor was she ready to tell him—everything. For a long time, they sat in companionable silence, each with their thoughts.

"There's pie," she said suddenly, jumping up to refill his empty coffee cup. "And I need to see if Tansy needs anything." She hoped she hadn't discouraged Ash's visit, she was not ready for him to go. She brought out a golden-crusted wedge of pie oozing purple blackberry juice onto the plate. She held it out to him, "Unless you'd rather have sliced peaches? Tansy asked for both, a positive sign she's on the mend."

"Peaches? Are you joking? Just the pie, please."

Laila smiled to herself in satisfaction. His words were just what she wanted to hear. She wanted every last one of those peaches for herself and Tansy.

For the next hour or two, Ash and Laila discussed everything under the sun, or rather, under the climbing moon. Laila went inside to tuck Tansy in, and when she checked later, the child was asleep for the night. Back outside, a thousand brilliant stars filled the sky; a resin sweetness arose from hillside shrub. Firelight flickered, coals popped and whispered as Ash told Laila about the hotel in Portland that he left in the hands of capable help, that he needed to oversee only now and then. She talked of books she'd read in her room at night, from the Saugrain library, described original paintings by well-known artists, art she'd seen in the Saugrain home. She would have liked to have talked of plays and music but her life had been devoid of those. Now and then, they laughed together at one of his stories. Full dark came too soon.

"The hour is late, Mr. Corbett, you'll be wanting to find a place to stay," she told him finally.

"Good grief!" he exclaimed, pulling out his pocket watch and examining it by the light of the fire. "Where did the time go? I had no idea it was this late. Laila, I apologize. If anyone realizes I'm here so late—well, I hope there's no gossip."

"It's all right, Mr. Corbett—uh, Ash," Laila laughed softly. "You're right, in polite society an evening like we just spent would ruin my reputation for a lifetime. But this is a very different place, and I think that's one of the things I like about it. We did nothing wrong. I'm not worried, and you needn't be either." She was just glad to be where she was, who she was, with him, if only for an evening.

Ash stood up, tall frame unfolding slowly, stretching. "Okay, and thanks Laila, for a nice evening. I have a friend over at Venture who'll put me up for the night. Want to leave first thing in the morning so I'll say good-bye now." From the shadows where he'd tied his horse, he said, "You didn't get a real good look at my place when you were there. Come see Kate, and let me show you my peach trees, the whole operation. I'll put a muzzle on Pa if necessary."

"I'd love to! Tell Kate I'll come soon. And, Ash, I think I like your father a lot." She laughed. His laughter, echoing from down the trail, was more derisive.

Next morning Laila was dressed, had barely finished fastening the rope of her dark hair to the back of her head when Ash Corbett was back, pounding hard on her door. "Gracious, what is it?" she asked, taking in his dark, sober expression. A frown creased her own brow.

Chapter Eight

Ash's mouth was a tight white line, his voice raw-edged with feeling, "Found a man bad hurt off the trail as I was starting home around dawn. He was pinned under a tree he'd cut down for stove-wood. Brought him back to Venture to Thornhall's store. Don't know if he'll survive, it appears he was pinned for a day or two. Thornhall says you have a medicine kit. Can you get it and come with me?"

"Of course, just give me a minute." Laila turned to Tansy, who had dressed just moments before Ash's arrival, "There's warm oatmeal in the pot on the back of the stove for your breakfast, honey, and you may eat one of the peaches Mr. Corbett brought yesterday. Please wait for me here in the cabin. When you're finished with breakfast, you can wash our dishes and make your bed, and practice making your ABCs on the slate—remember how I showed you? I shouldn't be gone long."

Tansy confidently climbed on a chair for a small crockery bowl from the cupboard, while Laila found her bag of medical supplies and the little red medical guide, "First Help In Accidents" although, for lack of reading material she knew the book by heart. Looking forward to a time she might be called upon, she'd bought extra bandages and other medicinal items through the Venture store and had added them to her kit. She threw her brown shawl over her shoulders.

Ash took her elbow in a gentle grasp. "Hope you don't mind riding double on my horse, it's important to hurry. S'long, Tansy, be a good girl, and I'll bring Miss Mitchell back as soon as I can." Tansy was busy scooping oatmeal into her bowl but took a second to wave goodbye to them.

Outside, Ash helped Laila into the saddle. The billowing skirt of her mouse-gray work dress caused his horse to shift and snort nervously. "Whoa, fella, whoa there." Ash leaped up behind Laila, arms around her to control the reins.

The horse clambered down the rocky slope of the hill, sending a tan rabbit bounding across their path to cover elsewhere. Grasshoppers *chirred* into the air from the yellowed grasses and chokecherry bushes. Within minutes, Laila and Ash were making their way swiftly along the sandy riverside trail toward Venture. The gorge wind whipped Laila's cheeks. Her anxiety over what lay ahead was somehow eased by the strong arms encircling her.

Inside the general store, with Ash at her heels, Laila parted the small group of men and went to the injured miner who lay atop the main counter. His groans came in soft, animal-sounding sighs; he seemed to be hanging onto consciousness by a thread. His hair was matted with dirt and debris, his hands and clothes were stained with dried blood.

Laila smothered a gasp at sight of his mangled leg where his jeans had been cut open. There was a long jagged tear in the flesh and the leg, knee to hip, looked like a dark, fat sausage. Except for a fresh red seep at the main point of injury, his thigh was caked with dark blood mixed with pine needles, bits of bark, and dirt. Jagged ends of white bone protruded from the blood-crusted injury.

Dear God. She was expected—? Laila took several deep breaths, pushing uncertainty from her mind by strength of will. Her shock was followed by a deep wish, almost *eagerness* to help the man, be of good use. "I'll need soap and hot water to wash my hands and to clean his leg," she told Thornhall. She'd spotted Ginther in the corner of the room and she told him, "Mr. Ginther, in a few minutes I will need you, and one of the other men, to help hold the gentleman down, please."

As she took her scissors and cut away the remainder of his pants-leg, she further explained to the men, "I'm not sure the amount of laudanum I can safely give him will be enough to deaden the pain. We must hold him as still as possible while the bone is being set and the wound sewn up. Mr. Corbett—um, Ash, when I tell you, I'd like for you to gently but firmly pull the patient's leg down while I guide the broken splinters together."

He nodded that he understood. "If you need me for anything else let me know."

She asked as she lay out soap and cloths to cleanse the wound, "Does anyone know his name?"

"Joe Pelling," Mr. Thornhall, the grocer, told her in a voice thick with concern.

"Mr. Pelling, can you hear me? This will cause you pain but I'll take as much care as possible and do this as quickly as I can. Then we'll leave you alone."

In the next half hour Laila became so engrossed in what she was doing everything else faded from sight and mind. She washed the injured leg carefully with warm, soapy water; with pincers she picked out bits of debris from the wound. She spoke to the injured man in a gentle, encouraging voice with every move, "You'll be fine, Mr. Pelling. Try to lie still, please."

She nodded to Ash and Hutton Ginther when she was ready for their assistance. They stepped forward. The room grew quiet. She quietly repeated her earlier instructions. With her own jaw set, and a forced steadiness in her hands, Laila slowly and strongly guided the two ends of the broken bone together at the same time Ash drew gently and steadily on Pelling's leg. The grating sound seemed extraordinarily loud as the two roughened surfaces of the broken shaft were matched. The man let out a long raw moan of pain, but seemed too weak to thrash much, and the stronger men held him.

Tears for his pain stung Laila's eyes but she quickly blinked them away. The ragged edges of the rest of his wound were red with infection but there was no sign yet, of gangrene, no grayish dead flesh. Ash, reading her mind as if they were a team, hurried to the stove centering the store and brought the thread and a needle that she had ordered sterilized in a pan over the grate.

Pelling had passed into unconsciousness. For a time that felt like an eternity, she could hear the men's heavy breathing behind her as she mended the torn flesh with slow, patient effort. Finally, she was able to swab the closed wound with cold water and bind it in clean white bandage.

"There," she said with a relieved sigh. "Now, we must splint the leg so it will remain rigid, the bone held together while it heals."

Under her direction, Ash and Ginther prepared splints of wood shingles, a shorter splint for the inside of his leg and longer for the outside. Pads of folded flannel were fitted between his bandaged leg and the wood splint. Pelling stirred but didn't try to rise or struggle.

By the time she was finished gently belting the splint to Pelling's thigh, Laila felt as exhausted as if she'd spent the day climbing mountains. Her insides felt quivery. She wiped her perspiring forehead on the back of her arm, made her voice steady as she spoke to the waiting men, "As bad as it is, I'm afraid his injured leg is the least of his troubles. He's lost blood and he is dehydrated from lack of water. . . ."

"We gave him a big shot or two of whiskey when Corbett, here, brought the feller in," Mr. Thornhall wheezed.

She nodded. "Good. Spirits will keep his system stimulated but aren't enough. He needs *water,* and nourishment from broth and soups to build his strength up if he's to heal and—live."

Rather than take Pelling back to his tent several miles upriver, a decision was made to let him rest a bit and then put him to bed in Desper Thornhall's cabin behind the store. Laila would be close at hand to attend Pelling for the several weeks it would take him to heal. Desper said, wrinkling his nose in a frown, "My wife, Opal, is due home from her sister's any day." He added stoutly, "She won't mind Pelling's bein' here." There was less conviction in his expression than in his words as he watched Laila.

"I'll be glad when your wife does come," she answered in soft abstract, as she carefully finished up, tucking a blanket around her unconscious patient. "It'll be so much nicer to have another woman close by." Scarcely aware she'd spoken, on shaky legs she went out to the store's porch to sit down. She rested her forehead on her arms folded across her knees. She felt sick to her stomach, and as though she had run a race without remembering to take a breath.

The world around her faded, she was not aware she was rocking back and forth until strong hands grasped her shoulders and held her still. Lifting her head, she saw that Ash Corbett knelt in front of her, deep concern and something more etched in the granite planes of his face. His broad chest looked strong, steady, very inviting. She fought the urge to throw herself into his arms and cry. She must be strong, herself, to continue this kind of work. She leaned her head back, closed her eyes.

She felt him still watching her. He caught both of her hands in his. "My God, look what this has done to you. Will you be all right?" She met his tender, protective gaze, and nodded. He looked less than convinced as he said, "You're white as a sheet. I'm so sorry. We shouldn't have left it up to you, but Thornhall said you wanted nursing jobs. He made out you have a medical background and would know what to do."

She breathed deep, managed a smile and steadiness in her voice. "He told the truth, I did ask for medical work. And I'm fine, I really am. I've had years of experience caring for illness, I know something about medicines—a very wise apothecary taught me, but this was my—" she shrugged. That she had had no true professional training and this was the first time she'd handled a serious wound was obvious, so why moan about it? There had been no one else around to take on the task.

Ash shook his head vigorously. "I'm not faulting how you handled the situation, you did a beautiful job setting and treating Pelling's leg. I can't imagine anyone doing any better. It just seemed to take a lot out of you and I wasn't sure you'd be all right—"

"I will be and I am." She continued to draw fresh, pine-scented air into her lungs. The world was righting itself again. She had a strong urge to leave her hands in Ash's comforting grip for as long as he was willing, but, flustered, she pulled them away. With a brush at her hair to tidy loosened tendrils, she stood up to go back inside to her patient. "Don't worry, Mr. Corbett—Ash. I *do* know what I'm doing."

Or did she?

"*Opal!* Mrs. Thornhall," Laila's temper snapped, "please put that blessed broom away!" Her shout caused poor Joe Pelling to start in his bed and she was instantly sorry for her uncharacteristic explosion. With his head barely off the pillow, he looked about in glazed confusion. Laila pushed him back gently, patted his shoulder, drew the quilt back up over his shoulders. Her face heated with guilt for losing her temper.

Desper's wife, Opal, a stout ash-blonde several years younger than Desper, had returned from the valley a day or two after Joe Pelling had been found hurt. From that moment, Mrs. Thornhall had attacked the cleaning of their home with a vengeance.

Laila couldn't believe she had yelled at the woman in her own home, even though she had good reason. Her patient, Joe Pelling, had only last night broken another infernal fever. She hoped finally to get the upper hand over the infection that raged in his body. He'd been about to drift off to sleep in response to his medication.

Across the room, Opal's round face was pinched with anger and disbelief below the scarf tied over her hair. Frozen in place, wearing a pink-checked gingham dress, she held her broom tight against her burgeoning apron front. "I have to clean, Miss Mitchell. Desper hasn't touched the place decently in all the weeks I've been gone. I don't know why you say I can't sweep." Her fleshy chin quivered and her eyes flashed. The small caramel and white terrier she'd brought home with her came to sit at her feet and whine in sympathy.

Opal had every right to be upset and to want to clean her home. At the same time, her cleaning methods could possibly kill poor Mr. Pelling. "Of course you're right," Laila agreed, her voice low so as not to disturb poor Pelling who looked to be drifting off again. "But there must be another way to sweep." *Not so vigorously for one thing.*

"Another *way?*" Opal's lip curled in question. "To sweep is to sweep." Her expression indicated that Laila was out of her mind. Marigold, the rat terrier, flopped down with her head resting on the toe of Opal's high-buttoned shoe and gazed at Laila accusingly.

"I know you don't mean harm, but you throw dust into the air," she told Opal gently, "bad dust." Every time Opal, Desper, or one of their visitors, or she, sneezed or coughed, thousands and maybe millions of streptococci were sprayed into the air. The good doctor who tended old Mr. Saugrain had taught her about such things. In Laila's mind, she could see the microbes floating, drifting, settling until the dirt-fighting Mrs. Thornhall sent them flying into the air again with her busy broom.

Laila was herself clean and efficient. She always washed her hands before treating Pelling. She used spotlessly white bandages. Until now she hadn't figured out how her patient was becoming constantly re-infected. Dust-borne germs had to be the answer.

She smoothed Pelling's pillow around his waxen-white face, and turned to tell Opal regretfully, "I shouldn't have yelled at you."

"You want the dirt just left to pile up?" There was deep disgust added now to the disbelief and anger in Opal's pale blue eyes.

"No, no, of course not," she said softly, "the dirt has to go, but I have an idea. Could you sprinkle damp sawdust on the floor before you sweep? That might contain the dust and keep germs from going every-which-way into the air. Maybe disinfectant could be added to the water to wet the sawdust? If you have some bleaching powder or carbolic acid that would do it. We'd all be better off," she encouraged.

Opal looked grievously insulted that her cleaning efforts practiced over a lifetime were regarded as less than exemplary, but she nodded. "I suppose I could do that if you think I have to."

"Really, I'm sorry for snapping at you and I'd like to explain further. Let's go in the other room and sit for a while, and have some tea. Could we?" Over tea a few minutes later, she spelled out in uncomplicated terms the dust/germ theory as she'd heard it from Ben Saugrain's doctor. "Of course you want your house clean, and Mr. Pelling's infections aren't really your fault. But we must do whatever we can to help him. The sooner we can get Mr. Pelling well, the sooner the both of us can be out of your way."

Opal's face brightened at the last remark and she nodded. She reached down to pet her rat terrier's head. "We do the best we can, don't we Marigold? But our house really is small, and *not,*" she said with emphasis, "meant to be a hospital." The terrier licked her hand, then cocked her head and looked at Laila with large expressive eyes.

Laila smiled. Another time she would like to convince Opal that the water dipper used by everybody who came into the store wasn't necessarily clean because it was in the *water* bucket and didn't *look* dirty. She'd heard that debilitating diarrhea was common thereabouts especially during the summer months. The drinking water ought to be boiled and the common dipper replaced with clean drinking cups.

"I need to be getting back to Tansy," Laila said, taking a last sip from her cup, "although for such a small child, she's very trustworthy when I have to be away." She caught Opal's deep frown, and hesitated at the door, "Is anything wrong?"

"I don't know why you'd want to take that dirty, wild ragamuffin in with you."

Laila turned slowly, "I beg your pardon?"

"That girl, that Tansy. She's an ungrateful whelp, nasty and mean. Every time I've tried to put a helpful hand to her, she's run away. Nearly kicked my shins to pieces when I tried to take her with me to Salem this past spring. Ran and hid, made me late for my departure. She'll grow up to be just like her mother, that tramp, Minnie Sellers, I vow. Ornery little scamp!"

Laila's jaw was tight as she fought to hold her temper, "I don't agree with you at all about Tansy, Mrs. Thornhall. She's very smart, she's catching onto her ABCs and learning to count very quickly. She does chores for me. She's a very good little girl who only needed loving attention. How was a child so small to adapt to her father's death, her mother's abandoning her? And having no one to truly care about her?" *Hauling her off to an orphanage isn't a sign of true caring.* "She's afraid, hasn't known who to trust. It wasn't simple for me to win her over."

Opal was adamant, "I still think you're making a mistake." Her nose twitched. "From what I gather, you're barely able to take care of yourself, Miss Mitchell. Why take on the extra burden? The girl must be fed, clothed, looked after. In your shoes, I'd be finding a husband to take care of *me.* But what man wants a woman who already has a child, someone else's child at that, and with the background Tansy Sellers' has?"

Laila had rarely been so angry. She said tightly, "Please don't concern yourself with my personal affairs, Mrs. Thornhall, or Tansy's, if it bothers you so. I love Tansy, I hope I never have to give her up. And I'm not looking for, nor do I need, a husband."

Opal Thornhall just shook her head, unconvinced.

Laila's backbone was rigid with fury all the way home.

In the days that followed, Laila determined to get along with Opal Thornhall if it killed her, but under no circumstance would she ever again let the woman bad-mouth Tansy so unfairly.

When Laila wasn't tending Pelling's injuries and infection, both of which were showing improvement, she helped Opal set her house to rights to the satisfaction of both.

Pelling's injuries continued to heal rapidly and he was more and more alert, and starting to eat with a grand appetite.

All seemed to be going well, until the day Laila was changing his bandages in the small bedroom and they heard a terrible commotion coming from Opal's kitchen. She was screaming, her little terrier yipped wildly, furniture crashed to the floor.

"*What the bloody hell?*" Pelling questioned. "Sounds like the damn world is ending."

"Wait here, I'll go see." Laila headed on the run to the headwaters of sound. Opal was standing on a kitchen chair shrieking her head off, springing up and down and shouting something that sounded like "get 'im." Laila watched open-mouthed as Opal leaped off the chair, scooped Marigold off the floor, opened the flour bin, and threw the little dog inside. She closed the bin and leaped back up onto the chair. A terrible thumping, bumping ensued from inside the flour bin. On the counter above, raw biscuits were rising in snowy rows on a floury board.

"Dear heaven," Laila asked, "what are you doing?"

Suddenly, the kitchen went quiet. The thumping in the cupboard ceased. With an expression of satisfaction and panting heavily, Opal got down from the chair. She opened the flour bin and lifted the dog—covered with flour and a mouse in its jaws, from the bin. "That's the end of that mouse!" she declared.

Laila sagged against the door frame. She really had to get out of this place. Thank heaven Pelling was ready for release. At the sound of giggles behind her, she saw that Tansy had been watching from the open kitchen door. Tansy's hand covered her mouth and her hazel eyes danced. Laila, bursting into laughter herself, ran to the door and caught Tansy in a hug, ignoring Opal's frown of disapproval.

Chapter Nine

Deep summer came to the Snake River canyon. The mountainsides, seared golden-brown by the sun, more than ever resembled the rippling scaly hides of gigantic beasts. Down in the bottom of the canyon where the few residents had their shacks, it was a baking oven for days on end, with only an occasional breeze off the river for relief.

One day at Thornhall's store, Opal handed Laila a rumpled and slightly dirty envelope addressed in her own handwriting to her grandparents at La Grande. The words, *Undeliverable as addressed* were scribbled across the face of it. Her disappointment was acute. For weeks she had looked forward to an answer from them, telling her they were alive and well and welcomed her into the fold of the family. She would take Tansy with her, the little girl would have grandparents . . .

Laila felt Opal's probing gaze, her curiosity wanting to know what the letter meant. She was afraid if she tried to tell her she would cry, and she didn't want to do that. Instead, feeling bereft, she made her selections in silence, paid cash, thanked Opal graciously and quietly, then left the store.

If only she could get away, maybe she could learn what had happened to her grandparents. She wouldn't give up hope completely, yet. They could be still living and had perhaps moved to another location and someone at La Grande could tell her where they'd gone. When she found them, she could tell them how her parents died; it would sadden them but they would want to know.

She reflected that she must face the very real chance that both grandparents were dead. But that was something she couldn't accept until she'd made her own search for them.

It was impossible to guess when she and Tansy might have an opportunity to leave the canyon and go to La Grande. After successfully treating Pelling, Laila was in almost constant demand for her nursing services. There seemed to be no one else willing or able to take on the medical problems that cropped up from time to time in the remote area; she had the most experience, knowledge, and willingness to simply use her commonsense in treatments. And she of course needed the work.

It was particularly hot and smelly inside the huge wall tent referred to as the "Ironstake Miner's Boarding House" on the hillside above Venture. Laila's dress and apron were soiled from men's vomit, her back ached from hours of nursing stooped over a half-dozen sick miners' cots and pallets. When she stood up, the sun beating through the canvas was like a hammer to her head.

"Mr. Riley," Laila addressed the mine boss, who'd entered the tent moments before and hulked over her like a bad-humored grizzly bear, "your men have food poisoning and are very badly off." She wiped her hands on a clean cloth she'd brought. "I've spoken with them and to be precise, tainted meat—venison—has made them deathly ill." Worn down as she was, she could scarcely contain her anger over what had happened, her disgust with this man's infernal attitude. The only thing that seemed to matter to him was the break-down in mine operation.

"How long they going to be down? Days, hours? Do I need to be looking for new help?" he'd wanted to know. In other words, *would any of them die and cause him to lose money and time?* She stared at him, and strived to bring her anger under control.

Close up, the skin of Hobart "Hob" Riley's concave face was pitted and scarred, his features hard. His brown canvas pants and khaki shirt were too clean for the kind of man who worked directly with his men. His manner toward her was as superior and brutish as ever.

She didn't expect him to apologize for his earlier rudeness to her, when she'd gone to him seeking work as a cook or laundress. She accepted that hiring her services now would be the limit of respect she'd see from him. What she couldn't understand was how he could worry more over the workings of his darn-fool mine than the personal welfare, the lives, of his men. Who did he think really ran his mine?

She slapped an insect biting the side of her sweat-sticky neck. "If you'd supplied your men with fresh meat, they'd be at their jobs now. It'll be days before any of them can be back on their feet and able to work. We're lucky the rancid meat didn't kill them."

She had dosed each man with a sharp emetic of calomel every fifteen minutes until she was sure the offensive contents of their stomachs were completely ejected. Two of the men, faint and near death when she came, had fallen into a worrisome sleep and she was afraid they might not come out of it. Her glance kept turning their way. The others still twisted and moaned in agony in spite of warm flannels, the mustard poultices she had applied over the site of their severe pain.

"Well, hell!" The nostrils of Hob Riley's broad nose flared. "The deer ain't come down to the low hills for winter, yet," he excused himself. "I couldn't spare nobody to go huntin' so far up after 'em, shorthanded like I've been, and—now!" He threw up his hands and his ebony eyes glittered as his glance swept over the beds of ailing men. He swore darkly. "We had meat, dammit! Cook figured the venison we had in camp was all right. Supposed to last 'til the weather turned cold, 'til it snowed up high and the deer and elk herds moved down to graze the lower levels."

"I was told that two hindquarters of venison had hung for weeks in hot sun here in your mine camp. Maggoty as I hear the meat was, I doubt the kill was properly dressed in the first place! Great God, Riley, couldn't you have bought beef, or fed your people potatoes? Anything but rotted meat? What about fish? The river swarms with salmon, and sturgeon."

"We fed the men fish, too. And," he waved a blunt finger in her face, "you are bein' paid to get these men back on their feet, not to wag your tongue at me, Miss!" With a last scouring look at her, he flung his bulk out of the tent.

She ran after him. "These men are severely weakened. It will take decent food to make them strong again!" She added in a fierce whisper, "I'll get them well and on their feet, but it will be for them not for you, Mr. Riley!" At a sound, she turned. One of the men tried to sit up, shoulders heaving, and she ran for the bucket just emptied.

As she had with Joe Pelling and his crushed leg, Laila saw to the poisoned miners until she was sure of their recovery. In the end, Hob Riley paid her well in cash for her time and services, but never voiced thanks, or appreciation. Business, with him, was business.

Whenever possible, Laila took Tansy with her on her nursing rounds. They had seen a half-starved Sparta family of newcomers—a man, his wife, and three sons—through a bout of scurvy. Laila had treated them with sugared lemon juice, bed rest, and all the calcium-rich potatoes she could get down them. She had extracted three abscessed teeth for an elderly bachelor prospecting on Herman Creek. He had anesthetized himself with a generous dose of whiskey. A wizened rancher from across the river, up on the Idaho rims in the Windy

Ridge area, had come for her by boat to attend his wife who had sliced her leg while scything hay. By a narrow margin the woman hadn't bled to death, her husband had the presence of mind to apply cold water and pressure to stop the bleeding. But, later, infection had set in and days of applying linseed meal poultices had been needed to draw the infection out.

Laila made her rounds by boat or wagon as called for, usually accompanied by the party hiring her services. Sometimes, her destination could be reached on foot. Other times she borrowed a mount that Hutton Ginther kept in a corral behind his wagonshop and rode double with Tansy, along narrow, treacherous trails to check on patients.

More than once in her past she had been in a position of desperate need, and she was glad to ease a person's pain, to help however she could. Seeing folks to recovery and renewed strength gave her brand new feelings of self-worth. Actual payment in gold dust, coin, or in goods, was simply a welcome bonus.

The few times Laila's trips took her to the vicinity of Conner Creek and Corbett's Ruby Gold Ranch, she went out of her way to visit. She enjoyed seeing Kate, and more and more, she looked forward to those brief occasions in Ash's company. He was a delightful host, he told wonderful stories that made her laugh, and he seemed equally glad to see her. Behaving almost like a young boy, he would dash through the orchard playing tag with Tansy; he would give her small gifts he'd found: an abandoned bird's nest, pretty stones from the river. Those good times added further richness to Laila's days.

Then one day, the atmosphere at Ash's peach ranch was very different. Laila, Kate, and Tansy were filling baskets with late-crop peaches for Laila and Tansy to take home with them. Laila rested a moment, tucked a tendril of hair behind her ear, and making furrows in the dirt with the toe of her boot, asked Kate, "Is there something bothering Ash? He seems awfully preoccupied this afternoon, he's hardly come out of his office. Do you think he minds our being here, Tansy and me?"

"Pshaw, no, he don't mind havin' you two around. Matter of fact, he's mentioned how much he enjoys it. He says your little Tansy is better behaved than his Pa, and a lot more fun! A blind man can see he's fond of you." Kate wiped her hands on her apron and smiled broadly, "And I'd say it's more than in a neighborly fashion how he sees you, Laila."

"That's nonsense, Kate." Laila's face warmed and she looked off into the distance. "You're imagining things." She turned again to face Kate, "But if it isn't our being here that bothers him, what is wrong?"

For a long time, Kate didn't answer, but went back to filling her basket, her usual placid face wrinkled in a frown. "You won't think I'm a snoop, or a gossip?" she asked after a few minutes, frown lines smoothing out but a look of red-faced guilt remaining.

"Goodness, no. I could never think badly of you, Kate." Laila scratched her elbow where an insect had bitten. She instructed Tansy in an aside, "Just pick the firm peaches, honey, the gold-pinkish ones that are only a little soft to the touch." She turned back to Kate, her head cocked to listen.

"From what I see," Kate began with a sigh, "Ash gets upset when *letters* come from a lady. Name on the envelopes is Miss Claudine Galen. Last letter, from Paris, was brought down here to the ranch by the mail rider yesterday. Later in the day, that sheet of paper was layin' open on Ash's desk as I was dustin'. Just layin' out there plain and open," she waved her arm, "so I don't think nobody'd blame me for readin' it. This Claudine wrote all happy in her letter about buyin' *art,* and house furnishin's. She carried on about buyin' a 'trousseau' at *Worth's,* some fancy store there in Paris sounded like."

"Trousseau?" Laila's heart sank. "Then—then Ash is planning to *marry?* And this person is his intended, his fiancée?" Her disappointment was sharp. She wanted to flee from the suggestion, wave it out of existence, wished she'd never heard. She struggled to feel indifferent, yanked at a peach and nearly squeezed it in two. She had no right to feel a loss, be angry. Ash and she were only friends; there was nothing more than that between them. She said in a thin calm voice, "Of course a man like Ash would be attached; I suppose I just never thought about it."

"I didn't neither. Then I saw how he got out of sorts and worried-actin' when these letters come. Curiosity killed the cat, an' maybe it'll get me, but I just had to know what was in the letters to bother him so."

Laila looked at her, felt a flush of guilt, but Kate had her curious, too, about why the letters would upset Ash. She waited expectantly for Kate to explain.

"This Claudine person don't want Ash stayin' here in the canyon. Because Ash is here on his Pa's account, she says to 'just move his Pa to the city, to Portland, where she needs Ash to be'." Kate's eyes narrowed, "She expects Ash and his Pa to be out of the canyon and livin' in Portland by the end of summer, when she finishes her 'tour'."

"Ash's father would never be happy in the city. All the people, the buildings crowded together, the noise—would be terrible for him. He can barely tolerate what civilization there is here in the canyon." Laila considered, and said slowly, "It's late summer, now, is Ash making preparations to move?"

"None that I can tell. No," Kate shook her head, "I don't think Ash has any intention of movin' his Pa to the city, or goin' off himself without him, either. But Ash is an honorable man an' he wouldn't be one to fail his bride's wishes, either. I think he's just plumb tore in two over the whole situation—not knowin' how to fix it—and that's what's eatin' him."

"That's understandable. I feel sympathy for his predicament." As for her, she must get used to the facts: that Ash was taken and another woman—who bought her clothes in Paris—held his heart, was the one who'd share his future. And she was a silly goose for ever allowing herself to be attracted to him to any degree.

Chapter Ten

Laila's new lever-action, .30-30 Winchester rifle had come from Joe Pelling who claimed she saved his life. Most certainly she had saved his leg, too. Hutton Ginther taught her how to load and shoot the rifle, and after many lessons they agreed that her score, four tin cans out of six popped off a boulder at fifty yards, was more than adequate. She now also owned a lovely trunk, a walnut clock, a pewter water pitcher and matching glasses—goods as payment for her nursing. The homey additions added to her love for the cabin, the first place that felt truly her own. Should the true owner come by and find her there, she was prepared to pay him rent so that she and Tansy could stay as long as necessary.

Desper Thornhall had been paid off at the store, and she took satisfaction now in being a cash customer for her needs.

It was hard to live in the canyon and not think about Ash, but she told herself that her foolish feelings were simply a sickness that she'd have to get over, and it wasn't as though she didn't have enough other matters for her attention.

One day in September, Laila hurried along the east trail toward Venture and Thornhall's store. Twittering wrens and sparrows harvested seeds in the brush along the riverbank. The fall sky was turquoise-blue, the air warm on her skin. Tansy had begged to stay at home at the cabin rather than endure Opal's disapproving eye, her constant refrain that Tansy should be placed with other children in an orphanage where she could also receive proper schooling. Laila was teaching Tansy her numbers—she could count to one hundred and write numbers to twenty—and Laila had ordered a few small books so that she could teach her to read.

Laila started to step over a rock as she walked along. On second thought, wanting to smooth the path, she took time to boot the rock out of the path in the direction of the water. The rock contained copper, she knew from its greenish cast. She and Tansy had learned a lot about their surroundings over the summer. For instance the tall yellow spikes of flowers that bloomed on the hillsides were called Golden Banner.

There were so many things to like about the canyon, but Laila regretted that she couldn't count her association with Opal Thornhall as one of them. Her excitement at having another woman for company in her part of the lonely canyon had dimmed considerably in the days since their spat over Opal's ferocious activity with the broom, not to mention their disagreement about Tansy's welfare.

Following their discussion about germs, Opal had become a real pest. She developed imaginary symptoms every week or so and insisted that Laila check her over. She pleaded for medicines which she didn't need. Laila tried to convince her that from every available sign she was healthy as a horse but Opal couldn't believe it.

Opal claimed enough ailments that, had they not been imaginary, would have long since killed her. Her list of female complaints alone were enough for ten women. Because Laila wouldn't dispense from her precious stock of medicines at Opal's every demand—on top of their differing opinion about what was best for Tansy—their relationship was cool and strained.

The sound of industrious hammering came from the store as Laila approached. She opened the door and gaped. A large crate, flat lid askew, was centered on the floor. Pine-scented sawdust was tracked here and there. Marigold romped and raced in the wood shavings. Desper, hammer in hand and nails clamped between his lips, was in the process of building a set of shelves around the east window. Opal, robust and bouncy, seemed everywhere at once and much of her grayish blonde hair had escaped its combs. Surprisingly, her smile for Laila was beyond convivial.

"Heavens, what's going on?" Laila's own smile faded when she moved into the room. The crate was marked with flamboyant red scroll, *Dr. Shoop Family Medicine Company, Racine, Wisconsin*. Below that, *Good for Man Or Beast—Shoop Celebrated Medicines. Saves Money, Saves Lives. Ask for No Other.*

Such wild claims! She felt prickles on the back of her neck, her heart thudded in dread, and she silently cursed the useless nostrums.

Desper, perspiring and grunting, thumped and bumped an arrangement of shelves against the wall below the window sill.

Opal motioned at her husband's work, cried out happily to Laila, "You're just in time to see Venture's new—*venture*. A pharmacy!" Lunging then to the crate, she snatched up one amber bottle after another, filling her plump arms. She repeated in grating singsong: "Favorite Prescription, Cascara Syrup, Catarrh Cure, Cough Cure, Diphtheria Remedy." Her eyes glittered. "Fever Cure, Lax-ets, Night Cure, Pain Panacea, Preventics." She held a last dark bottle high, "Nerve Pills!" Her smile for Laila was gilded with triumph. If Laila would not treat her, she would treat herself and likely anyone else who wanted to buy the nostrums.

"I hope," Laila said through her teeth, "the medicines are safe and effective." *Good for man or beast?* What good would nerve pills do a cow, a hog? She resisted the urge to snatch

Desper's hammer and destroy every last dangerous tonic. The day would come, she hoped, when a "pharmacy" such as Opal's—the wide-open making and peddling of so-called medicines—would be under severe scrutiny from the government and under regulation by law.

Personally she could continue to try and educate Opal, present her with facts she had gathered from professional papers and knowledge gained from her apothecary friend in St. Louis.

Setting aside the matter, too agitated to be calm and tactful on the subject at the moment, she remembered her reason for being there and she asked Opal off-handedly, "Do you have some fig preserves? Tansy and I are going to make some bar cookies."

"Figs? Oh, yes fig preserves, we have some. Did I tell you, Miss Mitchell, I have a whole crate of Lydia Pinkham's Vegetable Compound Tonic on order?"

Laila sighed and shook her head. There weren't enough women in the canyon to need the tonic; if it were worthwhile, which she doubted wholeheartedly. A tonic that was mostly alcohol might make a woman feel better temporarily. But there was no single tonic so miraculous that it would aid digestion, build up the nervous system, fortify the reproductive system, ward off anemia, prevent miscarriages, allay the threat of dropsy, rheumatism and obesity, control hysteria and chase away the blues during the "change of life"—all of which its maker so strongly claimed.

The episode at the Venture store was still very much on Laila's mind on a cool morning a week later, her thoughts running amok as she headed for the creek with her bucket for water. She had to find a way to keep Opal from hurting anyone with her pills and tonics.

A proprietary medicine was only that. It was a tonic sold over the counter after having its name and trademark registered in a kind of copyright. It was thus *proprietary*. Exclusive rights to a patented formula would expire at the end of seventeen years, after which anyone could appropriate both the formula and the name. But of safety regulations and government approval it had none.

She guessed, beginning to simmer down, that if she spoke out too vigorously against Opal's "general store pharmacy," and named it a danger to the community, many would just presume that she was unfairly trying to destroy competition. If people treated themselves, they wouldn't have to pay Laila for treating them.

What the canyon needed, above all, was an honest to goodness real doctor. In the long run, maybe she could help find one. And if he was agreeable, she could act as his assistant.

Approaching the creek, her mind busy, at first Laila paid little heed to the odd snuffling and crunching sounds that came to her ears. Then she stopped short, stiffening. She stifled a sharp cry.

At the creek's edge, the cougar that had interrupted so many nights' sleep for her, and sometimes woke Tansy, too, the same animal that caused Laila to carry her Winchester anytime she went more than a few paces from the cabin, was feeding greedily on the carcass of the yearling deer.

Laila gripped the bucket's bail tightly in her hand. Protest rose in silent waves inside her, *no, no, no!* Almost tame, the yearling hadn't gone to the high country, but had stayed around all summer. Last time it visited, the enchanting creature had the nubbins of antlers, was showing signs of becoming a magnificent buck. That it was a yearling fawn was likely all that prevented its being shot by a hunter. Now, it was dead, anyway. Laila strode back to the cabin and placed her empty bucket on the floor just inside the door.

Tansy looked up from where she sat in the middle of the floor cutting pictures of people from a ragged old magazine, making paper dolls. She jumped to her feet at sight of Laila's face. "What's wrong, Laya?"

"Stay inside, Tansy, please." Laila grimly grabbed her rifle from the rack over the door. Trembling, she made sure the weapon was loaded. Outside, she went as close as she dared, and then fit the walnut stock into the curve of her shoulder. She slipped the lever, and sighted along the blue steel barrel. Hearing a rustling behind her, she looked over her shoulder. "Please go inside, Tansy!" Her voice shook, "Mind me now! I don't want you hurt." Tansy retreated back up the hill and the door thunked softly after her.

The cougar went on eating *their yearling.* Laila choked, then she squeezed the trigger. The cougar tumbled, then clambered up, only stunned. Laila whimpered in dismay, she wanted the animal instantly dead. Her heart pounded as the animal minced toward her, muscles rippling under its tawny hide, a spot of red appeared on its right shoulder. The cougar was almost on her when she fired twice more and finally the animal lay still, a heap of tawny gold.

Laila felt queasy and cold sweat blossomed on her flesh. She sat down suddenly on the ground, with her head between her knees and the rifle across her lap. Tansy quietly joined her a few minutes later and put her arm around Laila. "It's all right, Laya, don't cry. You were brave, and you had to shoot him."

"Y-yes, I had to do it." Laila leaned toward the child. It was several minutes before Laila's shaking stopped. A feeling of sadness obliterated whatever triumph she might have felt. If it was going to happen anyway, she wished the cougar had taken their deer far from their sight, where they might never have known. Or that the deer had been killed to feed the miners without their knowledge.

For weeks the big golden-eyed cat had prowled dangerously close to her cabin, hissing, spitting, yowling in the night, it was true. As often, Laila had worried that she or Tansy would be attacked. But what the cougar had done to the yearling fawn was part of nature's plan. Did men feel as she felt now, after killing a wild creature? Or did they hoo-raw and head for the nearest saloon to brag, as she suspected? The answer didn't really matter. How she felt was all that was important to her. She was thoroughly sorry for the whole mess.

The sound of clattering rock later that day made Laila look up from her yard where she was amateurishly but determinedly skinning the cougar. It had taken no small effort to drag the carcass home. She intended to at least salvage the furry skin and put it to some practical use. The raw, rancid smell of the beast clung to her as she stood up, feeling wary. The sun was beginning to come out from behind the clouds.

She held her bloody hands at her sides as first a hat, then the shoulders of a man came into view on the brow of the hill. Her heart leaped with hope, thinking that it might be Ash, that they might have a friendly visit. Then she had full view of the rider and his dark bay mount clambering up the rocky trail her way. She didn't know the stocky, dark bearded man in a brown corduroy suit and tan Stetson. She wondered if it had been a mistake to take her rifle back to the house?

"Miss Mitchell?" he called out as he rode up.

She nodded in answer. "I am Laila Mitchell." She frowned as a second man on a tired-looking roan rode into sight after the first. He was a rangy, hawk-faced fellow in worn, dusty garb and a battered black hat; he led a loaded pack mule.

They were taking long enough to survey her, the whole place. What on earth could the pair want?

She followed their gaze and took in the rustic cabin that now had her touches, the crude homemade benches, rock gardens, the straggle of late-blooming blue petunias in the window box she'd made. Tansy's wood toys scattered in the yard. *Their* things, *their* home.

The bearded man in brown stated, "You've made some changes, Miss. This old line cabin never looked like a home before." Then he asked, "You do that?" He motioned at the half-skinned mountain cat as he wrapped the reins about the horn of his saddle.

"Yes."

Approval filled his face as he leaned to take a closer look. "That's the same bugger, I can tell from that scarred hind paw, that's been taking some calves from me and some other ranchers up above the rim-rock. Tried tracking him several times, with no luck. I'll pay you bounty, right now." His saddle creaked as he shifted to reach inside his coat for the money.

"No thank you. I'm keeping the skin."

"Keep it, I'll still pay you." He held a closed hand toward her.

"You haven't stated your business, or your name," she told him, as five silver dollars *chinked* together into her upheld palm.

"Kittrell is the name, John Kittrell. I own the ground you stand on, and the cabin. I'm afraid I have to ask you to clear out and move on."

It took a moment for his statement to register. Dismay filled her. A chill traveled her spine before she closed her mind to recollections of being displaced in past times.

She had nearly forgotten that the cabin belonged to someone else, someone she'd never met. During her time in the canyon, the place had grown to be home to her. "You want me to cl-clear out?" she stammered.

Although from the beginning she had seen her time in the canyon as probably temporary, she had come to like it there very much. No where else on earth—since she left the Emporia farm as a child—had felt so much like home as did the little cabin. Further, she felt needed and worthwhile in her work providing nursing care to the scattered inhabitants of the area. She had friends there, *Ash, Kate,* others. For a second she wondered if Ash was behind the man's asking her to leave, then she reflected that Kittrell was the owner and acted on his own regard. But she wasn't ready to go. Couldn't go, not yet. Not only would it break her heart to leave, there was no other place for her to go to. She was responsible now for Tansy. If things had turned out differently, she might have gone to her grandparents in La Grande, but now . . .

"I want to winter a few head of my cattle here in this basin," Kittrell was saying, "and I'm putting my man, Mackenzie, here, in the cabin to look after them." He reached inside his coat for tobacco and commenced to roll a cigarette. He took a moment for introductions: "Miss Mitchell," he smiled at her and then back at the other rider, "Mack MacKenzie." He then went on, "Sorry about this. They told me about you down at the Venture store. Mrs. Thornhall says you've been here all summer, as my guest?" He smiled without mockery or resentment.

"I've been living here," she admitted, "and I appreciate that your cabin was available." She frantically searched her mind for an answer to the problem, a way she could stay. She asked without preamble, ignoring MacKenzie and speaking directly to Kittrell, "Is there any reason why I can't stay on here and look out for your herd? I'd add a little cash to that for rent of the cabin." Nervous perspiration rolled from her brow to drip off her nose and she wiped it indelicately on the back of her sleeve as her heart pounded in desperation.

Kittrell took a long pull on his cigarette, seemed to size her up. "You know I can't do that." He motioned over his shoulder, "I've already given my word to Mack that the job and the cabin are his. But—seeing that cat, there, and what you've done to the place, makes me think that maybe you could have done the job—if I hadn't already found somebody else. I'm real sorry, but you have to go."

She felt numb all over, still not quite believing what was happening. She asked in a thin voice, "How long do I have, to find another place, pack my things?" *Prepare the child who counts on me for everything . . . ?*

"Mack was planning to stay here tonight. He's got everything with him, we didn't know 'til we got here that you'd taken over the cabin."

"Tonight?" she asked, aghast. "I have to be out by *tonight?*" Anger and frustration gripped her until it felt like a sickness. She had no say, however. Kittrell owned the cabin and she was trespassing, a squatter. But how could they do this to her? Where could she and Tansy go? What did these men expect, that she could just suddenly make a home under a tree? She gave both of the men a look meant to chisel them to nothing, then she said, "Please leave for now, give me a chance to—When you come back tonight, I will be gone." *To where,* God only knew.

Chapter Eleven

Desper was sympathetic and readily agreeable to giving Laila and Tansy a place to sleep that night and he helped them to tote their things. They could stay as long as necessary, he promised, until such time as Laila found another place. His wife concurred with far less enthusiasm.

Tansy cried in Laila's arms, "Those men took our house, they took our house! I don't want to sleep in the storeroom anymore."

"This move is only temporary, my little sweetheart," Laila hugged Tansy, her own heart aching for the child, the disruption and loss she was feeling. "Don't worry, I'll take care of you. We'll have a place of our own again. Soon!"

A second cot was crowded into the small storage room next to bins of potatoes, apples, and bags of beans, flour, and sugar. Most of Laila's things were placed under a tarp in the yard in back of the store and would be ruined if she didn't find another place for them.

"We'll not be here long," Laila promised Opal.

News of Laila's ejection from the cabin traveled fast. Ash arrived on an unseasonably cold night three days later, pounding on the door of the store and calling her name. The Thornhalls had closed up and gone to their cabin. She and Tansy had retired to their storeroom quarters and Tansy was asleep after curling into an unhappy little ball on her cot.

Laila lighted a lamp, stumbled barefoot through the store, and met him at the door with her wrapper hastily tied over her thin nightgown. "Ash, for goodness sakes—!" she scolded lightly, a finger to her lips to stop him from calling out her name again. She was hardly able to conceal her unbidden, under-riding joy at sight of him, even at that late hour, and in spite of what she was sure was his mission. She just hoped he would understand what she was going to have to say to him.

"Laila, you shouldn't be here," he stated flatly, to the point, the light from her lamp reflecting the disturbance in his eyes. "When Kittrell booted you out of that cabin you should have brought the little girl and come to stay with m—should have come to stay with Kate at my place," he corrected. "In the morning, you're coming back with me to the ranch. I can give you your own rooms, the whole house if you want. I'll be damned if I'd stick somebody like you in with spuds and beans! Made me mad as hell when I heard these folks had done that. Opal could have made a place for you two in their cabin with them."

She held the door and spoke quietly, "We're fine where we are! The Thornhalls have been very kind to give us a place to stay at all on such short notice. And for pity's sake, I've never had any intention of being here very long."

"Good, then you will come with me," he said on satisfied sigh. "Kittrell's cabin wasn't a place for you any more than Thornhall's storage room is. In the morning, we'll get your things and we'll head back to Conner Creek."

"No, I won't. I can't."

He threw his head back, gave her a keen, startled gaze. Then for a second he seemed distracted as his glance took her in, head to toe. Her hair flowed loose about her shoulders, her nightwear was nowhere near proper covering on her slim figure. Little lights danced in his eyes in the glow from her lamp.

"What do you mean, you can't?" he asked softly. "Of course you can."

"No."

"Why not?" his voice was near a shout again.

"Ash! Shhh," she cautioned. "Come inside before you wake the Thornhalls and Tansy." She clasped his arm and drew him in with her, closing the door, leading him to the chairs placed around the potbellied stove where a few coals still gave a little warmth. "Sit down and I'll explain."

Her senses were acutely aware of everything about him: The fresh air emanating from him, the stiff way he sat that showed his determination to come to her rescue, his bedeviling good looks in the light from the lamp. She was aware, too, of herself: that her feet were bare, the rest of her not properly dressed. But hang it, there were things she had to say to him to his face, late hour or no, properly dressed or not. She just wished he hadn't come so far, thinking he had to help her.

The thing was, she didn't want saving, didn't need saving. She was not going to accept charity, certainly, or pity, from a man she was worrisomely attracted to, who belonged to someone else. She had too much pride for that. She had too many plans she wanted to accomplish on her own as well. His concern for her, certainly, was misplaced.

She tried to explain as best she could, leaving out the part about her feelings for him, but he scarcely listened. His eyes flashed, he shook his head.

"It doesn't make good sense. I have all the room in the world, you'd be a lot more comfortable at my place. Kate is your friend, you'd enjoy one another's company every day. I'll bet my bottom dollar that Opal isn't exactly making you two welcome even in their storeroom."

She wasn't, but that was partly her own fault. The second day after she'd moved in, a customer was about to buy a bottle of Carlson's Colic Relief for Flatulence when Laila intervened and explained that the tonic was forty-five percent alcohol, or ninety proof, and dangerously addictive. Although it promised to produce a "warm, soothing sensation to stomach and intestines," a better aid would be a teaspoonful of bicarbonate, kitchen soda, in a glass of plain water. The customer's wife had thanked Laila and led her husband from the store without the purchase. Losing the sale made Opal furious. It was only to Desper's credit that Laila and Tansy hadn't been tossed into the store-yard, with the need to find another place to sleep right then and there, again.

"This is only temporary," she tried again to tell Ash. She halted, suddenly hearing what his brusque voice was telling her so confidently:

"—And you wouldn't have to go chasing up and down the canyon, these hills, to care for the sick, either. There's no need for you to do that."

He might as well have struck her. For a few seconds she sat in stunned silence. In the next moment she was awash with fury at him. She was deeply disappointed that he wasn't aware how much her work meant to her or that she was filling a real need there.

"I beg your pardon. I *like* 'chasing' after the sick. They need me. If you must know, they are quite desperate for my skills around here, due to this country not having a real doctor, close. What do you want these people to do, go back to folk-charm cures?" She spelled some out for him: "Are they to cure backache by turning a somersault upon hearing the call of a whippoorwill—hang a bag of live bugs around their neck, or drink white-ant tea, or wear a stolen blue ribbon to cure whooping cough? Or maybe the sufferer can be passed three times through a horse collar for a cure?"

She stood panting a moment while he looked shocked, then she told him, "I don't need your assistance, as I've been telling you all along. I am making my living and doing just fine, thank you. I have prospects, I have plans."

"Laila, please—"

She rushed on again, her anger making it impossible to still her tongue, "I have talked to Mr. Ginther and he's going to sell me one of the lots he owns." She pointed in the general direction. "Right here in Venture, over by his wagonshop. I'm going to build myself a new cabin, maybe even an infirmary, a hospital of some sort, and engage a doctor. I thank you for your kind invitation, Mr. Corbett, to come live with you—" she took a breath, rolled her eyes, "my, what a scandal that would make!" She mocked, " 'Young single woman moves in with peach rancher and takes his charity in exchange for—' *For what* do you suppose folks would think?" Her face was hot as fire. She had resolved to not worry too much about propriety but there were limits. The fact that he was already betrothed to yet another woman wouldn't improve the picture any. *Harem*, it would look like.

He tried for the third or fourth time to respond but she didn't let him. She leaned toward him. "I'm sorry that you don't see that I can take care of myself without your help, but that is your fault, not mine!"

She had never felt so hurt, so angry at anyone, before, and it stunned her. His disapproval hurt all the more because she liked Ash, admired him very much, cared for him probably more than she should under the circumstances. In the next moment, before she knew what was happening, and possibly an impulsive act without thought on his part, he had reached over and pulled her from her chair. A moan of desire came from his throat as he drew her to her feet with him, into his arms, his body pressed into hers.

"Ash, no!"

He ignored her protest, held her tighter. "I'm so sorry," he whispered against her temple. Her thin garments, his outerwear, were as nothing between them. He kissed her hard, a long kiss that stirred her deep inside. Responsive emotions made her want to kiss him back, curl into him and let her racing feelings go. Instead she pushed herself out of his arms while she was still able. She stood breathless, trembling, unable to speak.

It was hard to hold him off, but she had to, because of his bride-to-be, and myriad other things. And him . . . ! "Don't you have enough in your life to worry about?" she demanded to know.

He stared at her strangely, "You're referring to the woman I'm betrothed to, and my troubles with Pop? Don't know how you found out about that, but it doesn't matter, it's no secret."

"You have someone else and you—you kissed me like that? And you—you butt into my life? No one asked you to!"

"I'm sorry," he said again, grimly this time. "It seems I've overstepped in more ways than one tonight. I wish I hadn't hurt you, I didn't mean to belittle your nursing work. The truth is, I hear constantly about the good you do. Nor would I do anything that might ruin your reputation. I just pictured you here—these conditions—" he waved around him at the crude interior of the general store, "and I—" He hesitated, then went on husky-voiced, "Forget it. You obviously don't need or want anything from me. Next time, I'll mind my own business."

"But I—" She hadn't wanted to anger him, hurt his feelings, or appear ungrateful. But he ought not to have said what he did about her work. She chewed her lip that was still warm and bruised-feeling from his delectable kiss. She watched him pull his hat down tighter and turn for the door. "Where are you going to stay tonight? You can't start back home now in the dark, and it's cold out there."

He glanced at her briefly over his shoulder, and she winced as he told her, "It's *cold* in here, too. Friends will put me up." With that, he went out, slamming the door.

Laila waited several breathless moments, worried that the Thornhalls had been awakened and would rush to the store and she'd have to explain. When they didn't appear, she went to the storeroom and her bed. Tansy hadn't stirred, she still slept soundly with her mouth slightly open.

For a long time after Laila blew out the lamp and crawled onto her cot, she stared into the dark, her eyes dry and aching, her heart heavy, her mouth still able to feel the imprint of Ash's lips.

What had she done? Ash had been a good friend, she had enjoyed his company more than that of any other adult human being she'd ever known. Now, she would be lucky if he ever spoke to her again. He'd been wrong to say what he did, but she needn't have gotten up her dander so, either. She'd ruined everything. Everything except her dreams. And he ought to have tried to understand the good she was trying to do, understand her, better.

Ash would be hard to forget, especially now that she knew what his kiss could feel like, knew how it felt to be in his arms. But the kiss was an accident of the moment and it was just as well she put him totally from her mind.

For the next half-hour Laila's thoughts gave her no rest. She churned in her bed, her blanket knotting around her. She had wanted Ash in her life as a simple friend, no more than that, why couldn't she make it work?

She supposed she could take part of the blame that he had taken her in his arms and kissed her the way he had. Any man might have reacted the same way to a half-dressed woman in the middle of the night. Although, if he were really in love with someone else, would he?

None of that mattered, in any regard. She had truly angered him and she doubted even a plain, ordinary friendship could be salvaged from the ashes of their disagreement.

Ash's horse-drawn carriage passed through wrought-iron gates and sped clip-clopping along a curved drive into the forested hills of the Galen's Portland estate. Moments later he drew up before the residence, a spacious Queen Anne mansion surrounded by acres of well-kept lawn and rose gardens, the roses fragrant in the fall mist.

Upon alighting, he removed his hat, smoothed his hair, straightened his tie. Welcoming Claudine home was supposed to be a joyful time but she wasn't going to like it that Pop was still in the canyon, that nothing was changed. Minutes later, Ash waited in the marble-floored vestibule while the Galen butler, Fernald, announced him. Then Claudine, startlingly beautiful in sapphire blue, her usual elegant bearing forgotten, rushed down the curved stairway like a child. He moved to meet her in the entryway and she threw herself into his arms.

"Oh, Ash, my dearest darling, I've missed you so this summer! I could hardly wait to come home to you, and now you're here!"

"I'm here." He kissed her rosy lips turned up to him, and lightly touched her blond hair, remembering not to muss it. She considered her natural curls low-class and struggled to keep them controlled in a sleek bun at the back of her head. "It's good to see you, Claudine. You're especially gorgeous in that gown." The fashion was the latest "hourglass", the ballooning sleeves and wide skirt made her tiny waist even smaller. The rich fabric was the same blue as her eyes.

She laughed, catching his hands in hers. "I nearly emptied

the shops in Paris! It was such fun. Daddy scolded but I don't think he really minded."

"Claudine, could I have a brandy? My throat's dry for some reason, the long trip, I suppose."

"Of course you can, darling. And I'll have a sherry. Come with me. I have so much to tell you." She hooked her arm through his and led him into the drawing room off the left of the entry.

Ash had been in the room many times, and it still took him off guard, made him slightly uncomfortable. It was a woman's room, brightly lighted and decorated in soft blues and rose, with an abundance of gilding in woodwork, the wallpaper, the frames of many enormous mirrors on the walls. Claudine's piano stood at one end of the room, at the other huge windows flanked the fireplace. He crossed the carpeted floor, strewn with gargantuan roses, to look out on the floral gardens but not really seeing them.

He turned, feeling perspiration pop out on his brow. "Claudine, we need to talk—" He doubted it would feel any worse to face the gallows, but to be fair to Claudine, he had to explain his position and the sooner the better.

She joined him at the window, handed him a brandy in a fragile crystal glass. "Darling, let me go first, all right? I've been bursting." And she began to prattle about the social engagements ahead of them, the parties, dances, receptions that would be held in their honor by her family's many friends, and his. And of course they would reciprocate in their new home, as soon as they were married.

He took her hands, and looking into her lively eyes with regret, told her, "Claudine, we may not be able to get married as soon as we planned."

She halted in mid-sentence, something about a painting she'd purchased for their parlor, and the blood drained from her heart-shaped face. "Ash, what do you mean? Of course we'll marry before Christmas, just as we decided. The arrangements are made. I bought my wedding trousseau, some lovely things for our home. All my friends expect—"

"I can't be here in Portland just now, not for any length of time, not to work on our house, or to be here for the parties." At the look on her face, guilt flooded him. He was being very cruel, but to withhold the truth, to put off telling her the facts, would be more so.

"You're joking, Ash." Her tapered fingers crept up to her throat and she sat down on the sofa facing him. "Is it your father? You did do as I asked, didn't you? You did move him to Portland? He's here in the city?"

He took a long swallow of brandy. "No, I'm sorry, Claudine, but Pop is still in the canyon. And for now I need to be there with him as much as possible."

A maid came in with a tray of desserts and Claudine waved her back out of the room. She kept her voice carefully modulated, but her eyes blazed blue fury, "I need you, too, Ash."

"I know, and I feel badly about this Claudine, I really do."

"Then convince your father to move here to Portland. You can do it, if you want to. I can't imagine anyone preferring to live in that dreadful country, anyway."

Some people like it, though it's hard for me to imagine why, myself. Ash pushed thought of Laila from his mind. Laila was an odd, stubborn female who had nothing to do with this.

Claudine was saying, "—and your father would have wonderful care, here, and every advantage. We could go ahead with our plans."

He fought inner turmoil that would lead him to say something he'd regret. "Pop isn't like you and me, Claudine. He's probably not like anyone else we know. The canyon is where he's most content and I can't uproot him." As Ash looked at the room, and at Claudine, recalling what she'd said about the parties, the socials, the shopping in Paris, he realized how little that sort of thing meant to him, really. Somehow, sometime over the summer, he had changed. As he hesitated, a truth he hadn't faced before flooded into his consciousness so powerfully he couldn't dismiss it. He had to say it, "This is not only about Pop, Claudine. Everything I've said about him is fact, and I can't bring him here. But this is also about me. I need more time. I'm not ready to get married." He felt like a louse, wouldn't have blamed her if she grabbed the bronze statuette from the table beside her and beat him bloody with it.

In spite of her struggle for polite control, Claudine's voice trembled with indignation, "What do you mean, not ready? You were ready four months ago, before I left for Europe. You were ready when you put this ring on my finger," she twisted it furiously. "It was all I could do to keep you out of my bed, you were in such a hurry for us to—to—" her face pinked, "to be together *that way*. You asked me to marry you."

Because I was blinded by your beauty, your lovely charm, your qualities that I believed were what I wanted in a wife. I know better now, although I'm not sure what brought the change, maybe it was just an awakening, a coming to my senses.

He ran a hand down his jaw. "If we went on with our plans, I'd only make you unhappy, Claudine. I'm not ready for any of this. I'm truly sorry I didn't see it earlier, before we went ahead with intentions to marry. Forgive me."

"Never," she said tonelessly, frost in her glare. Then her eyes flooded with angry tears. "I'll look like such a fool to our friends—I assume the wedding, our relationship really is off, then, permanently?"

He didn't answer, finding no new words to express his

regret at what he'd caused her. He said on a sigh, "I have to be going, Claudine, I'll see myself out."

"I want to keep the ring," she called after him, icily, "I deserve it, for what you've put me through!"

Ash turned slowly at the door, amazed that in a moment like this, she could think of the ring. "Of course, I want you to have it."

Driving from the estate, he felt lighter, and yet he hated himself for destroying the feelings of yet another woman, in such a short time, who really didn't deserve it. His fault, both instances. Better to stay away from women altogether! Forget any serious intent!

Chapter Twelve

The warmer river bars barely whitened in December in the canyon, but snow clung deep on the trails and in places ice formed on the creeks.

The day was in evening shadow as Laila rode the river trail homeward on Jenny Wren, the nimble-footed brown mare Ginther often loaned her. She'd left Tansy at the store to play with her paperdolls and picture books close to the stove, ignoring Opal's look of displeasure when she gave Tansy her orders.

Laila had been to see Joe Pelling, who was once again her patient. Getting around on crutches had been difficult and he had slipped on a patch of ice and had broken three ribs. Pleurisy followed his fall and she had been treating him in a battle to prevent pneumonia. He had decided that the canyon, and mining, were bad luck for him. As soon as he was strong enough to travel, he meant to move further inland, possibly to the Willamette Valley. Opal was delighted at that news, saying Laila should seize the opportunity to send Tansy with Pelling, to Salem where she belonged. In no uncertain terms, Laila let Opal know what she thought of that idea.

"C'mon, Jenny Wren, almost there." Horse and rider puffed steam into the chill air. A pewter sky hung low over the canyon, over the small community of Venture ahead.

She would liked to have been wrapped snug and warm in the coat she intended to make from the cougar skin, but with help and instructions from one of the miners on how to care for it, the skin was still curing. When made, the garment would hardly be fashionable in cut, it wouldn't smell like perfume, but it would keep out the cold she was feeling intensely today.

She minded less and less the fact that Kittrell's man and his cattle had taken over the old place, the cabin that she had considered so much her own. Her new cabin was nearly ready, it would truly belong to her, and she was eager for the move. Tansy had stopped fussing about being back in the storeroom, when she saw their very own new cabin being built. As soon as the weather warmed, they would plant a small garden, even if the cabin wasn't finished completely.

Their cramped quarters at the Thornhalls, Laila's ongoing feud with Opal over quack medicines, had made that situation nearly impossible. It was a relief for her and Tansy to be away from the store, to ride out on nursing chores or to give Hutton a hand in his wagonshop, or just to keep him company.

A couple of times Laila had wished she hadn't been so high-handed in turning down Ash's invitation to stay at his place. It would have been so much more pleasant. Distance to some of her patients would have been further, but others would have been closer. She could have boarded until her cabin was built, paid her own way and kept her pride.

In spite of the chill of late day, her face heated as she asked herself if—on the other hand—it would have been romantically safe to live under the same roof with him a month or two? Her heart skipped a beat as she considered the prospect. Now that he had kissed her, implanting a pleasurable memory in her mind, she doubted that such a thing would be a wise idea.

She was strongly attracted to Ash Corbett, and giving in to that attraction would be wrong, not to mention that it would get in the way of other things she wanted to do.

No matter, she reflected. It was altogether likely that he

wanted nothing more to do with her. He'd been clearly angry and hurt by the way she had rebuffed him that night he had charged so gallantly to her totally unnecessary rescue.

A frown creased her brow. She had heard that he had left his father in Kate's care twice this fall to make trips to Portland. Necessary trips, since Miss Galen was there, as was his hotel business that needed to be overseen.

A buff-colored grouse flew up suddenly from beside the frosty trail, others in the flock rustled away in the shrub. Her mount danced sideways, almost unseating her.

"Whoa, Wren, you're all right. There now." She settled herself more firmly in the saddle. She had ridden horses as a small child on the Kansas farm, but she was re-learning. She leaned forward to pat Jenny Wren's neck. The mare blew, stepped lively, hooves crunching in the snow. To Laila's right, the Snake River was a cascade of iron gray, rushing to join the Columbia River miles distant to the north.

At the edge of the settlement, she rode slowly past her nearly completed cabin. Her heart filled with longing to have her own place again. Hutton worked on the small structure whenever he could get time away from the wagonshop. Occasionally he got a helping hand from some other fellow from nearby, and from her. Today there was no activity in or about the structure. She could hear Hutton at work inside his wagonshop.

Her cabin was not the only new one. Venture was growing and changing, though not at the speed of some mining towns. Not like Canyon City in the John Day River Valley west of them, which, due to a rich strike a few years back, had grown by five thousand residents overnight. *Overnight!* Other boomtowns had grown similarly, but not Venture. The area was remote, and perhaps no "big find" would ever be made.

Even so, small mining operations cropped up from time to

time. Most were started by folks left in hard straits by the depression, men struck by mining fever and hoping to strike it rich. Sometimes a single man came by himself, or two or three men would come there together.

Some men brought families. Several claims, for both copper and gold, had been taken north of Kittrell's cabin. Mine names, Blue Swan, Gilded Lily, Duck Creek, Big Boy, and the like, salted nearly every conversation in the store and at the wheel-shop.

"Whoa, Wren, whoa." Laila swung from the saddle before the open-fronted shed next to the Venture Store. After caring for her horse, she stomped the snow from her boots and headed inside. Opal hummed noisily as she dusted shelves of canned goods while Tansy helped dust the lower shelves. Tansy whirled and smiled her relief that Laila had returned and Laila went to hug her. Desper was at the counter with a customer, a miner, who hoisted bags of flour and beans onto his shoulders and headed for the door. He nodded greeting to Laila.

She smiled in return. "My, but it's cold out there," she said to all of them, "it's nice to come in where it's cozy." Marigold slept behind the potbellied stove in the middle of the store. Laila released Tansy back to her dusting chore and hurried to the stove. She tore off her gloves and rubbed her cold stiffened fingers together. She pushed her shawl back from her head and onto the shoulders of her thin coat. Opal kept a pot of coffee on the stove for customers. Laila lifted the lid, and sniffed, decided against a cup of the tarry brew.

"You run out of the last medicines you bought from me?" Opal wanted to know, her smile guarded, careful. "You've been taking care of a lot of folks." Opal was bending a little, ordering and stocking safer medicines that Laila had suggested—such as Essence of Ginger for colic, Peroxide of Hydrogen to disinfect open wounds, Pepsin for upset stomach, Zinc ointment for burns and wounds. She had even shipped back to the company tonics heavily portioned in opium and whiskey.

Opal had put a lot of money into her pharmacy and was disappointed that it wasn't turning out to be as profitable as she'd hoped. Most canyon-ites continued to depend on Laila for diagnosis and prescription for treatment. Making matters worse, Opal had humiliated herself by overdosing on Lydia Pinkham's Compound, giving folks pause about the nostrums she pedaled.

Drunk from too much of the alcohol-laden tonic and near naked, Opal had climbed to the roof of the store one evening "to see the world." She had danced around the chimney while her red-faced husband and Laila begged her to come down, and Marigold yipped concern at their feet. Tansy, giggling in shock, had begged to watch but had given in to Laila's insistence that she go to the storeroom and stay there.

Later, Opal claimed that it was female stress, *not* intoxication, that had taken her temporarily "out of her mind." But since that time, she had been more willing to heed some of Laila's precautions about proprietary medicines.

Now, Opal had ceased her dusting to wait for Laila's reply, her eyes lit and hopeful.

"I am well-stocked, thank you." She avoided the disappointment in Opal's eyes and added, "But I suppose I could use some toothache plasters and—Vaseline."

"Say, Miss Mitchell," Desper said suddenly, "there's a letter for you, came today." He added, nosey and friendly, "Looks like it is from Ash Corbett, up to Conner Creek."

Her hand, starting to brush back a tendril of hair, froze in mid-air, her breath came in a rush, her heart pounded.

A letter from Ash? She reached for it from Opal. "Yes," she struggled to sound calm, to keep tremors of joy from her voice as she read her name and the return address written in large, masculine scroll. "Yes, it appears that it is from Mr. Corbett." She subscribed to a newspaper now, and a couple of magazines, but she almost never received letters. Her only true correspondence was with John Ryland, the apothecary in St. Louis, whom she wrote to now and then with a question about medicine.

She smiled at Desper and Opal, at Tansy. "Will you excuse me?" She nodded her head toward the storage room. "I need to get out of my coat and boots, change my clothes." What she really wanted, of course, was to read the letter in private. Maybe he had written to apologize but, she realized nervously and with a touch of defiance, there was an equal chance he wanted to bawl her out some more.

In her room, she didn't wait to remove her coat and shawl but tore the note open with nervous fingers. She scanned the words quickly, saw no mention of their disagreement of several weeks ago. Rather, the note was an invitation, the words rather impersonal and cool, however.

At least he had written to her, she thought with a sigh of relief. He was back at Conner Creek for Christmas. Kate had asked him for one special present: to have her friend, Laila, and the little girl, Tansy, join them at the ranch for Christmas. He wanted to grant Kate her wish but Laila's decision to come or not would be, of course, entirely up to her.

She sat for a long time, thinking. Of course she wanted to go and Tansy would love it—it would be a real Christmas for her. Personally, she could think of nothing that would be so enjoyable as a holiday at Conner Creek, of spending time with Kate, and with Ash, too, as a friend. She wished their argument had never happened, but at least he didn't hate her so much as to refuse Kate her Christmas wish. They might be friends again. That's all she really wanted.

It was nice of him to write that he would come and get them. But she and Tansy would make their way upriver on Jenny Wren, on their own, barring a blizzard. That way Laila could choose her own time to come and go, without being a nuisance. She would write to accept the invitation and let him know she and Tansy would come by their own means.

Chapter Thirteen

Right after Laila received Ash's invitation, the mining community suffered a spate of colds and flu, and one man broke his wrist. Laila was kept busy, with hardly time to think about the holiday ahead.

Then, a few days before Christmas, she woke at dawn, realizing with relief and joy that all her patients were on the mend. She was free to turn her attention to Christmas at Ash's ranch. The afternoon before, she had gotten along reasonably well with Opal as the two of them baked fruitcakes in Opal's kitchen. She helped Tansy make gingerbread cookies. The aroma of apple, cinnamon, molasses, and raisins had filled the cabin and had spread outside over the frosty white landscape. The Thornhalls and nearly everyone who came into the store, seemed to be in an especially festive mood.

Laila had ordered a new turkey-red calico dress for herself and a red and green striped frock for Tansy, from the Sears Roebuck & Company catalogue. Tansy was so proud of her new dress she could hardly wait to wear it, and Laila felt the same about her own. Red calico was a serviceable dress, but pretty, too. She had a new doll and puzzles for Tansy, small gifts for Kate, Ash, and for Ash's father. Kate's gift was a porcelain puff box, for Ash she had a French calf cigar case, and for Old Tom a Swiss pocket watch figured with an elk head. Nothing very expensive, but presents none the less. She thought Opal and Desper would like the mantel clock she had wrapped and put under the Christmas tree in the store for them. There was a small leather toy for Marigold. Hutton Ginther would receive one of the fruitcakes she had helped bake and some of Tansy's cookies.

Laila sang as she washed up and dressed and later built up the fire in the store's potbellied stove. She made fresh coffee, and then woke Tansy and directed her to wash at the small bench in the storeroom, and dress. The Thornhalls would come to open up any minute. She and Tansy would be on their way to Conner Creek soon after. A sudden knock at the front door of the store interrupted Laila's thoughts.

A tall, older man, a stranger, waited on the icy porch. He turned his tan felt hat around and around in his hands.

Laila smiled and stood back, opening the door wider. Cold air rushed in. She told him, "The store isn't open yet, but you're welcome to come inside. Opal and Desper will be here any minute, but maybe I can help you in the meantime."

He stood there, silent, the wind riffling his hair and tangling in his graying beard. He had honest eyes, a worried look. "I didn't come to buy nothin'," he finally spoke. "Are you Miss Mitchell? The doctorin' woman?"

"I do home nursing." *Drat.* Would she be called out now, with Christmas but a few days off? She motioned him inside and closed the door. She waved him toward the stove that was just beginning to heat up.

"Name's Joseph Bolton. I own the hotel at New Bridge?" His statements came out sounding like questions. "Mrs. Bolton don't like botherin' you right on Christmas? But she needs you to come, right away, if it ain't no bother?"

"What's your wife's problem, Mr. Bolton?"

"She'll be tellin' you, herself?" His eyes examined the ceiling while a slow red crawled up his craggy cheeks.

She frowned. "Mr. Bolton, if your wife has a medical problem, why didn't you go for a doctor nearer your home? The town of New Bridge may not have a doctor, but Richland must have one, and that's closer than here. Surely there is a doctor available in Baker City, more than one. You would have had a quicker, easier trip than coming all this way to get me, so I don't quite understand. I'm not a trained doctor, you know. Is her problem serious?"

He answered with a single statement, "She wants a woman."

"She's having a baby, then? Her time is close?" She felt a touch of panic. Surely he wouldn't come so far for her if his wife was already in labor.

He shifted nervously, shook his head. "Not a baby." He repeated, "She'll tell you her problem when you come?"

Laila still hesitated. "It's at least twenty-five miles to New Bridge." *And twenty-five miles back, not leaving enough time to get to Conner Creek for the holiday.* "I had Christmas plans . . ."

He nodded reluctantly, snugged his hat back on down to his ears, and turned to leave. A cold wind blew in the open door.

"I'm sorry, Mr. Bolton." The chill wind whipped her skirts as she followed him into the store-yard. She addressed his back, "You will get your wife a regular doctor from Baker City or Richland, won't you?" A few feet away was his waiting rig, a dark bay hitched to a small buckboard.

He shook his head. "She said to get you, or nobody? I'll tell her you can't come."

A few minutes later, Mr. Bolton was back in the store beside the stove, sipping fresh coffee, and eating some of the store's bread and jam while Laila prepared to go with him. She put cash on the counter for what she'd used for their breakfast, and for a small lunch of bread and cheese to take along. When the Thornhalls came to the store a few minutes later, she told them that she would be gone for a few days.

"And the child?" Opal asked, eyes glinting and a frown making rivers of wrinkles in her plump face. "It's a busy time here in the store, I don't know that I can look after her."

Tansy stood by worriedly, her eyes wide and expectant. Laila took a deep breath, "I wouldn't burden you, Mrs. Thornhall. Tansy will be going with me. Get your coat and mittens honey. We'll try not to miss Christmas, but I—can't promise."

"Thank you, Laya, we'll have Christmas where we are. St. Nicholas will find us!" Tansy hugged Laila tightly, then raced to get her things.

"I hope he will, but honey," Laila called after her, "don't count on it, please."

The sky was a cloudless blue, the sun bright and giving off a feeble warmth the better part of the day as they traveled. Toward evening the sky turned the color of gun-metal, the air grew brittle cold and intermittent snowflakes fell.

It was probably eight or nine o'clock that night when they traversed the last icy ridge and rolled down into the settlement of New Bridge, the town so named for the bridge that was built some years previous over Eagle Creek, Bolton said. In night-time gloom, the Bolton Hotel appeared to be a crude structure, but pale lamplight glowed from the half-dozen or so windows facing the rutted street.

Feeling half-frozen and hungry—the bread and cheese she'd brought with them had long since been consumed—Laila was more than relieved to have arrived. Tansy, buried in robes, had slept for the last two hours or so and now stirred awake.

Mr. Bolton, as it turned out, was not a taciturn man. He had gabbed away, filling hours with his talk, the whole long and rambling journey. He and his wife, Gladys, he had told Laila, had come to Oregon from the midwest several years before. This was after they'd lost their small furniture factory in Osage City, Kansas, to fire. At New Bridge, Oregon, on the acreage behind the hotel, they kept a cow, chickens and pigs, and grew a garden; they had put in an orchard. All the milk, butter, cheese, eggs, pork and chicken, vegetables and fruit, that went into meals served in their hotel's dining room, they produced themselves. The work of it all was not so easy now that their children, three boys and two girls, were grown and scattered. And so on.

Although he talked enough to fill a book about everything else, the man remained silent as a rock about his wife's medical problem. Laila gave up trying to get him to reveal his reason for bringing her to New Bridge, other than that his wife wanted her. She could only wonder how serious Gladys Bolton's situation might be, and why it had to be such a secret.

The Bolton Hotel lobby was empty, quiet except for a small fire that hissed and crackled softly in a stone fireplace. A mixed scent of furniture polish, tobacco, and wood smoke met Laila's nose. Beyond lamp-shine in the window, the room was cast mostly in chill shadows as she followed Bolton and Tansy trailed after. They skirted white-clothed tables in the empty dining room, crossed through a tidy, delicious-smelling but empty kitchen to another door marked PRIVATE.

A woman in blue gingham and a crisp white apron rose from a chair by the stove in the small, well-furnished sitting room. Mr. Bolton introduced his wife. Gladys Bolton was an attractive older woman, slender and tall. She lay aside her needlework and took Laila's hands in her own. "Miss Mitchell, thank you for coming. It can't be at a good time for you, and I'm sorry." Mrs. Bolton's graying auburn hair was shiny, luxuriant. She had the loveliest hands Laila had ever seen.

The rosy coloring in Mrs. Bolton's cheeks might be due to the warm fire, or from a mild fever, Laila reflected. There was an equal chance her high color was her natural skin tone.

"I hope I can help." Whatever the woman's problem, it wasn't outwardly evident.

Gladys Bolton took their coats, letting her hand rest for a moment on Tansy's head. "You're looking forward to a visit from Santa Claus, I imagine?" She smiled when Tansy nodded vigorously. Gladys turned to Laila, "I've got supper ready as soon as you three have warmed up here by the stove. Nothing fancy, I'm afraid. Hot potato soup, graham muffins with fresh butter. Will that be all right, Miss Mitchell? If not, I can fix something else . . ."

"What you've fixed sounds wonderful. But I've come to take care of—to treat whatever . . . ?" She shrugged, lifted her hands, and smiled encouragingly.

Mrs. Bolton flushed a deeper red. "My problem can wait a few minutes. You've come a long way and deserve a rest and a bite to eat first."

"All right." Even with Mrs. Bolton, Laila decided, she must wait the matter out. Gladys Bolton was as reluctant to tell her her problem as her husband was.

Finally, the women cleared away the dishes from the kitchen table and Mr. Bolton went out to put his horse in the barn and see to their other animals. Tansy was put to bed on the sofa in the sitting room. Then Mrs. Bolton picked up a lamp and led Laila into the couple's tiny bedroom.

She turned to Laila. "I'm not normally a stupid woman, Miss Mitchell. But I have done something very foolish." With trembling fingers she began to unbutton the bodice of her dress, then let it drape down over her hips. She unlaced her corset, opened the chemise beneath it and removed a pad of bandage to expose her flesh.

Laila stared. "Dear Heaven! You're still being foolish, Mrs. Bolton, if you don't see a regular doctor right away!"

Mrs. Bolton's stoicism finally melted and quiet tears coursed down her cheeks. "I'd be too embarrassed to have a regular doctor look at me. Surely you understand. You're a woman, Miss Mitchell. You must help me." Her hands fluttered about, as though she wanted to cover herself but also wanted Laila to see and understand.

The woman's left breast was swollen and discolored a bluish-green. Below the nipple was an oozing cavity Laila could have put her knuckle in.

Dear God. "I want to know all about this, don't leave out a thing." Laila tried to contain her shock. If this was an ulcer from a malignant cancer what could be done? There were claims for cancer cure—removal of the tumor in early stages, bleeding by way of leeches or lancet, change in diet. Silly creams, proprietary nonsense. A real doctor might know what to do—if only Mrs. Bolton would see one.

"May I?" She reached out to touch Mrs. Bolton's breast. "There seems to be a bit of fever around the abscess. Is it painful? Here? Or here?"

"Y-yes," Mrs. Bolton winced, "a little tender." Her face grew rosier, her eyes looked away in embarrassment.

"You must, absolutely must, see a regular doctor."

"Listen, please," Mrs. Bolton resisted. "The sore might not be so bad as it looks. I tried to clear it up on my own, but I think I've only succeeded in giving myself a worse sore that just won't go away. Help me, please." She slipped the last tiny button through its buttonhole, straightened her clothes, sat on the edge of the bed and motioned for Laila to sit in the rocker nearby, her eyes all the while pleading with Laila.

Laila sighed as she sat down. "All right. Tell me how this came about." Not that it would make a shred of difference.

Gladys Bolton had to see a doctor. A real doctor and a good one.

"I found a lump in my breast." Fresh tears started. "Not until much later did I remember how I got it. But by then it was . . . too late."

Laila motioned for her to explain.

"I'm positive I got the lump when I'd gone out to milk our cow and was giving her hay. She tossed her head and her horn struck my breast, hard."

"But that would only cause a hard bruise, if the skin wasn't broken. Such a lump would go away in time. You'd not have this open sore."

"Yes. But I wasn't thinking clearly when I first noticed the knot under my skin. The lump frightened me, I'd read some advertisements about—cancer. I didn't want to think that's what I had. I tried to rid the lump by rubbing it with camphorated oil, and liniment. There was no change and I became truly frightened. I'd seen a newspaper ad for Dr. Pitt's cancer medicine and the store in Richland had some."

Laila's brows rose in question.

"The advertisement said Pitt's Cancer Cure would *eat* the cancer, remove the growth at the roots. The flesh would grow back as though the cancerous growth had never been. I would be totally healed in ten to thirty days."

Laila sighed. "But it wasn't a *growth,* from what you're telling me, but a hard bruise, caused by the cow striking you." She had read about fat necrosis and hematoma—conditions resulting from injury to the breast, a hard blow. There would be destruction of some fat tissue within the breast. Or the blow could lead to the collection of a blood clot as the result of hemorrhage from a blood vessel within the breast. Either could result in a lump resembling cancer. But such a lump would be absorbed into the tissue, eventually, and would disappear.

"If you thought it was cancer, why didn't you see a doctor right away?"

"I am a modest woman, Miss Mitchell. Doctors available hereabouts are men, all of them. Besides—I was afraid they would cut me, leave me deformed. Vanity, I suppose, made me want to believe in the advertisement. Dr. Pitt's advertisement said he had successfully cured more than *sixty-thousand* cases of cancer with his remedy, and that he was currently treating one hundred and seventy-nine *physicians* afflicted with cancer."

"For heaven's sake, Mrs. Bolton, we cannot believe everything we read, no matter how convincing the claims sound." Laila shook her head. "I'm sure it's the acid that has done the harm, eaten this nasty hole in your flesh!"

"I'm positive of that now, too, and I've stopped using Pitt's Cancer Cure. The thing was, I wanted to take care of the matter without anyone else ever knowing. Not even my husband. The storekeeper's wife who sold me the medicine might have suspected something, but we didn't discuss it. The ad made me believe I could take care of the matter myself. When I said I would see only you, now that the damage was done, my husband insisted on going for you right away."

Laila felt sad for Mrs. Bolton, but it was hard not to show impatience with her, too. "If you'd gone to see a regular doctor, he would have checked you over, kept you under observation to make sure of your problem. You would have healed by now, I'm convinced." She reached over and grasped Mrs. Bolton's arm. "I believe I can ease your discomfort and some of your concerns, but not without your help. And I must have some guarantees from you." She sharpened her tone, "Do you agree?"

"Yes." Mrs. Bolton slipped a wadded handkerchief out of her sleeve and dried her tears. "I'll do anything to take care of this, be done with it once and for all." She sat up straighter, and her eyes locked hopefully with Laila's.

"The area around the abscess looks essentially healthy. The sore itself doesn't seem to be secreting a great deal of matter. I'd like to apply a warm water dressing to draw out as much discharge as possible, and repeat as necessary. Then, I'll apply a drying astringent, a zinc lotion or calamine. You'll see improvement rather quickly, *if this is* a normal abscess."

Mrs. Bolton smiled in relief. "That sounds fine."

"However," Laila said sternly, "I won't lift a finger to help unless you promise me you'll see a regular doctor within the week. Are we of the same mind?"

The woman looked distressed.

"I mean it!"

"All right, I will. The day after Christmas, I'll ask Charles to drive me to Baker City. The Richland doctor is a drunkard, and not—not very clean."

"It's agreed then. And Mrs. Bolton—Gladys, please don't believe the claims you read about medicines in the papers. An enormous percentage of the claims are false. I believe there may be a way to have this remedy you used, this so-called 'cure' investigated! If you told your story, and it turned out that others have had similarly unpleasant results, with luck the patent medicine company can be put out of business."

John Ryland, her apothecary friend in St. Louis, and a journalist friend of his, had recently taken on that very battle: to tell the truth about fraudulent medical treatments to the public in a series of magazine articles. They hoped to force the making of new government laws against medical quackery.

"Oh, I don't know about that, Miss Mitchell." She shook

her head. "I couldn't let the world onto how silly I've been, I couldn't." Her hands twisted in her lap.

Laila leaned forward and took her hand. "I know some people who would look into this, I trust them, and your name wouldn't have to be revealed, only the verifiable facts. You'd be helping other women like yourself, Mrs. Bolton. When people's very lives are in the balance, their well-being, they deserve the truth, not dangerous lies." She got to her feet and lifted her medicine kit to the bedside table. "Now let's get busy. We need some warm water. I'll have to ask you to please undo your bodice again . . ."

Mrs. Bolton nodded, saying over her shoulder as she headed for the kitchen, "I appreciate your coming to see me, Miss Mitchell. I really do." She hesitated, heaved a sigh. "I feel so much better after talking to you. I'll do what you ask. Please name your fee, and be plenty fair to yourself."

Laila smiled, and was thoughtful for a moment. "I'd be grateful, if by way of payment I could be taken on to Conner Creek in time for the Christmas holiday. Friends there are expecting Tansy and me."

Chapter Fourteen

A bright Christmas Day sun had begun to melt the light snow that lay on the ground at Ash's Conner Creek ranch. Laila, seated next to Bolton in his wagon, felt further welcomed by the sight of smoke curling from ranch-house and bunkhouse chimneys.

Tansy stood up in the wagon behind Laila, held Laila's shoulder for balance as they bumped along, and pointed ahead, "What's Mr. Corbett doing?"

"For the love of heaven, what *is* the man doing?" Laila caught Tansy's hand in hers as Bolton drove them in the direction of the house, past orchards where naked branches webbed artistic silhouettes against the blue sky. Ash Corbett was dancing like a whooping crane on the whitened lawn below the wide veranda. "Oh." As they drew close, Laila saw he stomped last flames from a small smoldering pine tree.

On the ground around him strands of garland sent off thin tendrils of smoke. Beautiful glass ornaments lay shattered. Small wax candles with blackened tips were everywhere.

"His Christmas tree burned!" Tansy said sadly.

"I'm afraid so," Laila squeezed her hand.

Ash looked fit to be tied and Laila gave him a perfunctory smile, a quick wave, in greeting. He touched his hat, then tipped it to the back of his head, waiting with hands on his hips, a scowl on his face. Laila had forgotten how long-leggedly handsome he was.

Pursing his lips and drawing in a long slow breath that chilled his lungs, Ash stared at Laila. The others in the wagon faded from his sight, mind, and thoughts. Laila's head covering had slipped to her shoulders and tendrils of dark hair surrounded her pretty face. She got down off the wagon in one graceful, fluid motion, her smile over her shoulder enchanting. In that moment, the real reason he'd wanted her to come to his place when she'd been ousted from the cabin, the reason he had been more than eager to invite her here for Christmas—a truth he had blocked from his mind 'til now—hit him hard. *He was falling in love with Laila Mitchell.*

Which made him the world's biggest fool, just asking for trouble. Feeling this way about a woman *again*—actually he'd never felt quite like this in his life before, not even with Claudine—was stupid.

He had told himself he was being thoughtful, a gentleman, offering her a place to stay when she had been turned out. He considered it a neighborly kindness to go ahead with the Christmas get-together for the two women. Kate had few women-friends. Except for the company of the little girl, Tansy, Laila had to be lonely as hell in her crude existence down canyon.

But he'd gotten the Mitchell woman here *for himself* first and foremost and he was a fraud to think anything else. He had wanted to feast his eyes on her, and given half a chance, to kiss her again and hold her. Behave the fool he was fast becoming, as she cast him in her spell, making shambles of his promise to himself to avoid serious feelings about any woman, after Claudine. Laila had been on his mind almost constantly since the salmon supper she fixed for him, the long evening they had shared at her place.

That night was the beginning of the end of his feelings for Claudine, and the attraction she held for him, he realized now. Although, from the moment he received Claudine's ultimatum that he move his father, before he ever met Laila, he had—at least subconsciously—seen the order as a way out of a relationship he shouldn't have been in, in the first place.

Now that Laila was here, he fairly itched to lope to her side and hold her hand like a schoolboy, stroke her hair, kiss her tender-sweet mouth again.

Hell, he was smarter than to get his feelings all tangled up over another beautiful woman, one who really didn't want him anyhow, so what the devil was going on?

"The doctorin' woman," as Laila was called, was nowhere near his kind of female, anyhow. The stories that sifted his way about Laila told him that. Claudine had been closer to his ideal, although she had turned out not to be the *right* one. He'd always liked 'em soft, sweet, and fragile—not tough, obstinate, and so darned independent. For damn certain, if and when he was ever fool enough to again consider marriage, settling down, having kids, it would be with a woman far different from Laila Mitchell. It was neither here nor there that she was as beautiful as Claudine, the rest of Laila's character, her personality, didn't suit him at all.

"Laila!" Kate burst from the house, arms stretched wide, huge white apron aflutter. The two women flew together, and hugged.

"Oh, Kate, it's so good to see you. Merry, merry Christmas! Say hello to Kate, Tansy."

Tansy came forward with a shy smile. On earlier visits she'd gotten on well with Kate. "Hello."

"Ah, my little darlin'!" As Kate buried Tansy in a big hug, Kate whispered confidentially, "We had a little accident with our Christmas tree, but we still have stockings to hang by the fire and I'm a'bettin' Santa finds us, tree or no!"

Then Kate and Laila hugged a second time.

Ash yanked his hatbrim low to block out the scene, but that didn't stop his aching to be in Kate's place, with that wild woman's arms wrapped around him, her feminine curves pressed against him. *For Christ's sake!* He stomped over to shake Charles Bolton's hand. The two of them had met a few times before. "Bolton," he growled.

"Howdy, Ash. 'Pears you had a Christmas tree fire?"

"Yeah."

"Everyone's all right, then?" Laila asked.

Ash glared in the direction of the ranch-house door Kate had left ajar. Barely showing there was a tuft of white hair and one peeking blue eye which suddenly vanished. *Old Tom.*

The newcomers were assured by both Kate and Ash that no one had been hurt. No damage done except to the tree, a burned spot or two on the parlor rug.

Laila explained she'd been seeing to a patient in New Bridge and Mr. Bolton had been kind enough to bring her and Tansy on to Conner Creek. True to her promise, she didn't reveal that her patient was Bolton's wife, Gladys, nor a word about her problem.

"I'm afraid I've come empty-handed though. My gifts for everyone are at Venture, along with fruitcake I made to bring."

"You wouldn't have needed to bring anything, we're just glad you're here," Ash Corbett said bluntly. His jaw was set in a hard, sideways twist, an imitation of a smile. His eyes held an expression that was more wary than friendly.

Laila was disappointed, but not surprised at his demeanor. He'd been really angry the night she refused his offer to move from the storage room to his place with him and Kate.

"Thank you, but I do want you all to have my gifts." She spoke mostly to Ash, fell silent as a current of unvoiced thoughts and sudden, magnetic feelings meshed between them.

Heavens! She liked Ash, very much. But he was set to marry another woman, a woman she guessed was very like his mother, a fine lady. And she likely only imagined that he was sincerely attracted to her. One stolen kiss would be meaningless to a man like him, and even if he had been free, Laila had no time for a romantic interlude of any sort. It was obvious he was still angry at her, almost to the point of being unwelcoming. She'd do well to remember the invitation was for Kate's sake, the simple act of a gentleman and kindly employer. Given any other choice, he likely would never have had anything to do with her again.

Even so, he was quite appealing as he stood there so stiff and arrogant, his jutting jaw streaked with ash, his brows looking tangled as if from a tornado. Suddenly, she had to smile.

His glance veered from hers, and he said huskily, "Miss Mitchell—Laila—it's cold out here. Why don't you ladies and the little girl go on into the house. Kate, keep an eye on Pa, will you? Old devil will burn the house down yet, if we let him." He nodded toward the huge barn, motioned to Bolton, "We'll put your horse up, Kate's got Christmas dinner all ready for the table."

"Can't stay to dinner, the wife's awaitin' on me to get back? But I'd be obliged to have my horse grained and watered, given a bit of rest? I'll have a cup of coffee and a little somethin' strong in it to warm me? For the trip home, if you got it?"

"Sure thing." Ash caught the halter of Bolton's bay and led the way to the barn. "We'll be right in, ladies." He glanced covertly back at the younger woman. God only knew what she'd do to a man fool enough to fall in love with her, but that wasn't going to be him.

He could bless his bones he'd figured things out, saw

where his heart was headed, before getting in too deep.

Hell, they were saying Laila had shot and killed a cougar that had been prowling around her place! He hadn't believed that at first, but he'd heard it from enough people now to guess that it was so.

Kate herded Laila and Tansy into the delicious smelling house, and took their coats. "Go on in the parlor if you want, Tansy," she said. "It's all Christmasy in there, think you'll like it." Clasping Laila's arms she said, "Lordy, it's good to see you." Kate's eyes glistened. "I feel I'm alookin' at a daughter of my own I ain't seen in too long a while. How are you doin' dearie, down there in the canyon? You don't stop to see us half often enough. Ash says you and the little girl got throwed out of your cabin, been sleepin' in a storeroom at the Venture store!" Her mouth pursed, "I been so worried."

Laila laughed. "We're doing fine, aren't we, Tansy?" She hugged Tansy's small shoulders and Tansy nodded before slipping away to stroke a fat gray cat that slept in front of the kitchen fireplace, and then move toward the other room. Laila told Kate, "We'll be in a place of our own again before spring. And you, Kate, how have you been? You look wonderful." Kate wore a handsome, high-necked russet gown, long sleeves ruffled at the wrist. Small garnet earrings adorned her ears. She looked healthy, happy.

The two women chattered away as they set the dining room table with fine china, crystal, and silver on a white tablecloth. Kate boasted that she had the best of everything in life. "Except a man," she chuckled behind her hand. "I'm still alookin' though."

Laila told her, "I have someone down my way I'd like you to meet." Hutton Ginther was a wonderful gentleman, and lonely. If she could pair the elderly Australian with Kate, it would be grand.

"You bring the fella here, or maybe Ash will take me on down your way. He's been meanin' to." She shook her head. "Lately, though, he's been so out of sorts it's hard to know what he wants. There's a burr under his saddle for sure. Whatever's eatin' him, it took him off to Portland in a huff last fall and he ain't acted real happy since. Not that he's not nice to me, he is. I suppose partly it's his Pa he's worried about. And I know for a fact that he'd like to spend more time in Portland, seein' to his hotel business, rather than bein' here babyin' Tom."

In all likelihood, he'd rather be in Portland with the lady of the letters, his intended, Laila thought. She said aloud, "I'm sure it's difficult for him, not to be able to spend more time in Portland with his bride-to-be, Miss Galen, too."

Kate shook her head, hesitated in her efforts to center an enormous bowl of red and white roses mixed with juniper and incense cedar on the table. She lowered her voice, "It's just a feelin', mind, but I think that love affair is over, that Miss Galen gave Ash the glove, or maybe he called the marriage off, himself. Just things I've overheard Ash sayin' to his Pa." Kate's eyes twinkled as if her news should hold special importance for Laila, then Kate flanked the flowers with white tapers in scroll-etched silver candle-stands, then lit them. She winked, "Ash ordered these hothouse roses special for us womenfolk and the child to enjoy today. Drove clear to Huntington to pick 'em up."

"How very kind of him. He has nice taste." Laila felt a warming rush of blood to her face. *Bless Bess,* why couldn't she have been better dressed for the occasion? She must look like a—a dowdy milkmaid! The calico, even in pretty red, wasn't suitable, really, for a holiday in Ash's lovely home.

Any woman who traveled to Europe and bought her clothes in Paris would probably laugh at the likes of Laila Mitchell in her calico. Laila tried to put from her mind Kate's supposition that Ash's marriage plans were over. Kate could be wrong. And what woman engaged to Ash would give him up easily? The romance probably wasn't over at all. Laila sighed, and wished her thudding heart would be still. She made an effort to focus on her surroundings that for a moment after Kate's announcement were a happy blur.

The walls of Ash's dining room were beautifully decorated with garlands of cedar and bristly brown pine-cones tied with red ribbon. The garland continued into the parlor, Laila saw through the open door. A fire glowed cozily in the fireplace of each room. In front of her, candlelight danced off the china, crystal, and silver place-settings. For an instant, she yearned to surround herself with such fine things again, as she had been those years in St. Louis at Mr. Saugrain's. *Ah, well.* With the circumstances of her life such as they were, she was lucky to have a place to live and could provide care to Tansy. Laila was fortunate to have a line of work and be independent. She could be glad to be alive at all.

As the women drifted into the parlor, Kate explained to both Laila and Tansy about the Christmas tree: "Ash said only him or me was to light them Christmas tree candles. That made the old man mad. He don't like bein' treated like a child even if he does act like one most times. Anyhow, Old Tom ups and tries to light the candles his ownself, meanin' no harm, though. His hands just natural shake like a couple cottonwoods in a windstorm, and that caused the fire."

"Ash seems pretty upset," Laila said with a frown.

"Well, Tom could've burnt the house down, truth to tell. Or at least he could've gutted it, stone on the outside wouldn't have burned. Mostly, it scared Ash that the old man coulda' hurt himself. We do got to watch him." She chuckled. "Ash says if he ever has kids of his own, he'll be plenty practiced dealing with children after mindin' his Pa."

"Oh?" Laila returned softly. When her own life was settled, she could give thought to marriage and more children to raise with Tansy. But certainly not now. Not for a long time. She wanted family, though. That was one of the main reasons she had come to Oregon to try and find her grandparents. She still hoped to find them alive wherever they were, had to know in any event what became of them.

Back in the dining room, Kate handed Laila a cut-glass water pitcher with a circling nod to fill the water goblets. "Ash loves his Pa," Kate said, "it's just that the old man is such a trial. It's hard for Ash to admit even to his ownself that he cares as much as he does. I rightly don't know what it's going to come to, between them two good men."

Death, Laila thought, remembering her parents. If she could bring Mama and Papa back, she'd want them even if they were "a trial." Maybe she should talk with Ash about his father, urge him to be more patient, more understanding for as long as he had the old gentleman with him. She would remind him that the devilment of advanced age couldn't be easy for anyone.

Of course, he might feel his problems were none of her business, and they weren't, really. She hoped they could be better friends, though. Whatever would be, would be. Today, the way he was so scowly and grouchy, she could hold scarce hope for even mild friendship.

At dinner, Ash had little to say, his eyes hardly ever meeting Laila's. Maybe, disturbed about his father, the fire and the Christmas tree, not being in Portland where he'd surely prefer to be, he was put out with the world in general. And again, he might be regretting he had invited her, even as a special gift to Kate. The way he was behaving, he only wanted the day to be over.

Old Tom, at the opposite end of the table, ate his ham and corn pudding noisily, not bothered by anything. At one point, he tossed a half-eaten roasted potato back into the china serving bowl. Ash looked too disgusted to say anything, but sagged deeper into his chair and looked the other way. Tansy covered her mouth to smother a giggle and Laila shook her head and smiled for Tansy to mind her manners.

It was Kate who plied Laila with questions about her life in the canyon. Laila briefly described her new cabin going up. "I think I'll be able to move in by February. The cabin will be roofed by then, and I'll have painted the inside. We've been waiting for a shipment of window-glass." She talked about her medical work, stories that were fit enough for table talk. She said with a solemn shake of her head, "A real doctor is needed in our area, badly."

At her last remark, Ash's head came up, hope and acknowledgment flashed in his eyes.

So he did believe her medical work was not adequate, that someone else, a real doctor ought to be in her place? She felt let down, but at the same time she could hardly argue the fact. In spite of the good she had done, the lives she had saved, she was not a trained professional and she was treading on thin ice. She spoke aloud, "I do the best I can, but one day a medical situation could come up that I'm not equipped to handle. The results could be tragic. I mean to do what I can to get a doctor established in the canyon before that happens. I could never forgive myself, otherwise."

"I could try to get a doctor to bring his practice here."

This time it was Laila's head that popped up, to look in hope at Ash. "You could?"

"I'll ask around in Portland."

"You're going back?" Her voice sounded so hollow and forlorn, she was momentarily embarrassed. She must be careful or everyone around the table would know her true feelings for Ash. Particularly him, even now he was giving her a strange look.

"I'm going back to Portland as soon as the holidays are over, for business and personal reasons," he said quietly. "I have plenty of friends there, someone might know somebody with good medical credentials, a man willing to set up a new practice. Although," he grimaced, "it won't be easy. To most folks, this canyon is the end of the earth, the hellish end. We'll be damned lucky to find a doctor willing to relocate here."

In defense of the area she had come to love, Laila maintained, "This canyon *is* far away from anywhere else, but it's also beautiful." She went on, ready to defend to the end what she believed. "Maybe there is a good doctor who is like—like Tom, here, who appreciates living in the wild. Maybe he will be quite glad to come."

For the very first time, Tom looked at Laila as if he liked her. The skin around his eyes crinkled and there was a sparkle in their depths.

"I think he'd have to be a fool, myself," Ash ground out. "But maybe such a doctor is out there, somewhere. We'll just have to find him."

"Yes," Laila replied, her own eyes flashing. "We just have to find him."

Frustration tore at her. Why was it that she and Ash were on the verge of argument any time they were in one another's company anymore? They both wanted a doctor. Why didn't they just leave it at that, why must they argue the disadvantages and advantages of the canyon? Clearly, a friendship wasn't going to build if they were always at odds on matters.

She took a sip of water against a thickening in her throat. It couldn't be more obvious that he was sorry to have her there, couldn't wait to deliver her back to Venture, and be shed of her.

Her consternation must have showed in her face. Kate said abruptly, looking worriedly from Laila to Ash, "Now, who is ready for some pumpkin pie?"

"Me," Old Tom grunted, then he hesitated and waved his fork at Laila. "No, serve the young lady her pie, first. My boy," he looked at Ash, "can wait."

Laila felt like blowing him a kiss. At least there was one Corbett at the table who didn't hate her.

"I want pie, please," Tansy said.

"Yes, you do, and it's a'comin'!" Kate replied with a wink and a smile at Laila's young charge.

The long trip back to Venture next day was an even worse nightmare than Laila expected it to be. And not only from the treachery of the narrow, icy, rock-strewn semi-road along the river's edge that kept the horse and buggy Ash drove—and them—in constant peril.

He hardly spoke the entire journey, and when he did, it was polite conversation as cold as the air around them. He stayed on his far side of the seat, made pains not to touch her. To please him, Laila sat well away from him. Which made her colder, and put her in danger of falling off the side of the buggy each time a wheel struck a rock. Her fury, her sheer unhappiness at both the physical and emotional distance between them grew with every chilly mile.

She turned to look now and then at Tansy, curled in blankets on the buggy's backseat. Tansy looked so drowsy and sweet, Laila almost wished to be riding in back with her.

It was a relief to reach Venture and the Thornhalls' store.

It was well after dark, snowflakes swirled around them, fairy-like in the light from the buggy's lantern. Without waiting for his assistance, Laila jumped down from the buggy, slipped and almost fell on her bottom. Her glare at him stopped him from getting down to make sure she was all right. "Come, Tansy," she said gently, helping her down. "We're home, angel."

Laila didn't invite Ash in. He said grimly, "I'll get some hot coffee at my friend's, and he'll give me a bed for the night."

"Do that!" she said. She added with icy politeness, "And thank you again, Ash, for inviting us to spend the holiday with Kate." Holding Tansy by the hand, Laila stomped away on legs numb with cold. She had never been so glad, as at that moment, to be shed of such disagreeable company, wanted nothing so much as to put this day and his bad mood behind her. She didn't look back.

If she had, she would have seen the look of deep longing on Ash's face as his eyes followed her through the falling snow.

Chapter Fifteen

Ash Corbett snatched a monogrammed towel from a shelf and stalked to a slatted bench in his hotel's steam room. The next twenty minutes damn well better loosen the perplexities of his soul as well as rid the canyon from his pores. He sat with his head back against the wall, towel across his lap. Blistering fog swirled around him and his hard flesh dripped with sweat. He willed his mind to go blank, and failed.

His life was out of his control, could no longer be called his own, and it was hard to know where to put the blame that it had happened. He didn't have to be beholden to Pop. The old man never should have planted all those goddamned peach trees in that godforsaken canyon in the first place.

He had his own work to do, or what was his degree in architecture for? Pruning peach trees, building more fruit sheds? Dammit, no, he was supposed to be *building hotels.* Leading his own life, anywhere he wanted to be. His choices.

He ought to haul the old man over here to civilization whether he wanted to come or not. His employees here at the hotel would love to spoil the old man silly, tend his every need. Forget that woman in the canyon, nursing Pop and the others. Claudine was right when she said they had real doctors and decent hospitals here in the city and his father would be better off here.

Claudine. He had received a couple of messages from her, suggesting that perhaps they'd been hasty and should meet and discuss resuming their relationship. As kindly and politely as possible, he had declined. Recently he had heard she was seeing Brick Nixon, a debonair, middle-aged financier worth millions, and looked very happy as she made the Portland social scene on Nixon's arm. Ash was relieved and in his mind he wished them well. He had enough problems of his own.

Like what the hell did he, Ash, think he was doing, inviting Laila to spend Christmas at Conner Creek even as a favor to Kate? For all the rest of the damn winter, he hadn't been able to get her image—slender yet curvy in that pretty red dress—out of his mind. Her beauty had a grip on him he couldn't shake and from Christmas on, through sleet, snow, and wind, the slightest excuse had him returning from Portland to the canyon, just because she was there. Later, in spite of having plenty else to do in the orchards as the weather improved, he'd gone chasing to get her to check over his Pop each time the old man so much as sneezed!

Ash rolled his head back and forth against the steam room wall, remembering how the caring touch of her hand on his arm, when she wanted to tell him something about his father, nearly reduced him to jelly. The clean, flowery scent of her, the rich, round tones of her voice, the liquid magic of her laughter, had seeped into his soul, become part of him. No matter how he battled to forget, and cussed the state of his heart, tried to reestablish his intention to forget women, she had a hold on him the likes he'd never felt before—not with Claudine, not with any woman.

God knew he had tried hard to end his feelings for Laila, list her as an attraction well over, as had happened with Claudine. He failed because of the loneliness over there in the canyon, the isolation, sure as hell. A man just naturally desired a woman. Why, there wasn't a dozen women in his part of the canyon under the age of fifty, and half of them were married. Kate Boston would look good to him if Laila wasn't there grabbing his attention.

No. No. He was lying to himself thinking that way. Laila, in red calico and later wrapped in that damned cougar skin, was the most beautiful woman he'd ever laid eyes on. His problem wasn't loneliness, or residual pain from ending his romance with Claudine, or any lack of other courtable women. It was Laila, herself. She was his trouble. Without the least effort on her part, she made him want her so bad he thought he might die if he couldn't have her.

He had to get hold of himself, though, because she didn't share the feeling and damned if he'd force himself on her.

Anyhow, he was better off without her. Laila—*damn!*—even her name was pretty—only looked like a gentle flower—lovely, cultured, refined, his type. He'd been wrong assuming on first meeting that she was delicate and out of place as his mother had been. He didn't want any woman who could kill big cats on her own, treat the ills of half of Eastern Oregon as good as a professional doctor, and live self-sufficient as if she had no need of another soul, no need of a man for anything.

Unless maybe it was an act that everything was fine and dandy with her? She had to be pretending when she insisted she loved the canyon, didn't she? No woman could be happy with so little. Every woman he knew wanted everything a fellow could provide them, and more, and more.

A man could enjoy taking care of Laila, giving her beautiful things, providing her a fine life here in Portland more suited to a woman. But Laila acted so damned happy, like she had everything she ever wanted, and no needs outside the damned canyon.

To hell with it. Too bad he had ever laid eyes on her. If he had never met her, at least he would be sane! Even before Claudine came into his life, he had always had his pick of available women—desirable, beautiful young ladies—here in Portland. And he'd been strongly attracted to some of them.

When those relationships didn't work out, he managed to forget them, to the point he couldn't bring their faces to mind six months after they parted. That same thing could happen again, this time with Laila. He could and would forget her. It just might be a little tougher, take a little more time.

He took the towel up and wiped at the steam dripping from him, buried his face for a moment in the raspy cloth. That woman in the canyon, the loneliness, thirty acres of peach trees, and responsibility for a nutty old man had him on the edge of losing his mind. Well, he could stop that, now, today.

A few minutes later he dried off, reached for his robe, smiled to himself. Back in his well-furnished room, he dressed carefully, relishing his fine city clothes: merino undershirt and drawers, lisle half hose, pleated front linen shirt. On went a Burnaby collar and cuffs, satin Glendale tie in stripes of grey, black, and brown. He thrust muscled legs into trousers, fastened silk suspenders, got into the trousers' matching cutaway coat of imported worsted the color of rich, black coffee. Shoved his feet into walnut brown Wellington boots. Already he was feeling better, a new man.

He sang in lusty baritone as he brushed his ashy-brown hair,

"I've a secret in my heart, Sweet Marie;
A tale I would impart, love for thee.
Every daisy in the dell
Knows my secret, knows it well
And yet I dare not tell,
Sweet Marie!"

He found Otis Halliday, his manager, downstairs in the lobby. Halliday, though slight in stature, nevertheless struck an imposing figure, and was commonly referred to as

"Count." He was a dark-complexioned man, immaculate in a black cutaway evening suit and black and silver tie. Ash was grateful for The Count, a man who loved his work and did it well, allowing him to be away so much of the time.

"Otis, do me a favor."

"Yes, of course, sir." The congenial Count returned Ash's smile.

"Invite Miss Marie Jessup to meet me here at the hotel, this afternoon if she can make it. There are a few things I need to discuss with her." The lovely Miss Jessup had directed the most recent refurbishing of the hotel and had done a smashing job. He ought to tell her how he felt about it, maybe give her a bonus.

The yellows and tans of the previous decor had come to look dirty, and Ash had never cared for the heavy, stiff Empire furnishings stained black. Miss Jessup had introduced red draperies with white under-sheers against white walls. Deep Axminster carpet patterned in greys and reds. There was new Chippendale furniture in mahogany, sparkling new light-reflecting chandeliers and wall sconces, and gilt-framed landscape paintings by Inness, Van Dyck, Goya.

Ash himself had insisted on having large upholstered sofas in the lobby, and smaller versions in the rooms. Glittery elegance was all right as long as it was accompanied by comfort.

Redecorating had cost him a fortune but business had picked up thrice-fold. The Corbett Grand had become *the* place to stay in Portland. Local merchants chose his lobby for meeting out-of-town business associates. Ladies met their friends there, before turning to the dining room for tea. For some the Grand was a residence, a few permanents having lived there from the day it was built. On any given day those men could be found in the lobby reading newspapers, their ladies employed in people-watching.

"Anything else, sir?"

Halliday had waited patiently while Ash mused.

"If I was to take the young lady to dinner in our own dining room, tonight, what is the Chef recommending?"

"Fresh oysters to begin the meal. Pork tenderloin with apple jelly and crisp sauteed potatoes and fresh fruit. He's also offering partridge with bread sauce, or you might prefer halibut au gratin and potato balls. For dessert there is Raspberry Cheesecake, Nougat Cake, or Bavarian Cream. You'll want to begin your repast with champagne, or a fine Madeira."

No, he felt more like getting roaring drunk on straight whiskey. But he answered, "Sounds good, Count, and thanks." For the pleasure of Miss Marie Jessup's company he'd stick to wine. *Every daisy in the dell knows my secret, knows it well . . .*

"Any good theatre showing in town just now?"

Halliday nodded. "A traveling troupe of players are presenting *The Prisoner of Zenda* at the Willamette Theatre. The New market Theatre offers Italian grand opera. Miss Ada Rehan is in town playing in *The Taming of the Shrew.*"

Ash wrinkled his nose, straightened his tie. "We'll see."

Later, he sat across from the petite Miss Jessup at a table in a darkened corner of the dining room. Candlelight flickered across their facial features and touched on their moving hands as their evening together lengthened.

"Your father is a lawyer and rancher, you say?" Ash found it hard to hold up his end of their conversation. He'd eaten too much, he felt bound up in his city suit. He threw back a large swig of wine that reminded him of syrup, set his glass down, tried to show more interest in his dinner partner. The evening had not been going well for some time, and he had no idea why.

Miss Jessup was a pert, pretty woman with smoky blue eyes in a pixie-ish face. A few cute freckles dusted her nose. She wore small, gold-rimmed spectacles that were most often folded in her hand and waved to make a point. She was attentive, a good conversationalist. And yet, all evening, Ash had to remind himself of the damned song to even remember her name: Marie. The worst, twice he got carried away telling her stories of the canyon and almost called her "Laila."

"Yes, he's a country lawyer with a small practice down in the Willamette Valley, and he ranches on the side." Marie Jessup took a dainty sip of Madeira, smiled at him.

"Do you like Portland better than—wherever, down there?" Lord, but he'd like to prop his elbow on the table, lean his tired head into his hand, and just go to sleep while she talked.

"I prefer Portland over Lebanon, yes. For a time I thought I might study law and follow in my father's footsteps. But then I chose interior decoration and design instead. I'm not sure the world is ready for women lawyers and judges, but the day is close at hand. Don't you think so?" She wagged her spectacles at him, repeating, "Don't you believe, Mr. Corbett, that the world is about ready for women in the field of law?"

"Uh, well—" Ash fought a yawn, straightened his long, cramped legs under the table, bumped Miss Jessup's ankle hard, apologized. God, he was being a clod. He sat up straight, took her hand in his and put on his best smile. "It would have been the world's loss, if you hadn't become a decorator, uh, *Marie*. You made the right choice. You do excellent, beautiful work."

"You've complimented my work at least ten times already,

but thank you, Mr. Corbett, you're very kind." Her fingers surreptitiously, bravely, squeezed his in return while her smoky gaze clung to his with unusual warmth.

Every daisy in the dell knows a secret I can't tell, I'm in love with a woman not *named Marie.*

Like a determined dragonfly flitting from blossom to blossom, Ash saw a different woman nearly every evening for the following week and a half. He found none to his special liking, was bored out of his mind. Something was radically amiss. In the past he had always been able to enjoy a woman's company on some level, whether or not he was romantically involved with her. Now, he found himself being far too picky. He could not relax, but found serious fault in every female he spent an evening with. It took strong effort not to be rude, or a bore, himself.

There was Amy Forstairs, a banker's daughter whose innocent beauty hid an ice-cold brain. Next, Nettie Hammond, of the lumber mill and railroad Hammonds—in spite of his hopes otherwise, her wistful, fragile manner was clearly false, put on for his benefit like a delicate spider web meant to trap a fly.

Like a chain of paper dolls, other women followed Amy and Nettie. He was determined to change the fact that going out had become more work than pleasure.

On one occasion he had let himself be seduced by a hotel rounder, a friendly, midnight-eyed girl, a Venus de Milo with arms. She had no permanent address, but made the rounds, living in one hotel after the other. She'd seen him only as comfort for the night, as he had seen her. Then in the morning he had been more miserable than ever.

Twice again, he'd called on Marie Jessup, who was nice enough. Both evenings turned out as badly, if not worse, than the first. The next time he asked to see her, she turned him down. He'd felt intensely relieved, and had gone back to his private suite at the hotel to study drawings of a hotel he hoped to build in Seattle, and work over the Grand's account books until almost dawn.

While he could, though, he partook of the special benefits of his hotel: tonsorial parlor, fine food, light social interchange with hotel guests. On a couple of afternoons he made the rounds of museums, art galleries, took in a musical event or two, and was disgusted with himself when he found his mind wandering to the wilderness sights and sounds of the Snake River Canyon.

A half dozen strong drinks in the bar, afterward, was not enough to blur the image of the dark-haired, square-jawed, beautiful and competent woman who lived over there. *Oh, Laila.*

One morning at the beginning of the third week, Halliday knocked sharply at the bedroom door of Ash's suite and at Ash's request came into the room. "Sorry to wake you, Sir. But a wire has come, a quite urgent request for you to return to Eastern Oregon."

Yawning, Ash sat up slowly in the huge polished mahogany four-poster bed. He pushed his sheet and butter-yellow blanket down around his waist, rubbed his eyes, drove his fingers through his hair. "Who sent the wire?"

"A Miss Mitchell sent the wire, Sir. Miss Lolly Mitchell."

Ash froze, then he burst into action, nearly breaking his neck as he tried to untangle his long legs from the bedding and get up. He grabbed fresh clothes from the mahogany wardrobe. "Name's Laila, somebody got the name wrong. Her name is Laila."

Chapter Sixteen

Back at the canyon ranch, Ash paced the bedroom where his father—a pale shell of the man he used to be—lay in bed with his bound broken arm pillowed on the coverlet. Under the covers, his cracked and bruised ribs had also been bound. Old Tom slept restlessly, each slight movement he made caused him to wince with pain and gum his lips. His false teeth had been removed, making his mouth a collapsed cavern.

Laila sat close by the bed, her hand lay affectionately on Old Tom's other withered paw. From the distant kitchen came the muted chatter between Kate and Tansy as well as the fragrance of baking sugar cookies.

"What the hell was he doing in a tree, anyway?" Ash fought mixed emotions, remorse and sorrow about Pop, disappointment that Laila hadn't wanted his return to the canyon for herself.

"There's no need to swear or to look at me like that, Ash," she said quietly. "I've done nothing wrong and neither did Old Tom. One of the peach trees hadn't been pruned properly, he thought, and he was trying to fix it."

"He's too damned old to be climbing trees! And the orchards were pruned just fine in February. I saw to that before I went to Portland."

"Yes, he's too old to climb, but it's difficult for him to accept it. Try to be more understanding, Ash." She slipped from the chair and with skirts awhirl led the way out into the hall. She closed the door. "Put yourself in his place. Would you appreciate being told what you can and cannot do because of your age? How can it feel having other people think of you as useless when you want to live, when you're not ready to die?"

Ash's face heated up. "You talk like this was my fault!" He resisted the urge to grab her and shake her for being so calm and caring about his father, so sweet, and right. He shook his finger. "Listen, that old fellow in there can get around me, around Kate, and a whole crew of my workers when he wants to. That accident could have happened just as easy if I'd been there."

"Of course it could have. Ash, I'm not blaming you." She tucked a brown tendril of hair behind her ear, and backed away from his anger. "It would be good for your father, though, if you could spend more time with him." Since Christmas, he had made one trip after another to Portland. Not that those trips weren't important. He was searching for a doctor for the canyon, so far unsuccessfully, and his "other life"—his friends, his hotel, were there. But Tom was important, too.

Ash advanced again. "I've already done more for the old son-of-gun than he ever did for me!" That he spoke the truth didn't make him any happier for saying it. He was not a whiner and what he did for his father was his own choice. *But damn!*

"Oh, Ash, I know you've sacrificed your own life for him, to keep him happy." She caught his hand in sympathy. Distracted by the large size and warmth of his palm against hers, she hastily let go. "Maybe I shouldn't have rushed to call you home," she said, flustered. "His injuries aren't terribly serious, but with his age—you never know. It's just that he's lonely for you when you're gone, and he is hurt." She changed the subject, circling away from him, "Did you have success in Portland, did you accomplish what you wanted to do?"

He shrugged, scowling as he was reminded that his main mission in the city—to rid himself of her constant intrusion in his thoughts and bring order to his life, romantically and professionally—had been anything but successful.

At the moment, his heart thudded crazily from the simple touch of her hand. And he was tired of his part in this whole discussion about his father. He drove his fingers through his hair in exasperation. "Listen, I'm as sorry as you are that Pa got hurt. Should he be hospitalized, do you think?"

"I tried. We were going to take him to Baker City, but he wouldn't have it. Now, I'm not so sure, myself, that it's a good idea. I believe he'll recover faster here at home. Regardless of how much he grouses about the canyon, he likes it here better than anywhere else."

"I'm afraid that's all true, unfortunately." Otherwise, it would have been an ideal time to move the old man out into real comfort. "You're pretty busy," he said brusquely. "Will you be able to take care of him?" He half hoped not. She'd be within arm's reach too often and how could he resist her, then?

"I would like to." She smiled. "He's a dear, and I think he likes me, too. If you trust in my ability, why, then, yes, I'll do my best to see him recover." She was freer than she had been for some time. Canyon folks' ills and accidents had abated with the coming of spring. Kate loved having Tansy around.

Ash stared at Laila, his eyes on her pursed lips, her softly veiled hazel eyes that were intent on some vision beyond the room. *God she was lovely*. Her cheeks had the healthy glow of ripe peaches, she smelled like fine flowers, and it was all he could do not to reach out and caress her face, tangle his fingers in her hair. He had had this fever to touch her from the moment he got back.

To blazes, then. As he'd done a hundred times in as many

dreams but one more time for real, he reached out and swept her close. He brought his mouth down to hers, tenderly at first, then tasting, loving deeply. As he'd known would happen, the kiss reached every part of him, brought a fire to his blood.

Laila gave a small murmur of surprise against his lips. The ever increasing pressure of his mouth on hers, the close contact of his long lean body to hers, brought her a sudden, soaring tide of emotion. Surprising herself, she returned his kisses with a hunger to match his own. She realized how starved she had been for months to be in his arms again, she saw how foolish she was to have rejected such bliss. He was no longer attached, his marriage plans to Claudine ended. Would a brief, sweet romance be so wrong?

If this wasn't heaven, it was close . . .

Swept away with thought and dizzying feelings, she stumbled when he finally released her. He caught her again to steady her, held her away. What had she done wrong? she wondered, wanting to be back in his arms.

He said huskily, looking down at her, "I apologize for just grabbing and kissing you like that." His eyes glistened, the strong planes of his face filled with color, he seemed almost to tremble. "I couldn't help myself, but if you want we will just say it was me telling you thanks for taking such good care of Pop."

Just barely aware of what he was saying, she stared up at him, dumbstruck with knowledge at how much she really loved him, in spite of every effort she'd plied against such a thing happening.

She was sure he felt the same, and yet, standing just inches away from her, he showed little sign of it. His face was set in a hard frown, his intense blue eyes were sweeping the room, seeing everything but her, what he'd done to her. Only a thank you, that was all that wonderful intimate moment had meant to him? Or was he, for some reason, avoiding the truth of it?

Caught in a turmoil of feelings and unanswered questions, it was several seconds before she could reply. And then her throat was full, her voice husky, "In that case, I suppose—you're welcome."

She watched him turn and stride down the hall. Scarcely able to breathe, it was as though her heart marched with him, toward whatever turn his life or hers might next take. It was the oddest feeling of her existence, as though she had shed an old skin of herself. She had become someone brand new, and naked to all kinds of fresh, unfathomable possibilities.

Suddenly, she was overcome with feelings of excitement, an eager welcoming, her anxiety of just moments before vanishing.

That she was in love with his son had little to do with Laila's fondness for Old Tom. She liked him for himself, and she gladly added his care to her other nursing chores.

His cracked ribs made breathing difficult for him, and painful. She hovered over him the first weeks, seeing that he ate properly, drank plenty of water and nourishing broths, took his medicine to prevent infection, got lots of fresh air into his weak old lungs. She checked and double-checked that his broken arm was healing properly.

When she had to be away, she left instructions for Kate, or Ash if he were there, to watch for signs of a cold. She wanted to squash respiratory troubles before they became pneumonia which would kill him. Old bones took their time mending, but slowly, gradually, he improved.

By early summer, he was finally able to hobble about the

place, his good arm hooked through hers, telling her what the canyon was like when he came: wild, virgin country, game plentiful, with the only other souls around a few Indians who summered in the canyon. Then he would stop in his tracks and cuss the blooming peach trees a blue-streak, and himself for planting them.

With a quiet smile, Laila would remind him that the orchards were wonderful, provided work for many men, supplied food and treats for countless people. And he had a fine son looking after the place.

Had nothing to do with the growing of him, he'd tell her, Ash's mother did that.

All the same, Laila would pat his hand, feeling herself flush at thought of Ash, all the same.

They were having lunch at a small table moved out into the orchard one day: Ash, silent and withdrawn as he ate, his father busy gnawing at a chicken leg, Kate and Laila chatting, and Tansy tugging at Laila's sleeve and asking for another glass of lemonade. Laila, looking across the way toward the river, was the first to see the boat arriving at the dock. She poured Tansy's lemonade. "We should have fried more chicken," Laila casually suggested to Kate, "but there's plenty of ham and pie. Ash seems to have company."

Ash's eyes narrowed as he followed Kate and Laila's glance to the riverbank. His jaw dropped. "Claudine!" he muttered, "what the hell?" He stood up and strode to meet the woman being carefully assisted from the boat by a well-dressed older man, as the boatman, on the bank, anchored the vessel in place.

Laila's heart wrenched as Ash hurried to the visitors and embraced the woman. A woman who looked as beautiful and misplaced as a figure stepping out of a Monet painting into harsh reality. Ash's voice floated back as he shook the older man's hand, "Mr. Galen, Claudine, I wasn't expecting you, but welcome to Conner Creek." Ash turned to call, "Laila, Kate, Pop, Tansy, I'd like you to meet my friends, Mr. Galen and his daughter, Claudine."

"Come with us, Tom," Laila said, "you can take my arm."

"Nope," he answered, and continued to eat, unconcerned as the others stood up from the table.

"All right," Laila shrugged, and waited for Kate and Tansy.

"What's that woman doin' here?" Kate asked with a scowl, brushing a crumb from her plump bosom.

"She's beautiful," Laila responded in a hollow voice.

"Beauty is as beauty does! An' she's got no business chasin' after Ash when everything's over and done between 'em."

"We don't know any of that, why she's here," Laila admonished in a whisper as she and Kate walked forward, Tansy trailing. "The Galens and Ash are friends, and why they've come isn't really our business."

Kate's response was a derisive snort.

They reached the others. As introductions were being made, Claudine's eyes showed a glimmer of confusion, even resentment, taking in Laila, then she was smiling, cordial and polite, "It's very nice to meet you, Miss Mitchell." She was equally friendly to Kate and Tansy. As Tom stumbled up, Claudine rushed forward. "And you're Ash's father! It's so wonderful to meet you, Mr. Corbett!" She caught his chicken-greasy fingers in her own, then with a tiny frown, she released his hand.

Tom asked, leaning on his cane, "Where'd you and the gent come from?"

"Why, we came from Portland, Mr. Corbett. I asked my

father to escort me here so that I could visit Ash and have a talk with you."

"Can't have a talk, gonna take my nap," Tom said bluntly, and headed, stumbling, for the house.

"I'll help you!" Laila called out and started after him, worried that he could fall.

He waved her off, "No need. But if you can, get rid of them city people."

Claudine colored and bit her lip. Mr. Galen, a tall, handsome, gray-haired man, said, "I wouldn't mind a nap myself. That's a hell of a trip we just made, Ash, but Claudine wanted to see you." He nodded toward Tom, tottering away, "I take it that your father doesn't like company?"

"I'm very sorry, Claudine, Mr. Galen, for my father's rudeness." Ash fought amusement behind his sincere concern, his apology. He explained to the Galens, "I'd like to say that my father isn't normally like this, but I'm afraid that he is. It has nothing to do with you, he's like this with everyone. My Pop would live a hermit's life in a cave, given half a chance."

Claudine, with a warm confident smile, snugged her arm through Ash's, deliberately brushing her breasts against his muscled forearm, "I'm sure I can change your father's mind about that. And that's what I've come to do." Her expression and actions said she was equally confident about changing Ash's mind concerning their ended relationship.

Ash didn't answer directly, but suggested the Galens might appreciate some lunch, and a rest.

Mr. Galen nodded, commenting again about the uncomfortable trip there.

"If you'll excuse us," Laila broke in quickly, "Kate and I will clear away our picnic things, and bring you some sandwiches and drinks."

Tansy asked if she could play with Ash's barn cats. Laila, stacking plates, agreed, and Kate admonished with a shake of a fork, "Mind you don't get scratched, honey. Them cats is wild. Nice to meet you Miss Galen, Mr. Galen," Kate bobbed slightly at the visitors settling into their chairs, although she didn't bother to smile. "We'll bring you some lunch right away. After that, if anybody needs me, I'll be in the kitchen lookin' after supper fixin's."

It was a strange afternoon, Laila reflected later. She tried to guess if Ash was glad to see Claudine and her father, but it was hard to tell. Ash was an attentive host, as always. The Galens were served lunch, which Claudine hardly touched. Late in the afternoon, when the visitors came from their rooms, refreshed, Ash attempted to show them his operation, the orchard.

Laila, going to the barn to check on Tansy, overheard drifts of complaint from Claudine: the clods of dirt they stumbled over were ruining her shoes. She shrilled with worry that she would be stung by bees. Within five minutes, Claudine had seen all she cared to and begged for them to go inside.

Tom napped most of the afternoon and Laila approved. Since his accident, she wanted to see him grow stronger and stronger, and lots of rest was helping him.

After supper, Laila helped Kate tidy up the kitchen. Mr. Galen was graciously hearing Tansy's reading lesson in the parlor, a task Ash normally liked, while Ash and Claudine sat talking outside on the porch. Later, when Ash and Claudine's voices rose, Laila got up from the table where she and Kate sipped coffee, and started across the room to close the window.

"Don't take another step, Laila," Kate hissed, "this is my

kitchen, I'm the boss here, and I want that window open!"

"But—we can hear—them. And it's not polite to eavesdrop," Laila whispered back, mortified.

"Maybe yes, maybe no, but I'm gonna hear this." Kate grinned and motioned to Laila to sit down, then she cupped her ear and leaned forward.

Laila sat with her elbows on the table, her head in her hands, embarrassed, yet not able to take herself from the room as she should.

"I haven't changed my mind, Claudine," Ash's voice came from the porch. "I can't move Pop. For one thing, he had an accident, a fall, and he's still recovering." It was the third time he'd made the statement since the conversation began and his irritation was close to the surface as he spoke.

Claudine was persistent, confident, "If you'd just give me a chance to convince your father, explain how important it is to *our* lives that he move to Portland, I'm sure he'd agree."

"You don't know Pop, and he wouldn't agree." He sighed heavily, "Like I told you before, Claudine, this isn't only about Pop and my spending so much time with him here in the canyon. The main reason I called off our engagement is that we're not right for one another, and getting married would be a mistake. I'm sorry to have hurt you, but I can't make this any plainer."

There was a long silence, then Claudine said, "It's her, isn't, that made you change your mind, that young woman inside, Laila?"

In the kitchen, Laila's breath caught; Kate smiled and waited.

Ash didn't answer Claudine's question, only growled that Laila was there to look after his father's health.

"I knew it, I knew the minute I saw her, the two of you are in love, though you may deny it and make excuses about your father!" Claudine must have stood up suddenly, there was the scraping of a chair. When Ash said nothing, she continued, speaking bitterly, "I came here to give us one last chance, Ash. But it seems I've wasted my time. Brick Nixon has asked me to marry him. Fortunately, he doesn't have any complications in his life such as you have!"

"Bully for him, he's damned lucky."

"You make me so angry, Ash! It wouldn't bother you, then, if I consider Brick's proposal?"

"Like I said, he's damned lucky."

Chapter Seventeen

The Galens left very early the next morning. Laila wondered about the conversation between Ash and Claudine. Not once had Claudine said she loved him, that she couldn't exist without him, and that that was her reason for wanting a reconciliation.

Kate was probably correct when she said, as she and Laila washed breakfast dishes together, that Claudine likely hadn't heard the word 'no' in her entire life and was used to having her way. She might turn down suitors herself, but never, never had a fellow jilted her before, and that was the difficult hurdle for her this time. If an axe was swung, she wanted to be the one to swing it.

Kate, handing Laila a wet plate, chortled, "Now, my sweet girlie, you got a straight clear path to Ash's heart. See that you don't stumble along the way."

Laila just shook her head, but she couldn't help the smile tugging at her mouth.

Whatever Ash's true feelings were toward her, it was hard to tell in the period that followed. He seemed always out somewhere working on the ranch. Or seeing to the grading of the advancing road up on the rims, or the old trail along the river's edge that was being widened to take out the most dangerous spots. He made another trip to Portland. Claudine might be out of the picture, but Laila sensed that Ash saw other women there and the knowledge hurt. Those women would be beautiful and cultured—like Claudine, and like his mother had been. The kind of woman he made it plain he preferred.

She was not at all like that, was even very different from

Ash. He felt held back by the canyon, hated the area she had come to love. He was well-educated, she was not. His upbringing had been on a higher scale than her family's.

Of late, she sensed a push-pull of coolness and fire between them whenever they were in the same room together and she worried that it could end very badly. He would look at her with a hunger identical to that she felt, yet he would remain distant, treating her formally, as politely cool as he might have a stranger. She knew with certainty now that he was physically attracted to her. Yet, from his odd behavior she could only conclude that whatever his true feelings were for her, he was not happy in them.

If he cared for her as she was, he would say so. Instead he avoided her as if she were—toxic, or as if she might give him the plague. That knowledge left her deeply disappointed, feeling blue, and somehow guilty for being who she was.

From time to time she considered telling him of her change of heart, reveal openly that she was in love with him. She might suggest to him that somehow, they might make a life together, providing he felt the same about her. But she worried what his reaction might be. He already thought of her as something of a wild woman, daft to be where she was. If she were too bold, it might scare him off. Better to wait and see what might transpire.

Sometimes, she wished for the strength to not want him. And yet, his kisses, the way he had held her—particularly that last brief but intense time—had struck an unquenchable yearning in her. That taste of sweetness and passion had made her want a—a feast, fulfillment. Ash was *her* disease she couldn't cure, even though to him, it seemed, she was only his father's nurse, and a mild attraction. The fact that she stayed busy as a squirrel, and he avoided close proximity, made no difference. Ash was now so fixed in her heart he could have been there from the beginning. Perhaps he had been, she guessed, but she had made herself too busy making a new life to notice.

She decided that his disinterest—beyond the thanks he expressed for the care she gave his ailing father, and those few kisses—was for the best. "Honey-fussin' " as Kate termed courtship, would only bring new complications to her life when she already had aplenty if he really didn't want her.

It was a relief when Old Tom was well enough that Laila didn't have to keep returning to Conner Creek. Any more time in Ash's presence, she reflected, and she would be throwing herself at his feet. A scene that would be a humiliation to them both.

The day that Laila and Tansy had longed for had arrived; their new cabin was finished. They sang in unison as they carried Laila's things from where they'd been stored in back of the general store: "Skip, skip, skip to my Lou; skip, skip, skip to my Lou; skip, skip, skip to my Lou; skip to my Lou, my darlin'!"

Laila's black and chrome stove had been delivered from Baker City and sat royally in the kitchen. Because Ash had paid her well for the care she gave his father, she in turn had paid Hutton Ginther handsomely to build her lovely oak table and chairs, provisions cupboards, and two small beds. Hutton hadn't wanted to take payment, saying it was a favor to a friend, but Laila overrode his objections. She felt intense pride that the furnishings were paid for from her nursing skills.

Laila patted smooth the quilts on their beds. "Honey," she said to Tansy, who stood on a chair stowing white china plates and cups on the shelf near the stove, "I'm famished. The Thornhalls stocked a nice wheel of cheddar cheese at the store the other day. Would you run and ask them to give you a half pound and put in on my bill? We'll have a quick lunch of cheese and crackers and tomatoes."

Tansy scrambled from the chair. "Shall I get us some lemon drops, too?"

Laila smiled to herself, "Yes, lemon drops, too. We've both worked hard today and deserve a special treat."

While Tansy was gone, Laila unpacked food staples and placed them in the provisions cupboards that she'd curtained with a cinnamon pink print. Later, as she hung curtains of the same print at the window, she looked out to see if Tansy was on her way back. There was no sign of her. Laila, frowning, hoped that Opal wasn't causing the child difficulty. Laila wished now that she had gone to the store herself.

She scooted her large trunk into position at the foot of her bed, positioned her rocking chair, and then sat down for a few moments to rest. Above her bed she had fastened a shelf the length of the wall. She got up and put her few books on the shelf, as well as some papers, and her walnut clock.

The clock reminded her that Tansy still hadn't returned and yet she'd been gone much longer than the task would normally take; the store was only a few yards up the hill. Laila went outside and looked, but Tansy was nowhere in sight. *This was too odd. The child couldn't just vanish.* Laila grabbed her skirts in hand and ran up the hill. She burst into the store, immediately saw that Tansy wasn't there. "Where's Tansy? I sent her here more than a half hour ago for some cheese. Where is she?" The mystery of the child's disappearance sent her heart racing.

Opal's eyes glittered from her position behind the main counter. "Tansy's with her mother." Her plump chin lifted and she smiled with a mix of malice and triumph.

Laila went suddenly numb, "Her mother? What on earth

are you talking about? How can she be with her mother? Only a while ago I sent Tansy here to the store . . ."

"Now, Laila, don't get upset," Opal said with false sympathy, watching Laila's face, "but Minnie Sellers got to Venture last night. Hob Riley sent one of his men to meet her when she got in on the Huntington train and he brought her here horseback."

"Why didn't anyone tell me about this?"

Opal didn't answer but her look said that it wasn't Laila's business.

"I want to know what happened."

"Minnie came down to the store today and was talking to me when Tansy came for the cheese. Minnie nearly fell to pieces with joy seeing her little child."

"Where are they?"

"They went off up to Hob Riley's cabin. Real sweet, Minnie and Tansy's reunion."

"Hob's place?" Hob Riley had an intense dislike for Tansy, considered her a "stray cat", ran her off when the child begged food at the mine camp. Laila's head swirled and she grabbed the edge of the counter to steady herself. She repeated, "Tansy is with her mother at Hob's cabin?"

Opal nodded, "Minnie was Hob's woman for a while before she left, and now she's come back to him. Came back for Tansy, too—said she's not had a happy day since she left her little girl behind. She told Tansy that to her face, I heard her say it as she cried and held Tansy."

"Hob Riley's cabin is the last one up at the end of the trail?"

Opal nodded and Laila whirled for the door. Opal shouted after her, "Minnie's got every right to Tansy, the child is hers, Laila!"

No, the woman has no right at all to Tansy, she abandoned

her, she wanted to shout back, *Tansy is my little girl!* But of course, Minnie was the one who had a right to Tansy, she was her mother. Laila had no rights at all. Love, sometimes, didn't count for anything. It was her own fault for not suspecting this day would come, her own fault for the pain tearing her up inside.

Although Laila's impulse was to plunge into Riley's cabin, grab Tansy and run, she knocked lightly at the door. As she waited, she struggled for every ounce of composure she could gather.

She knocked twice more, and then the door opened. A frowsy young woman, her black hair worn in a tangled bun, the neckline of her wrinkled green dress undone and exposing the tops of her ample breasts, said, "Yeah?" Minnie Sellers stared at Laila from yellowish brown eyes. The flesh around her eyes was swollen as though she'd been sleeping. She yawned.

"I'm Laila Mitchell. I've been taking care of your daughter."

Minnie nodded back over shoulder, "Tansy saw you comin' out the window. I knowed who you was."

Laila looked past Minnie to where Tansy waited in the middle of the room, her expression bewildered. She held tightly to a large, beautiful doll in her arms. Laila smiled at her, and asked Minnie, "May I come in?"

Minnie shrugged and warned, "You're not to get any ideas about taking my little Tansy away from me."

"No, I won't."

Minnie slunk back out of the way and motioned for Laila to come inside.

Except for a messy pile of women's clothing falling off of a chair, and a pair of women's shoes kicked haphazard in the corner, the interior of the cabin was tidy. Hob evidently was one of those bachelor types who liked everything in its place.

It was easy to guess what he wanted Minnie for, but how long he would tolerate Tansy's presence in his life was anyone's guess.

"Are you all right, Tansy?" Laila asked.

Tansy nodded. "My Mama brought me this doll," she held it toward Laila.

"It's a beautiful doll."

"I didn't get the cheese, Laya. I'm sorry. But Mama came back. She came back for me, and brought me this doll."

"It's all right about the cheese. Do you want to stay here, honey?"

Tansy hesitated. "I wanted to live in our nice cabin with you, Laya. But then Mama—she came back. She wants me to be with her." The thrill of being wanted by her own mother was plain in Tansy's small earnest face.

Laila nodded, and said around the lump in her throat, "I understand. I hope you'll come to see me often, though, Tansy, in our—in the new cabin." *How could she walk away and leave her here, how?* "Minnie—Mrs. Sellers, if you ever change your mind . . ."

Minnie shrugged, "You're goin' to upset my Tansy, you keep talkin' that way. You better leave." She went to hold the door open, and admitted, "Tansy says you took good care of her, and Opal Thornhall says you did, too. But I'm her mother and now I'm back and I'll look after Tansy. You got no call to worry about her."

"Of course. But if either of you need anything, please come see me." Laila felt her feet were glued to the floor, it was so difficult to move. She forced herself in the direction of the door and then Tansy was flying after her, throwing her arms around Laila in a hard hug when Laila turned. Laila kissed her forehead, "Goodbye angel. Be a good girl. Come see me when you can."

Laila, making her way to the new cabin, alone, could hardly see the path for her tears.

A few days later, when Laila was in the store, Opal told her, "You should leave those two, Tansy and her Mama, alone! I see you going up to Riley's cabin time after time. That's only interfering with the mother and child getting on with one another. It's no help."

"I only want to be sure that Tansy is all right."

"And she is, isn't she? Why, she doesn't leave her Mama's side for a minute."

Tansy clings because she is afraid her mother will abandon her again. And it wasn't Minnie that worried her, so much as Hob. If he saw Tansy as a nuisance before, he likely would again. So far, though, there had been no evidence of trouble, beyond normal adjustments the three of them had to make. Hob argued for Minnie to clean up her messes. He preferred Tansy out of sight when he came home from the mine, insisted she go to bed early. Nothing pointedly dreadful.

"I'm going to be gone for a few days, Opal. If Tansy comes looking for me, or if someone needs my nursing care, will you tell them I won't be away long?"

Opal shrugged. "I'll do that."

Chapter Eighteen

Laila thought, upon arrival at La Grande, that Grandpa Leroy Chapin, of French-Austrian descent, might have picked his location for its French name. Most assuredly he would have appreciated the area's beauty. The town was nestled in a nook of the Blue Mountains, sheltered north and west, seated on a plateau overlooking eastward a broad lush valley and the Grande Ronde River.

Alighting from the train that she'd taken from Baker City, having taken a stage before that from Pine Valley where she'd left her horse, Laila picked her away along the Union Pacific tracks, her bag bumping against her legs while her eyes took in the sights. She was glad, excited, to leave her confusions, her troubles behind on this sweet September afternoon. Not that thought of Ash, or Tansy, was ever far from her mind.

She hesitated briefly beside an odd structure located a few yards from the train depot and just off the tracks. The top third of the narrow wood building sat like an oversized box-lid on the rest below. Except for a line of windows, the oblong structure, which she evidenced housed a free agricultural exhibit, was every inch covered with painted signs extolling the virtues of the Grande Ronde Valley. "PRODUCTS FROM FARM, FOREST AND FACTORY," proclaimed one huge sign. Another, "HOMES AND WORK FOR THOUSANDS. WE WANT YOU MR. HOMESEEKER," and so on.

Before she returned home, she would view the exhibit, and take time to read *all* the numerous claims. Wouldn't a "Miss Homeseeker" be welcome in that country, too, if it became necessary for her to move?

A half-hour later she had left her bag in a small room engaged at Mrs. Killey's Traveler's House on Depot Street. A bit after that she skidded around a beer barrel that thundered dangerously into her path off a horse-drawn wagon delivering to the Blue Front Saloon.

At Erickson's General Store, she found an older gentleman, bewhiskered and big as a bear, who knew of her grandfather, could tell her where the Chapins *had* lived. "That's the Estes place, now, though," he told her, with a shake of his grizzled head. "Leroy Chapin's been dead for years, and his wife, Mercy, she died a few years before him."

Her sadness and disappointment at his news drove deep and her last bit of hope about her grandparents slipped away. But she was hardly surprised. There had been no word from them in years. Now she had the facts: they were truly gone.

There was nothing left of them but their graves in a nearby cemetery, and the land where they once lived—which now belonged to someone else. Suddenly she felt obsessed to see their old place, no matter what. To touch the earth there, the farm they once tilled and called home; the only reality of her family remaining.

She hired a rig at the City Stables, and took the southeast road from town under a warm sun and a clear blue sky. The old gentleman had said she would find the six hundred and forty acre farm that once belonged to her Grandfather and Grandmother Chapin, about seven miles out. Her anticipation climbed as the road vanished under the buggy wheels and the place described to her at last came into view.

The tidy log-house was L-shaped; a vine-covered porch filled the inner corner at the front. A stone chimney clung to the left side. At the right back corner was a smaller side porch and steps. Carefully tended beds of late summer flowers—

zinnias, asters, and daylilies—bloomed in the yard.

Beyond the house was an orchard, a log barn and other outbuildings, corn and hay fields. Hawks floated above them. Fences were stake-and-rider style with corner posts of stacked stones. East of the fields was a wide lake. On the opposite bank of the sun-touched water, at the foot of a steep, treeless hill, was a long low building painted white. Whether lake and building were part of the property she couldn't guess, not being sure which way the property lines ran, but they looked interesting.

Laila called softly, "whoa." She took her time getting down from the buggy and looping the lines around a hitch-post in the yard. She must take in everything about this house Erickson said her grandfather had built himself, the fields Grandpa Chapin had cleared, tilled and planted; the chicken house and barn and garden patch where Grandma Mercy had gathered eggs, milked their cows, grew vegetables.

Suddenly seeing a slender form and a face peering at her from behind the lacy vines shading the porch, Laila smiled, lowered her parasol, and hurried up the flower-edged path.

"Hello! I hope I'm not intruding," she said to the tall, angular woman standing by the front door. She rushed to answer the woman's questioning look, "My name is Laila Mitchell. My grandparents were the Chapins, Leroy and Mercy, who homesteaded this farm years ago. I was hoping you could tell me something about them, how and when they died, perhaps? I know so little . . ."

The woman's querying expression vanished, she smiled briefly, stepped aside and opened the door. "I'm Althea Estes, Miss Althea Estes. Won't you please come in?" She gave her black hair, worn in a pompadour, a few tidying pats. In spite of her long nose, her features added up attractively: large brown eyes, high cheekbones, and a nicely-shaped mouth, in a slender face.

"Would you like some coffee?" she asked when they were inside.

"Yes, please, if it's no trouble." Anything, to stretch her time spent here, Laila thought, looking around. She sat down in the cushioned wicker chair Miss Estes motioned her toward. The room was pleasantly cool, smelled of lavender. *My grandmother's room, once upon a time.*

It was a room so filled with *things* that had it not been so tidily arranged and spotlessly clean, it would have been considered cluttered. Numerous fringed, floral rugs were scattered on slightly faded floral carpet. Large decorative fans, framed pictures, decorative china plates, and shelves of whatnots adorned the walls papered in dove grey stripe. The flowered velvet sofa held an array of fat, pretty pillows. Crocheted froth draped the walnut rocking chair, the two wicker arm chairs, and two small lamp tables. There were several bouquets of fragrant fresh flowers.

Neatly packed bookcases, and cabinets holding beautiful china dishes, crystal, and figurines, took up the corners of the room. An upright piano sat against the back wall. Laila was eyeing the ornate oak instrument, the top draped in fringed purple velvet, when Miss Estes returned to the living room.

She placed a cut-glass plate of sugar cookies on the table next to Laila's chair. "Do help yourself to the cookies." She handed Laila a cup of coffee cradled in a small saucer, then took her place on the sofa.

"Did you know my grandparents, the Chapins?" Laila asked, too eager to wait, or take more than a small sip of her coffee.

Althea Estes nodded, her thin lips formed a warm smile. "My father and your grandparents were good friends. I remember them, too, but my father, especially, knew them well. He represented them in their legal affairs, he was their lawyer."

"Legal affairs? Did they have troubles?"

"Goodness, no, not illegal or criminal problems, if that's what you mean. I was speaking about a time, I believe it was in the late 'seventies, when their health began to fail quite seriously. Leroy was losing his sight, Mercy had suffered a serious stroke."

Laila wasn't prepared for the sudden sting of empathetic tears in her eyes. She blinked them away. "Please tell me everything."

"Of course they had to have special care, but they also worried about dispensation of their property when they passed on. For two or three years, Leroy tried without success to locate their daughter in Kansas. She was missing from the last place they'd known her to be, on a small farm in the eastern part of the state. Would she have been your mother?"

Laila nodded. "She was Anna Chapin Mitchell, their only child." *Missing* wasn't the word to cover that terrible period after they left the farm. The cookie she held snapped in her fingers. She shakily scooped the crumbs from her lap and put them on her saucer. She gave herself a moment to recover then told Miss Estes, "Please go on."

"Your grandparents had hoped to have your mother come to Oregon to care for them in their last years," Miss Estes told Laila. "She was to have their—this property, Lark Springs Farm, after they were gone."

Her family had moved a great deal and would have been impossible to find.

Laila said simply, her mind evading memories of that period, "Had she known, my mother would have wanted to come, but she wouldn't want to leave my father, who was—ill. They've both been dead for some years." She felt stifled, wanted to rush out of the house into fresh air, but she sat politely, wanting equally as much to hear more about her grandparents.

Miss Estes said softly, sympathy shining in her dark eyes, "I'm alone, too. My father died five years ago." She was silent a moment, then burst out, "In all fairness, this property should be yours. I must tell you what happened." She leaned forward, "When your mother and father couldn't be found—after a great deal of effort on my father's part, I must say—the Chapins decided, in lieu of family, they wanted my father to look after them, to take charge for whatever their needs might be in their last years. Miss Mitchell, your grandparents, to the end, were given every comfort, the very best care my father could provide. That is the honest truth. They left their property to him in payment, he then left it to me."

"Don't let that concern you, please," Laila admonished. "You might say my parents led an invisible way of life. Grandpa and Grandma were right to follow the next suitable course of action when they couldn't locate any of us." And it gratified her no end to know they had received good care. The kind of care she would have given them if she had had the chance.

Althea Estes must have read in Laila's face some of what she was thinking. "Would you like to look around the farm? You know, there are some things here that belonged to your grandparents, and I'd like you to have them."

"Oh, I'd love to have a look. But their things are yours, I can't ask you to—"

"Please, Laila, it's the least I can do. Perhaps you'd like your grandfather Leroy's saddle, some of his tools? There are some lamps, a few linens, two lovely old quilts and other things your grandmother made, some dishes." She looked at the piano. "The piano was hers. I saw you looking at it when I brought the coffee. Did you know your grandmother played?"

Laila nodded, her throat so tight she could scarcely talk. "My mother told me that she did. When I was very small we sang songs together. The same songs, my mother said, that she sang at the piano with her mother. 'Wondrous Love; America; The Old Grey Goose; Lorena.' We sang hymns, songs of Christmas . . ." Remembering, she smiled around the pain in her throat.

"I would like you to have the piano." There was a faint note of reluctance in Miss Estes' voice, but she smiled.

"Goodness no, although I appreciate your kind offer. As much as I'd love to have Grandma Mercy's piano, I have no place for it." Whatever mementos she might take must be small, fit in her traveling bag with her clothes. She was ahorseback from Pine Valley to home. She explained briefly about her small cabin at Venture in the Snake River Canyon and her work there.

Althea Estes' relief was obvious. "I'll keep the piano for you, then, until you're able to have it. When the time comes, be assured that it is yours. Until then, I'll continue to use it, if you don't mind. I'm a schoolteacher at Ora Dell School. I also give piano lessons here in my home after school."

"Of course. I can see the piano is in very good hands!"

"Now then," Althea said when they were finished with coffee and cookies, "Let me show you around Lark Springs Farm. I believe your grandmother gave this wonderful place that name."

In the next hour or so, Laila discovered just how little Althea's description "wonderful" did the farm justice. The old farm was incredible, a dream of a place.

The two women wandered in and out of the musty, hay-filled log-barn, fed the chickens, picked and ate a sun-warmed tomato each from the garden, laughed at a noisy litter of half-grown piglets penned with an enormous mother sow.

As they crossed a gold-stubbled hayfield where hay cured in huge topaz stacks, Althea explained, "I hire the field work done, but I tend the garden, the chickens, pigs, and milk cow myself. With teaching, I hardly have time for more."

The breeze whispered in the corn stalks some yards distant, the stubbled hayfield crunched beneath their feet.

"Is the lake and the building over there part of the property?" Laila asked as they drew nearer. "Goodness! Is that vapor coming off the water? It looks—hot."

"Yes it's hot, that's steam. And yes, your grandfather made sure the lake, fed by a sulphur spring—can you smell the sulphur on the wind?—was included when he homesteaded the property. Around the lake the ground is too marshy to farm but songbirds and butterflies love the spot."

Laila murmured in pleasure, listened as Althea went on.

"Leroy was intrigued by the 'hot lake.' For hundreds of years and more, Indians, explorers, and later, immigrants on the Oregon Trail, stopped there to rest. Horses and cattle were put to graze on the grasslands nearby. Weary travelers bathed and relaxed in the geothermically heated pond. Most believe the waters are curative."

She doubted such waters could actually cure, but they would certainly ease the aches and pains of arthritis, rheumatism, a host of other ills that assailed folks. And it was such a pleasant spot. Her mind raced ahead to the possibilities such a place held. It was the perfect setting for a health resort such as she had read about, where folks could relax, enjoy themselves, and recover their health . . .

Althea was saying, "My father built the small hotel you see there, after the property came to him. He felt travelers needed more than a place to pitch their tents. I lease the hotel and bathing facilities to a man and his wife who manage them."

"This is fascinating," Laila said. She stood at the edge of the steaming lake, looked across at the small hotel, turned, and with a hand shading her brow, looked back at the rest of the farm. At the golden fields, the log barns and sheds, and the flower-rimmed house.

She was so overcome with yearning to have all she saw for her own, she felt guilty. Her heart hammered, she took a deep breath. "Miss Estes, have you ever thought of selling this place?" It was a stupid question. As much as she would love to have what had once been her grandparents' holdings, she didn't have the means to buy even a particle if Miss Estes wanted to sell.

Clearly her question left Althea Estes discomfitted. "I've been approached before, by people who wanted Lark Springs farm. But where would I go, what else would I do? It seems terribly unfair to say to Leroy and Mercy's own granddaughter, but I can't part with Lark Springs Farm. It's been my home for some years, now." In afterthought she declared, "But should I ever sell, I would assuredly give you first chance to buy." She seemed about to say more, but didn't. Whatever her thoughts, they brought a blush to her cheeks, a soft shine to her eyes.

"I understand," Laila said finally, nodding, although the look on Althea Estes' face left her mystified. She fought to hide the depths of her disappointment that the homestead, tangible proof of many years of her grandparents' lives, belonged to someone else. Yet, if the place belonged to her, she wouldn't want to sell, either.

Chapter Nineteen

At home again in the canyon, Laila was glad Miss Estes had insisted that she bring her grandfather's small leather trunk and the contents they'd placed in it back with her. Although, she recalled, it had been a bit of a trial to bring extra luggage along on the train, then on the stage, and finally to strap the trunk behind her saddle for the last leg of the trip, now it enticed her from where she had placed it on her table. She traced her grandfather's initials, LC, carved into the flat lid, and then, with a feeling of expectancy, she opened the trunk. A strangely appealing mixed-scent of tobacco, dried lavender and roses met her nose.

At a sound at her open doorway she turned to look and saw Tansy standing there. "Tansy!" They met for a hug in the middle of the room. "You're all right, aren't you honey?"

Tansy nodded. "Mama's at the store. I came to see if you were home." She was looking around her, eyes wide with wonder at the neatly furnished cabin, the cinnamon pink curtains, the wreath of cream and pink dried roses that decorated the door. Her voice was wistful, "It's awful pretty, the prettiest cabin in the whole world."

"I miss having you here with me, but you can visit as often as you like. We're just a short path apart, and that's not so bad. And you get to be with your Mama, too."

Tansy didn't reply to that. A shadow of a frown crossed her face and was gone.

"Everything's all right up at Hob's place, isn't it, honey? You're being treated well?"

"He doesn't like me. He yells at me if I sit in his chair, or if

I take seconds at supper that he wanted. I don't like Hob Riley even if he does like my Mama."

"Has he ever struck you, Tansy?"

"No, but I don't like him, anyway."

"Tansy, if Hob Riley ever strikes you, or threatens to hit you, or anything like that, you are to come to me immediately, do you understand?"

"Mama says for me to just try and stay out of his way and not rile him."

"Yes, but still, if you need me, you're to come here right away."

Tansy nodded. "I will."

"Now, come see the wonderful treasures I've brought home with me." Laila began to take objects one by one from the trunk, her heart filling with pleasure. She had already seen and touched these small homey belongings of her grandparents', but with every passing hour she cherished them more.

"This was my grandfather's moustache cup and shaving brush, two pipes, and his tobacco box," she told Tansy. She lifted out a tattered bible, with her family's names inscribed inside. "This old penmanship book was my mother's when she was a little girl, here's her name." She pointed at the childish, imperfect scroll inside the cover.

"Won't these linens make a lovely addition to the cabin?" she asked excitedly as she removed them. Althea Estes was confident that her grandmother had made the beautiful lace table runner, and a lavender cotton damask tablecloth embroidered in the corners with full-blown yellow roses and white trellis. "Look at this, Tansy!" She showed her an embroidered and framed picture of a young girl drawing water at a well with a family of brown rabbits at her prim feet. There were several embroidered handkerchiefs, two lacy fichu collars, and two stained, well-washed long unbleached aprons trimmed at the bottom with homemade lace. Laila decided she might keep the latter simply as sentimental souvenirs.

Tansy leaned forward against the table, her nose inches above the trunk as she tried to see inside.

"My grandparents' wedding certificate," Laila said, her eyes filling with tears. She held it lovingly, studied the declaration scrolled in lovely penmanship, the twining ivy and floral design around the borders. She would frame the certificate, she decided, and hang it on her wall. Maybe someday she and Ash—she abruptly halted that train of thought, with a quick look at Tansy to see if she had somehow read her mind. Flushed, Laila went back to removing the last of the treasures from the trunk. She was foolish to dream of married life with Ash. He was not interested in her seriously or he'd have let her know.

A shadow fell across the floor from the open door. Laila and Tansy looked up. Minnie stood there, her face was red and angry, her ample bosom heaving. "Tansy, you had no business runnin' off from me while I was at the store! I didn't know where you could've got off to, 'til Miz Thornhall said you probably come here."

"She was only visiting me for a few minutes," Laila tried to smooth Minnie's anger.

"Laya was showing me her treasures," Tansy said pointing at the objects on the table at the same time she hesitantly joined her mother at the door.

"And Hob will be showin' the both of us the back of his hand if we don't get on home with the tobacco he sent us for. Now come on." Minnie's hand fastened hard around Tansy's wrist and turning, she yanked her outside.

"Please, don't! Tansy wasn't doing anything wrong—" Laila tried to protest. But Minnie wasn't listening. Laila hurried to the door after them. Her hand covered her mouth, her heart was stricken as she watched them go. Tansy's feet hardly touched the ground as Minnie hurried her up the path through the tent and shack village.

Laila chewed her lip and uttered a silent prayer that Tansy would remember that she was to come to Laila at any sign of harm toward her. For almost a year and a half, Tansy had been her main concern; it wasn't a responsibility, a feeling, she could automatically turn off.

It was several minutes before Laila could continue her task, and even then, she wished Tansy was still there to see the beautiful things and decide where to place them. What had been such a joy moments before, was now a half-hearted chore. She made herself concentrate: The painted tin hairpin box and small covered basket of buttons would go on her dresser in the bedroom area. Someday, she must have a special cabinet to hold the covered crystal butter dish and vase, and the French porcelain tea set decorated with violets and trimmed with gold. For now she would put them on her open shelves where she could see them every day. The tea set—teapot, creamer, sugar bowl, and four tiny teacups with saucers—had very likely belonged to her grandfather's mother, her great-grandmother, in the old country.

She placed each item carefully, beginning to feel for the first time since she was small that she was truly planted and tied to people of her own blood. Her grandparents had used these things in the everyday flow of their lives. She was *them* and they were *her* and nothing could change that. She *belonged.*

She wiped a happy mist of tears from her eyes. Before Grandpa and Grandma moved away from Kansas there had been Sunday chicken dinners at her grandparents' Lyon county farm. One of her earliest memories was of a particular hot summer Sunday when the preacher's drone all morning in church had nearly put her to sleep, and, later, what a struggle it had been to keep her eyes open at the dinner table. She could still hear the gentle, chiding chuckles of her elders as they lifted her head from her plate and Mama brushed the mashed potatoes and gravy from her round childish cheeks. That day had become a funny, family story.

She had been surrounded with so much love . . . they were good times, her early childhood.

Laila placed the last cup and saucer on the shelf, admired the entire room once again, then prepared to leave for Thornhalls' store. She needed to buy a few groceries, but she also wanted to check for mail.

Along with a magazine and a newspaper, there was a letter for her with a St. Louis postmark, from John Ryland, her old apothecary friend. She made her grocery selections quickly, engaged in brief small talk with the Thornhalls, then hurried back along the path to her cabin, eager to read John's most recent letter.

She sat at her table, the letter propped in front of her, and, with satisfaction and excitement racing through her until she was giddy and light-headed, she read the letter through for the second, and then the third time. John's journalist friend, with the backing of the American Medical Society and aid of government chemists, had contracted with a national weekly magazine, *Colliers*, to write an expose about fraudulent medicines. Moguls of free-wheeling quackery would be called to account at last and exposed for the heartless, harm-wreaking bunco artists they were.

One of the anecdotes used would be about Mrs. Bolton's useless and frightening "cancer treatment." Thankfully, Gladys Bolton now saw a regular doctor. She was healed of the dreadful sore on her breast that might have led to blood poisoning and her death, and she had vowed never again to believe an advertisement that claimed, "in a woman's breast, *any* lump is cancer." Nor would she believe printed claims that she could cure herself with "miraculous creams."

Common folks were going to be shocked at the articles, but at last they would know the truth about the vast quantities of alcohol, opiates, and varied other drugs they commonly and innocently ingested, believing them to be simple, helpful, tonics. They would learn that another great evil of quack medicines was the delay of proper medical treatment.

John and his journalist friend's intention in doing the research and writing the articles, besides informing the general public, was to force Federal legislation of a pure food and drug act. It wouldn't be an easy matter to bring to pass. For one thing, newspapers and magazines, large and small, had for a very long time survived on the paid advertising from patent medicine kings. And folks had believed the advertising claims to the point of shelling out millions of dollars annually to the medical frauds. John believed that if periodicals refused the ads, within five years time the patent medicine industry would be history. The country would be "richer not only in lives and money but also in drunkards and drug addicts saved."

That was a day Laila would pray and hope for, and would contribute toward, in any way she could.

Tansy came to see her at the cabin again, a few days later, and she was alone. "Did you ask permission?" Laila wanted to know, thrilled to see her, but nervous. She didn't want Tansy getting into trouble.

Tansy's head lowered guiltily. "No. But Hob is up at the mine, and Mama was sleeping. I'll go back before Mama wakes up."

"I'm glad you wanted to come and see me, but maybe you should let your Mama know where you're going. And, honey, your Mama is welcome to come with you, anytime I'm not out on my nursing rounds. We could have a tea party, or lunch."

"Could we have a tea party now?"

"Maybe a quick one," Laila smiled and hurriedly set about the preparations, glad she'd made sugar cookies the day before.

Tansy came twice more in the next week, sneaking away each time despite Laila's insistence that she ask for permission so she wouldn't get into trouble.

Opal told Laila, one day when Laila was in the store, "Tansy came down to your cabin two or three times when you were away seeing to folks' medical problems. You shouldn't encourage the little girl to run off without her Mama knowing."

"I don't encourage Tansy to 'run off'. I've told her to ask permission, but I suspect when she does ask, Minnie refuses to give it. And I've invited Minnie to come with Tansy. For goodness sake, Tansy lived with me for a year and a half. She is used to being with me." *And I'm beginning to suspect Tansy prefers being with me, now that the newness of being back with her mother has worn off.*

"She'd be used to staying with her Mama if you'd stop interfering."

"I'm not interfering! Minnie should want Tansy to be happy, she should allow her to visit me now and then." Laila shook her head. Opal wasn't going to understand no matter what she said. She grabbed her parcels and left the store.

Laila had been up since dawn, choosing the early-morning

hours to white-wash the picket fence that Hutton Ginther had built around her tiny yard, then harvest the late summer vegetables from the small patch she had planted in the spring. She was perspiring in the warm sun, and dirty from the work. At the sound of a buggy approaching faster than usual, she looked up and saw that the driver was a young man she recognized as one of Ash's workers. Bob Garraty was a shy, slender young man with black hair. He looked unusually anxious as he drew the horses and rig to a halt, lifted his hat to her in brief greeting.

Her scalp crawled with premonition. Something dreadful had happened to Ash, or to his father, or to Kate. "Hello!" she called out, "what's happened? Is there a problem at Conner Creek?" Garraty nodded, solemn. Seconds later he was telling her that old Tom was very ill and was asking for her to come right away.

She was sure Tom had recovered from his fall, from the broken ribs, as much as a person of his age possibly could, so this malady was surely from another source. She took several slow deep breaths and shading her hand against the sun, asked Garraty, "Did his illness come on suddenly? What are his symptoms? He is going to be all right, isn't he?"

He licked his lips, fidgeted. "The old fellow took sick a week or so back. Just—sick, like being awful tired, some chills and fever. He's pretty bad off, now, though. Ash don't believe Old Tom is going to pull through, this time."

She stared at him another moment, anxious and disbelieving, her bottom lip caught between her teeth in concern. It sounded as though Tom might have lung fever, pneumonia. Was Ash not at home when his father first fell ill? If he wasn't there, didn't Kate see the seriousness of Tom's ailing? "He got sick a week ago? Why didn't someone, Ash, send for me right away?" Her tone was sharp, almost accusing, which she quickly regretted.

On the buggy-seat, Garraty seemed to shrink and he shifted uncomfortably. She wasn't sure he knew the answer, or if he did, that he wanted to give it. Being questioned was beyond the duty he'd been given.

"That's all right," she said in a moment, getting herself together in light of his distress. It was hardly fair to expect him to know Ash's mind, or to tell her things Ash might want to tell her, himself, if he did. "Will you please come inside and take a chair, and have a drink of water? Would you like something to eat? It will take me a few minutes to get this dirt off—" she examined her hands and arms, "and to get my things."

"I'll be changin' my horses for fresh ones over to a friend of Ash's, yonder just a ways. Got my own water with me, and some meat and biscuit. I'll be back shortly for you, Miss."

Washing up hurriedly in her tiny enclosed back porch, Laila felt warm tears starting down her cheeks. Her heart ached as she considered that Ash believed his father might not live. She cared a great deal about all of her patients, but she was fondest of Tom. She had come to love Ash's father almost as if he were family.

Whatever was ailing him, she must pull him through. He was such a delightful character, so much a part of the canyon and its history. So much a part, now, of her life. She was nowhere near ready to let him go, no matter that Ash believed his father wouldn't get better this time.

Later, seated in the buggy and gripping tightly the handle of the medical bag she held in her lap, she urged Garraty to hurry the team. She prayed to get there in time. She was cold with renewed fear that the illness was somehow a result of her treatment of Tom back when he fell from the peach tree. Something she had failed to see, or do. It occurred to her, not for the first time, that in a way, she was as much a fraud, treating folks medically when she was not a professional, as were the drug-cure fakers.

The improved river road made travel faster and easier, but still not fast enough and the hours dragged wretchedly. Several times during the day as they trundled along, Laila wiped the tears from her cheeks, and resisted the urge to leap from the buggy and run as hard as she could toward Conner Creek. At long last, the driver drew them to a halt before the main ranch-house; Laila leaped out and raced up the path to the door.

Kate opened to her swift knock and the two women went into a wordless hug. Then Laila whispered, "It's not too late?"

Kate's eyes were shining with tears as she answered, "No, but 'bout. He just don't want to live no more. He's got the pneumonia, he's wore out and can hardly breathe. He says it's his time. And I'd say he's just hanging by a thread as 'tis, waiting for you."

Ash appeared behind Kate. He looked distraught, his hair was uncombed, and his clothes rumpled as though he'd slept in them, but he was clearly glad to see her. His arm circled her shoulders. "C'mon. Pop is waiting to see you."

"What happened? How did he contract pneumonia, is he sick as a result of the accident, his fall from the tree? He seemed to be doing so well."

Ash just shook his head without answering. He took her medical bag from her and set it on a chair in the hallway. "You won't need this."

"Ash—!" She halted, pulled back to stare at him.

"Please, just come with me. Pop doesn't want your treatment, he just wants to see you. We've done our best for him."

She followed him into Tom's room that was filled with the sound of his labored breathing, the smell of sickness and disinfectant. Right away she saw the reasons her medicines, her ministrations, weren't called for. A man in his white shirt-sleeves, his white coat on the back of a chair, was listening to Tom's withered chest through a tube she recognized as a stethoscope. The doctor was shorter than Ash, and balding. When he moved, she saw that he was lame, one leg shorter than the other.

The second stranger in the room was a petite woman in white who, with practiced efficiency, was placing warm, towel-wrapped water-bottles under the covers at Tom's feet.

Laila was glad Ash had brought in a real doctor and nurse in this very serious instance, relieved that this was the reason she hadn't been called for sooner. Likely the medical team had had to come all the way from Baker City, and had excellent training. They would do their best for Tom, more than she could do, quite likely. She exhaled a breath she'd been holding for some time, and felt better.

"Laila, I'd like you to meet Doctor Carlton Stanfield, and his wife, Nurse Anna. They have been here looking after Pa for over a week." He told the Stanfields, "Until you came, Laila was our only medical person. She has taken excellent care of the sick in this country, on her own."

She smiled at the Stanfields, offered her hand to each in turn. "I'm glad to see you're here, looking after my favorite patient. How is he?" The doctor's brows knitted, he touched her arm and motioned that she follow him back out into the hallway. His solemn expression brought a deeper frown to her own face. It was hard to breathe as she waited for news she knew she wouldn't like.

Doctor Stanfield hobbled closer and told her quietly, "The old fellow is not good, I'm afraid. In spite of all our efforts—administering quinine in hopes of cutting short the disease, milk punch for nourishment and to aid expectoration—we haven't been able to break the grip of pneumonia. His lungs are filling rapidly now, his heart is very weak. From talking to him, I've learned that our patient has been hiding problems with his vitals—his lungs, kidneys, heart—for quite a while. He's dealt quite stoically with the ailments of advanced age, fought them like a tiger to tell the truth."

Laila nodded, and told him, "I'm a nonprofessional, but I've been treating him for colds, a broken arm, such as that. He never let on to me about anything more. If I had seen—"

Doctor Stanfield shook his head and said kindly, "If you had known of his general deteriorating state, or this pneumonia, there still would have been little that you, or anyone else, could have done. He was aware of that, himself, so he saw no need to especially worry anybody. He's lived a long life—"

Resisting where his statements were leading, she broke in, her voice stricken, "There must be something more that can be done!"

The doctor shook his head. "Old age isn't reversible, my dear, you know that. The best we can do is make him comfortable until the end. A small dosage of codeine will help him sleep, diminish the pain in his chest wall."

She supposed the doctor was right in his estimation that the end was near for Tom, but it was hard to accept. After another lengthy silence, she gave in, the fight going out of her. Through a pained daze she saw that Ash was urging her to join him at Old Tom's bedside. With tears burning her eyes, she went to stand beside him.

Anna Stanfield, a plain-featured woman with gentle amber eyes said, "Our patient has been asking for you repeatedly, Miss Mitchell. We're so glad you've come."

Laila sat down in the offered chair by the bed and took Tom's hand that lay on his chest. It was very cold, limp. She was shocked at how rapidly he had failed, at the way he looked. His flesh was gray except for his cheeks that were flushed and glistening, his breathing was labored and she could see that every breath hurt him.

"Tom?" His head turned slightly and his glazed eyes found hers. Around a thickness in her throat she chided gently, "What do you think you're doing? You need to get well and on your feet again! The fish are biting you know. And somebody needs to oversee the orchards out there. You'll do just what the doctor says and get well, won't you?" It was a demand more than a question. The others might give up, she just wasn't ready.

He struggled to speak, coughed slightly, and closed his eyes with the pain. His voice came faintly, "Not going to make it this time. But don't worry, Sweetheart."

"Of course you are! You've got a real doctor here to see to you, and a trained nurse. You're going to be fine."

He looked toward the medical pair in faint, childish disgust. In a few seconds he said, "They're no better than you, Lai—Don't matter, though. I—I don't have much time. Need to talk."

"All right, Tom," she said softly. If agreeing would keep him calm, at peace, she could at least do that. She asked around the ache in her throat, "What is it you want to tell me?"

"Private t-talk," he whispered, "with you and the boy." He dismissed the Doctor and Nurse with a weak glance, and Ash nodded politely for them to leave the room. After the door closed behind them, Ash brought another chair and moved it close beside Laila's so that they looked down on Tom together. Ash's arm was across the back of her chair and he leaned close to catch his father's labored efforts to speak.

Chapter Twenty

Laila held Tom's withered wrist and his pulse trembled under her fingers like the heart of a tiny frightened bird. Again and again he tried to speak, convulsing each time with fits of coughing that produced little or no expectoration. In her experience, this was often typical with tiny children, and the aged; he had to be miserable with the phlegm he needed to give up. His tongue was dry and coated, and she gave him a little water. "Maybe you should just rest, and not try to talk," she said. "I think we should bring the doctor back in and—"

Tom moved his head slightly to stop her, his eyes imploring her to let him try and say what was on his mind. Weak, yet determined, his glance edged from her face to Ash's and a feeble smile traced his lips.

His eyes held to Ash and his voice came like a whispered sigh, "She's *not* like your mother. Though Phoebe was my precious jewel." He took several raspy breaths. "You see that, s-son? I—I see it." The words came slowly, painstakingly, "Laila is a different gem, right for this place—right for you. D-don't let her get—away."

Laila stared at Old Tom in surprise and blinked at tears. So this was his reason in sending for her. Not only a last goodbye but to make sure she was paired with his son for the future? She didn't know what to think.

"Now, Pop—" Ash began but the old fellow continued, addressing Laila, this time.

She leaned closer to hear his faint words.

"My son will be good to you. He's a good boy. My Phoebe, his Mama, made him that."

"Yes, she did," Laila agreed, "but—" Maybe Ash wasn't interested in her in the permanent way his father indicated. He'd certainly shown an aversion to her a lot of the time.

Once more the old man's glance moved from one to the other of them. "Perfect for one another," he said more clearly this time as he strained to make them understand. "You'll see—give it a chance. Promise me—"

"Pop, I don't think—"

"We promise!" Laila said quickly. Ash could get out of the bargain later if he chose—if he didn't really care for her—but she wasn't going to make Old Tom unhappy in his last hours. She would promise him the moon if he wanted it. She stole a sidelong glance at Ash to see if he was angry at her declaration.

He seemed surprised but he didn't appear to be upset over either her promise or his father's request. He looked haggard and torn, emotions close to the surface that his father was dying. In wordless communication then, they agreed to promise Old Tom whatever he wanted if it would make him content, if it would make his passing easier. It would do no harm to agree, and arguing with him wouldn't help a thing.

"Okay," Ash said softly. He clasped Laila's hand tightly and lay the other over his father's. "You're right about one thing, Pop, Laila *is* a jewel like you say. She and I will think seriously about what you're asking. We promise to court and see where it leads." He released a soft sigh and it was echoed by Old Tom.

Laila's heart lurched with quiet joy. If it didn't work out, they would still have fulfilled their promise to Tom. She leaned forward to kiss the old man's forehead. "You just rest easy now, my darling."

As she stroked Tom's cheek, she was thinking that exploring a relationship with his son was far from an unpleasant prospect, was in fact something she'd dreamed about lately, against her better judgement. However, the immediate need for their attention was to make Tom's fading time as peaceful and pleasant as it could be. Or to save him, bring him back to health, if there was any chance of that.

Except for a few minutes at a time, she didn't leave Tom's side that night or all the next day. He lay in delirium at times, his breathing grew more and more raspy and shallow. The Stanfields were ever present, too, compassionate and professional in their ministrations, doing everything they could to make Tom comfortable and pain free. That included allowing Laila to stay with him, talk to him, sometimes sing to him gentle songs she'd learned from her mother.

He died quietly in his sleep that following evening.

The next day and a half passed in a blur, with the Stanfields staying on to prepare Tom's body for burial, Ash and Laila sending messages to those who might want to attend the funeral, Kate and Laila together getting the house and food ready.

Later, in the small ranch cemetery, with the wind blowing gloomily around them, Laila stood next to Ash to hear words of solemn farewell spoken over his father's grave. At one point she felt Ash's fingers graze her arm and he whispered, "Pa loved you."

She smiled at him through her tears; her throat was full. "I loved him."

That night after the funeral, Laila fell exhausted into bed in Ash's guest room. She slept soundly for several hours, then toward morning she was awakened by a sound from outside. She lay still for a second, coming more awake, frowning as she listened. Then she tossed back her covers and crept to her window. Down below in pre-dawn light a pair of riders were taking the lane toward the road. She recognized Ash, the other man she didn't know but he could have been a friend who attended the funeral today. When they reached the end of the lane, the pair turned their horses south and rode hard along the river toward Huntington. She watched them out of sight, wondering why they would ride out at this hour.

She poked her head out into the hall to learn if Kate was up and might answer her questions but everything was quiet. She shrugged, and—too groggy and tired to begin the day just yet herself—crept back to bed for a few more hours' sleep. Whatever Ash's reason for leaving, he would probably be back in time for breakfast. As she lay there, she found falling back to sleep more difficult than she thought it would be as her mind clung to the mystery of his leaving.

When she woke again, Laila discovered from the small bedside clock that she had slept until almost noon. Although emotionally and physically exhausted from events of the past few days, she couldn't excuse herself. Before closing her eyes last night, she had vowed to do what favors Ash and Kate might need from her this morning. She had planned to thank the Stanfields again for all they had done and tell them good-bye. Then she had intended to return home to Venture. Embarrassed for being a laggard, she dressed and crept downstairs. The house seemed almost empty, was eerily quiet. She wondered if Ash were back from his pre-dawn ride.

Kate had tidied the kitchen and was at the table drinking coffee. There was sadness behind her smile, but warmth in her expression, too, for Laila. She said, "C'mon, dear, sit down and let me get you some biscuits and jam, and pour you some coffee. You've been plumb wore out and no wonder. Can I fix you some eggs? Scrambled or poached?"

"Just coffee, thank you, and sit still, I can get it for myself.

You've had as much to do as anyone, and you must be tired, yourself."

"Well, I am heavy-hearted about Tom, I got to say that. But Doctor Stanfield said it was his time and wasn't nothin' anybody coulda done to change that." She wiped her eyes with her apron hem. "I come to think a lot of that old feller since you and me come here."

Laila nodded and smiled sadly. "I know what you mean, I feel the same. I think all of us will miss him for a very long time." She sat across from Kate and sipped her coffee. "Poor Ash. He seems to be handling Tom's death fairly well, though." She hesitated. "I saw him ride out last night just before dawn. Do you know why he left? Is he back? I feel horrible that I didn't wake earlier, give him a hand with whatever needed doing this morning before I have to leave for home."

"I been about to tell ya, he ain't here. He left this for us." She reached into her apron pocket and handed Laila a scrap of paper.

Laila frowned as she read the barely legible note, obviously scrawled in haste: *"Had to leave. Sorry no chance to tell Laila good-bye. Wire delivered to me last night. Serious emergency at my hotel—taking the Huntington train to Portland—don't know when I'll be back. Will explain later."*

For several minutes Laila sat in disappointed, puzzled silence. It was dreadful that Ash had been struck by trouble at his hotel only hours after his father's funeral. It was sad and unfair that he had to go. She did her best to ignore a niggling suspicion at the back of her mind—without success—that the emergency might not be a real one, but rather a way Ash could leave without going into a lot of explanation.

Surely she was wrong in her assumption, and yet, he had never cared for life in the canyon as much as his father had and now, with his father dead, he was free to go. There was nothing to hold him, certainly not the promise they'd made his father. How many times had Ash avoided her presence and not subtly, either? Why would their promise to Old Tom make any difference? Ash had said what he did to keep his father happy and—as much as it hurt her to think it—he had probably put the agreement out of his mind, deciding it held no real import.

Of course she could be wrong, she realized guiltily, and he'd left for a very real cause, a serious problem as his note indicated. In any regard, whatever Ash's reasons for going—and it could also be that he was returning to Claudine, although she couldn't quite believe that—his choices were his own business. Being mistrustful and *petty* made her uncomfortable, like a nasty extra skin that wasn't hers. She sighed. She needed to have faith and be patient. If Ash wanted to be with her, he would come home and tell her so.

"I'm sorry he had to go," she told Kate, "The timing seems awfully unfortunate for him. Whatever's happened, I hope it isn't too bad, and that he's able to take care of it without too much trouble. You weren't up when he left, were you, Kate? Did you have a chance to talk to him?"

"Sorry. I slept like a log and I figure Ash didn't want to wake either of us. What's in this note is all I know, honey."

"Of course. And Ash was thoughtful to leave it for us." Until they heard from him again there was nothing more to be done. She had hoped last evening that the two of them would have some quiet moments together today, sharing their sadness as well as their good memories of Tom. She thought that they might discuss their future, their promise to Old Tom. She wouldn't have expected anything to develop right away from that agreement, and never at all, if Ash wasn't in accord. But she had hoped that they might at least discuss the matter—it would have been a way to find out where she stood with Ash. That chance was lost for the time being due to the emergency.

He was probably not serious about the promise anyhow, and she would be better off not to get carried away with the prospect. He had seemed momentarily glad, but that would be for his father's sake there on his deathbed. Since last Christmas, except for when he needed her to look after his father, Ash had gone to extreme measures to avoid her. There was really nothing to hold him to the canyon, or to her, if it wasn't what he truly wanted.

She sighed, feeling genuine concern along with the letdown. "If it isn't one thing, it's another," she told Kate, getting up to pour each of them another cup of coffee. "Tom's death was enough for all of us." Kate knew that Tansy's mother had come back for her daughter and Laila had briefly confided her worry that Hob might mistreat Tansy. "I wonder why it is that trouble seems to come in batches?"

Kate shrugged, "One trouble at a time to work on seems enough to me."

Feeling the quiet again, Laila sat down and commented, "I suppose the Stanfields have returned to Baker City? I assume that's where they're from."

Kate shook her head, "They're not from Baker City, they come from Portland." She stirred a second teaspoonful of sugar into her fresh cup of coffee. "They went down to Venture, left right after breakfast this morning."

"Excuse me? They went to Venture?" Laila's eyes rounded in surprise. "Did someone there need their medical attention? Or did they have business there? Are they visiting someone?" She struck the table lightly with her knuckles. "I wish I'd gotten up earlier, I could have ridden there with them and not bothered Garraty to take me home."

Kate reached out to grasp her hand. "Oh, dearie, with all

that's been goin' on here, I reckon Ash didn't have time to tell you. Doctor Stanfield and his wife are here in the canyon to stay. They're not visitin' or nothin' like that."

"What? They are settling at Venture?" She sat up straighter, awash in curiosity and interest.

Kate nodded. "Some friends of Ash's sent them to take over the doctorin' hereabouts. You won't have to do it, no more. The Stanfields got here to Conner Creek just about the same time Old Tom took sick. I'm sorry Ash didn't tell you. I thought maybe you'd know, since both you and Ash been wantin' a real doctor to come."

For a second or two she was speechless. "Y-yes," she stammered after a moment, "we've wanted to get—get a real doctor in these parts for some time." As far as Ash not bringing up the matter to her, he had been preoccupied with his father and rightly so.

"The doctor and his wife thought you'd be stayin' on here to rest a few days, might even stay 'til Ash got back. They had to get on downriver, find a place to stay, get their practice set up. They said they'd be lookin' for you to come in a while. They want you to show them around down-canyon, introduce them to the folks you been seein' to, help them learn who suffers from what, who might be on the mend, or not."

She nodded dumbly, mumbled an answer, she wasn't sure what she said. She made an effort to gather her wits, feeling as though she were crawling from under a load of brick that had been tumbled on her. What she hadn't foreseen when she and Ash had discussed getting a doctor, was that he would employ a physician who would bring his own assistant, his wife—a professional nurse—with him! The Stanfields could handle quite ably the medical needs of the canyon and beyond without help from her.

Did Ash not care that he was putting her out of work when

he engaged the Stanfields as a team? If what he'd done was intentional, for heaven's sake, why? What did he expect her to do now that he'd put her out of a job?

Her chances of finding paid employment in the area, other than in nursing, were nil. And yet she must have a job to survive. Ash must have known what he was doing, must have wanted her to go, to leave the canyon and his life! Pain and shock when the truth hit made it hard to breathe, hard to think. She felt tears burning behind her eyes. He didn't care then, he really didn't care.

He had fled the canyon so hurriedly because he didn't want to face her with the truth about the Stanfields, he didn't want to be there when she had to pack up and leave. The Ash she thought she knew hadn't seemed to be such a cruel coward. But he was gone, and the Stanfields were there to replace her.

Evidence was clear that Ash's feelings for her didn't begin to match hers for him. Otherwise, he would not have put her in such a fix. She turned her head so that Kate would not see her tears, detect her devastating pain.

She had come to the canyon with such high hopes and she had made a good life there. All of it was over now, all of it done. And she must start anew somewhere else. Put Ash from her mind and heart, as well as Tansy, and get on with life.

Feelings of fury joined her hurt as she imagined what Ash was thinking: Eventually she would get over being angry at him. She'd find other work in Baker City, or in Huntington, or in La Grande, *somewhere*. Should their paths cross one day, he might even admit to his actions, arguing that he'd done her a favor getting her out of the canyon—where she had never belonged, anyway—the way he saw it. He would expect her to be grateful, wonder why they couldn't be friends, just friends.

She prayed to never lay eyes on him again! What he'd done

to her was terrible and she couldn't imagine any excuse in the world for it, not a good one that would take away the pain he'd left her with.

On the way back to Venture, Laila had a brief, rash inclination to follow Ash to Portland. She would face him, learn the truth of his mission there, insist on knowing his feelings—if he had any special feelings for her—and make him tell her what he was about contracting a competent team to replace her. But what was the use? Hearing the truth she suspected directly from him would truly be crushing, more pain than she already was feeling.

She closed her mind, ignored her aching heart. She focused in abstract on the miles passing beneath Garraty's wagon, in an endless-seeming trip as he returned her to Venture.

Chapter Twenty-One

When Laila lived in St. Louis, she had grown accustomed to seeing horse-drawn ambulance wagons so as to hardly notice them, but never in a lifetime did she expect to see one parked next to the Thornhalls' store. She knew, of course, that the big, blocky white vehicle belonged to the Stanfields, and that it must have been put away in Ash's barn while they were there because she hadn't known of its existence.

She wasn't surprised to find the whole community in a twirl of excitement over having gained the medical team. The Stanfields' ambulance wagon was the couple's bedroom by night, but by day Opal was their thrilled, gracious hostess at the store. Shoppers were invited to stay for coffee and cookies and get acquainted with Carlton and Anna. Pastured out behind the store was the Stanfields' pair of dapple greys.

"We're ready to get down to business," Doctor Stanfield told Laila when she paid them a call at the store. "We want to learn all we can from you about the medical needs of canyon folk."

"You've done a good job for us," Opal said to Laila, her mouth pursing in a coo, "but we have a real doctor, and a real nurse now. You won't have to work so hard."

I won't have any work at all, at least not here. "I'll introduce you to my patients right away," she told the Stanfields. "It's time I made a round to see my regulars."

Early next morning they drove up the mountain to visit a miner who had been stabbed in an altercation. As Laila suspected, he was still mending nicely, he had been well on the way to recovery when she was called to Conner Creek for Old

Tom. They went to check on the wife of another miner who was expecting her first baby. Before they went into the little cabin, Laila told the Stanfields, "Annie is young and a little frightened. She'll need lots of instruction about her health and the coming baby's." They traveled up to the rims where an old sheepherder suffered chronic 'knotted bowels'. The Stanfields nodded agreement when she said ruefully, "He needs to eat more fresh vegetables and fruit, but getting him to change his diet from dried mutton, bread, and coffee, is easier said than done!" Lastly, they went to see a case of dog bite—a child she'd been treating but who was totally recovered, and then a woman with chronic quinsy sore throat. Laila told the Stanfields, "I've recommended a chlorate of potash gargle, and it seems to do some good until her sore throat comes back."

Doctor Stanfield nodded, "It may be that she has an abscess on her tonsil. That can be determined by feeling inside her throat. Puncturing the abscess with a lancet will afford her great relief, but I'm afraid even then her quinsy will return if she's prone to it."

To Laila's relief, the Stanfields were warm and kind to her patients. The more time she spent with the doctor and his wife, the better she liked them. If there was a thing objectionable about either of them she couldn't discover it. Besides their gentle way with folks, they were as professionally wise and able as any two people she could hope to know, could hope to have replace her.

Both Stanfields held degrees from the Willamette University Medical Department in Salem, Oregon. They had become good friends and later had fallen in love when both were employed at St. Vincent's Hospital in Portland. More recently, they had their own practice, together, in Portland.

One evening when they joined her for supper at her cabin,

she told them truthfully how happy she was that they were the ones taking over for her. She admitted, "I'm not trained professionally and I would have hated to make a mistake. I suppose I believed, and believe still, however, that my experience in providing medical care qualifies me for practical nursing at the very least."

Anna Stanfield agreed. "Women, without formal training, for hundreds of years have nursed the sick and suffering by instinct and intuition. They have had to, when no doctor was present. Wasn't it Florence Nightingale who said that 'at one time or another, every woman is a nurse'?"

"We're just sorry we are putting you out of work," Carlton told her for probably the twentieth time. The three of them had already agreed that they would buy her cabin; the Stanfields intended to follow through on her plan to build a small infirmary. "You've done a fine job taking care of folks, we've heard nothing but praise for your efforts, Laila," he said, "we have seen for ourselves the good you've done. Maybe in the future, if the population in the canyon continues to grow as it has been, we can employ you in the infirmary."

It was a kind offer but she shook her head and gave them a quiet smile. "That could take a long time, and I can't wait."

"Where will you go, then, what will you do?" Anna's plain face filled with genuine concern. She lay her fork aside.

"The canyon has grown quite a bit since I came, but opportunities still don't abound here as I'm sure you can tell. As much as I love this place, I'll have to look for employment somewhere else. Possibly it will be in practical nursing. But I'll be fine, and you shouldn't feel sorry about taking over. The canyon has needed you for a long time, everyone here will be better off." She picked up the platter of sliced roast beef and passed it around for seconds.

"In mulling over my situation these past few days," she said as she put the platter down again, "I've decided that I'll seek work in La Grande." She took a bite of mashed potatoes and in a few seconds told them, "La Grande is a fair-sized city, progressive for a rural area. There will be opportunities there I'm sure."

She wasn't sure at all, but she put on a good face, "I hope to work with a doctor as his assistant, but if such a position doesn't turn up, I'll ask for a job as a domestic, or in a restaurant, or at a boarding house." There had to be something. She continued, "And it is a lovely area. My grandparents homesteaded there many years ago. They are gone now, but I like the idea of being near where they lived, if I can't be here."

"We truly hope you'll be happy in your new home, whatever your new position turns out to be," Anna said, taking a sip of coffee.

"I will be," she smiled. "Now, it's time for apple pie."

Although she was convinced of the Stanfields fine qualifications, and she liked them very much, she still had one concern. They had had a practice in Portland, a city much advanced compared to life in the canyon. How could they be content living and working in an area so difficult, with so few commonly accepted conveniences, or luxuries? There was no theater or opera, no fine restaurants, no well-equipped hospitals. Getting around was far from easy, good transportation and roads were almost non-existent.

As she served the pie on pretty dessert plates, she smiled to hide the very real worry she felt and asked, "Do you think you'll like it here enough to stay and make it your home? Life in the canyon is rough, very different from the city." She couldn't possibly abandon folks here if the Stanfields wouldn't be around long, if it turned out they didn't care for the canyon.

The doctor explained that their work previously was in some of the worst sections of Portland. Anna explained, "This country is heaven by comparison. Fresh air, nice folks to know, very beautiful surroundings."

"There are many doctors in Portland for folks to choose from," Doctor Stanfield explained with clear-eyed honesty, "and a lame doctor is usually the last choice if anyone else is available. It's hard for some folks to have confidence in a doctor unable to stand tall on two good feet. I'd have liked to have been such a doctor, but unfortunately I was involved in a train wreck when I was a toddler." He grinned. "What we most want to do is help, ply our trade, take care of people. We're an excellent medical team. We thought folks in the canyon might not be so choosy—if we're the only choice." His voice broke on a warm chuckle. He chewed for a moment, then told Laila, "My dear, this is the best pie I've ever tasted—next to Anna's, of course."

"You know I don't make pie," Anna scolded affectionately before turning to Laila. "All I know is medicine, although I try to be a good wife, too, to Carlton."

Laila felt envious of their obvious affection, totally confident that she was leaving the medical concerns of the canyon in good hands. "I think canyon folks are very fortunate that you've decided to practice here," she said from the heart.

Laila stared at Minnie in stunned surprise. It was a few days later and Minnie had showed up at Laila's cabin just at sunset, Tansy in hand, the child gripping her new doll.

"She don't like livin' with me," Minnie was saying, "an' she's afraid of Hob. Tansy wants to be with you, Miss Mitchell."

Laila felt strangled with joy but managed to say, "Well, of course, if that's what you and Tansy want, she's welcome to live with me." Minnie's news was like a glad new song to Laila's ears and she stroked Tansy's head, kissed her cheek, and felt a rising gratitude toward Minnie.

Tansy moved away to the small bed that Hutton had made for her. She put the doll on the bed, tucked the coverlet over her, and in a sing-song play-time voice told her doll that this was her bed now. They would be with Laila.

Minnie told Laila in a lowered voice, a glint of excitement in her yellow-brown eyes, "Hob is going to marry me and take me with him to a new mining job in Montana. But he doesn't want—you know—" she motioned with her head toward Tansy. "Kids get in the way, he says, an' they kind of do. But you and Tansy seem to get on well, and she wants to be with you." She beamed encouragingly, as though half-worried Laila would change her mind about taking Tansy.

"I love Tansy, Minnie. I will raise her as if she were my own child. You can count on that, and never worry about her. Thank you, Minnie, thank you from the bottom of my heart." Tears burned behind Laila's eyes and she embraced Minnie.

"Oh, I knowed you'd take care of Tansy like she's your own, or I wouldn't have asked. You'll be better for Tansy than I'd ever be. 'Bye girl, you be good for Miss Mitchell, now." Minnie appeared more anxious to get on with her life with Hob, than sorry to be leaving Tansy behind.

Tansy frowned as she watched Minnie leave, but she didn't cry. Laila went to hold Tansy close. "We'll be fine, honey, just fine."

Opal, with a surprising turn of heart, wanted to give Laila and Tansy a good-bye party, but Laila declined. She still grieved Tom's death, she missed Ash—although she'd sworn to forget *him*. She had to find a way to support herself and Tansy as soon as possible. She just wanted to go.

She bought Jenny Wren very reasonably from Hutton; it was hard to get him to take any money at all. Hutton, then, bless his soul, insisted she accept as a gift an old wagon he had repaired practically like new. He loved her like a daughter, he said, and she could bloody well accept a gift for all she had done for him and the rest of the community.

Finally, her things were loaded for the long trip to La Grande, for another new start. On the morning she and Tansy were to leave, there wasn't exactly a party, but nearly every soul in the community and for miles around turned out to tell them good-bye and godspeed. Many who came brought small gifts.

Laila fought tears, hugged her friends and former patients until she could hug no more for fear she'd break down. She wished everyone well, promised to come back for visits, then clambered into her wagon and took up the reins. Tansy wiggled with excitement on the seat beside her.

She had asked Hutton to accompany them as far as Conner Creek. It was the last chance, the best way she would have to introduce him to Kate, something she had wanted to do for some time. The pair could take it from there, themselves, if they were as well-matched as she believed they were.

Maybe because she was leaving the canyon, Laila had never seen the Conner Creek ranch so beautiful as when they approached in the golden light of that last, early autumn day. It was comparable even to springtime when all the trees in the orchards were popcorned with blossoms, or in winter under snow when it was a riverside wonderland.

Making up for her private unhappiness, was the reaction Kate and Hutton Ginther showed toward each other; like flowers to sunshine, discovering in a short time how much they had in common. Laila was right to bring them together.

Given time, she was sure they would become more than friends. Kate prepared a special supper, and later the three of them, after Tansy had been tucked in for the night, spent several hours in comfortable conversation in front of the parlor fire. Finally, wanting to get an early start in the morning for La Grande, Laila told Hutton and Kate goodnight and went upstairs.

She had hoped to find that Ash had returned to the ranch, so that she might talk to him, tell him good-bye, clear up the differences between them. But the only word Kate had had from him was that he was very busy and he was uncertain when he might return. It had not been uncommon in the past for him to remain in Portland for days at a time, a few weeks even, but she would have given almost anything to have had him back in the canyon for one last moment with him, a single day, the gift of a week or two. If she hadn't had to leave, and had been given half a chance, she would have gone through with her part of the bargain they had made with Tom.

Facing the truth of her heart as she prepared for bed that night, she knew that she would be in love with Ash for the rest of her days, wherever she went, whether or not she ever saw him again.

Laila and Tansy departed Conner Creek next morning at dawn for the long trip to La Grande. Laila snapped the reins over Jenny Wren's back, clucked her tongue beyond the thickness in her throat. Looking back over her shoulder she said good-bye to the canyon that she loved—her home, her haven—for two wonderful years. How could it be that she was leaving? Tears blinded her and it was hard to see where she was going. She reached over and tugged Tansy closer to her side.

Chapter Twenty-Two

They rented a room in Mrs. Killey's Traveler's House where Laila had stayed on her earlier visit to La Grande. Flora Averly, a widow, was the cook and housekeeper for the boarding house and lived there with her children in a two-room apartment. Her three tow-headed youngsters were playing hopscotch on the boardwalk out front on Laila and Tansy's first evening there.

Tansy watched in fascination, but scrunched shyly against Laila's side. The oldest Averly girl, Maybell, a thirteen-year-old, smiled at Tansy and motioned for her to join them. "Come on, it's fun. Jimmy, Lou, and I will show you how."

Pressed against Laila's side, Tansy shook her head, "no." But later, when Laila and Mrs. Averly sat in the porch swing, visiting in the twilight, Tansy made her way slowly to the children playing on the boardwalk. From the corner of her eye, Laila kept watch, glad when Tansy joined in the game. A smart child, Tansy caught on quickly and was soon laughing with the Averly children and enjoying the game.

"She's gonna be all right," Mrs. Averly patted Laila's knee. "My Maybell can keep an eye on your little Tansy right along with Jimmy and Lou, one more little child won't make much difference. Only be more enjoyment for all of them. An' you can go ahead and look for work without worryin' about Tansy."

"I truly appreciate this. I do need to find a job, and soon."

"Word of your fine medical work in the Snake River canyon has reached even here in La Grande," the stooped, snowy-haired physician, Doctor Carter, told Laila from behind his desk. His age-patterned face settled into a kindly smile and he pushed his spectacles back in place on his nose.

It was hard to believe anyone outside the canyon would have heard of her. "Thank you, Doctor." She sat forward in her chair, tense and hopeful, waiting.

He explained, "A few months ago I learned that a physician was needed in that area." His silver moustache curled up with wry grin. "For about a day I was feeling younger than I am and needful of adventure. I considered relocating there. Had my wife not brought me to my senses, I would have gone, and I would have welcomed you as my assistant."

Her spirits lifted higher still. "That's nice to hear, Doctor." If he had believed in her qualifications when considering a move, then surely he would welcome her as his assistant here in La Grande now. *If*, and a big if, he needed someone.

His expression became regretful as he seemed to read her mind. "My wife, bless her wise, caring soul, talked me into retiring instead of looking for a new challenge. She recognizes, even if it is a bit harder for me to see, that I'm long in the tooth. The honest truth is, I'm near wore out from almost sixty years of practice. It's time for me to take a rest and let the younger doctors take over. I would hire you in a whistle, my dear, but I plan to keep my practice open only a few weeks more."

Riddled with concern that this was possibly her last chance for work, she buried her disappointment and stood up, smiling, "Thank you, Doctor Carter, I understand." She gave him her hand. She would have enjoyed working alongside the old doctor, either in the canyon or in La Grande. But neither circumstance was to be. "I wish you well in your retirement, sir."

"And I wish you well, Miss, in your search for employment. We have two other doctors here in town, have you been to visit them? They will be taking over my patients' care, either one of them might need your help with the added work."

She nodded. "I wish that were so, but I have spoken to both doctors, without success." Doctor Turner was the first physician she had gone to see. His offices on Depot Street were very handily near Mrs. Killey's boarding house. Unfortunately for Laila, Doctor Turner had two competent daughters in their early twenties—one of whom had professional training as a nurse—and both daughters aided him in his work. The third physician, Doctor Grosvenor Urling, was a cold-faced but handsome young surgeon who wanted nothing but the best—a *professionally* trained nurse—at his side. He'd told her brusquely as she was leaving, "I suspect that eventually another doctor will come to La Grande to replace old Carter. Just starting out, the new man may have need of a practical nurse." She had thanked him. His information, though meant to be helpful, was of little use. She needed work right away.

Doctor Carter told her now, "Don't give up, Miss."

She smiled at him over her shoulder. "No, I won't."

She went back out onto the sun-filled, pleasant street, wondering where to look next. In the hour that followed she was turned down for work at two cafes, and in a hotel dining room. She tried for employment at a dentist's office, at a photographer's, and in a department store, but no one needed her.

As she walked the streets, tired and near panic, she told herself that it was useless to keep blaming Ash for her predicament. She had wanted a real doctor in the canyon as much as or maybe more than he had. It could have been just coincidence that the doctor he found was able to bring his own professional help with him.

As the day waned, and her head began to ache, she resisted the urge to return to her and Tansy's small, pleasant room, throw herself on the bed, and dissolve into tears. She had to make one more try before giving up for the day.

She would have pause to wonder many times, later, if it was good luck, or bad luck, that the Wisteria Laundry on Fourth Avenue readily hired her. The laundry had a pretty name, but its nicety ended there. The interior of the large, shed-like building was hot, steamy, and smelly. Her job, pressing linens for twelve to fourteen hours a day—depending on the workload—was mind-deadening and backbreaking. Standing all day made her feet and legs swell until they felt elephant-sized. But at least she now had means to pay for their room and meals at Mrs. Killey's, and a small sum to give Maybell for minding Tansy during the day.

Fortunately, next year, Tansy would be old enough to attend school while Laila worked.

There would be no money for extras, however, as long as Laila worked at the laundry. If a new doctor who might employ her was coming to La Grande, she prayed that it would be soon. Or, if not work with him, she hoped another, better job than at the laundry would come up. In the meantime, she would make effort to keep up her spirits in any way possible. It did no good to dwell on what might have been.

Each morning she rose early and drew wide her curtains, standing for several minutes at the window, admiring the broad valley and nearby mountains. True fall seemed indefinitely postponed and day after day was balmy under a deep blue sky. Foolishly, in spite of trying to keep a cap on her hopes, she would look hard at the road coming into town, trying to ascertain if whatever moving vehicle or approaching horse might be carrying the man she loved. Ash, wanting to explain, wanting her to forgive. But he didn't come.

Evenings, for a change of scene and a rare treat, Laila and Tansy twice took their supper at a café, rather than at Mrs. Killey's. Flora Averly was a decent cook, but unimaginative, her offerings unvaried. Laila especially liked the Palmer House restaurant for its pleasant atmosphere and inexpensively priced food. The second evening Laila and Tansy ate there, a tall handsome fellow stepped into the Palmer House, and seeing him, Laila's heart constricted and she thought, *Ash!* When she saw that the man was not Ash, but did resemble him, her disappointment was raw and the rest of her meal was like sawdust. She would have left most of it on her plate, but Tansy was more than happy to finish Laila's supper and her own.

That night in their room, after Tansy had fallen asleep, Laila got out paper, pen, and ink, to write Ash a letter. Her emotions were ragged as she wondered, should she begin *Dear Ash,* or *Mr. Austin Corbett,* or *My good friend,* or what? Her hand shook as she wrote *Dear Ash, I was sorry to hear of your abrupt but necessary departure from the ranch after your father's funeral. I pray the misfortune that called you to Portland has been rectified, or will be soon. I wish to hear from you, if you care to write. Because I had to leave Venture and find work elsewhere, you will find that Tansy and I have removed to La Grande. Address your letter, please, to me at Mrs. Killey's Traveler's House—*

Laila re-read the letter and sighed in dejection. He was not going to be impressed by her begging him to write. And it wouldn't be news to him that she had to leave the canyon due to lack of employment! She tore the letter to shreds. She had to maintain some pride after all. She wouldn't be hard to locate if he wanted to find her. Kate knew she had come here to La Grande; nearly everyone else in the canyon knew it, too.

Despite wanting to be content in the busy little town and in the pretty valley that had once been home to her grandparents—plus making a new life with Tansy who would now be her child for good—Laila was miserable. She could lay her state of heart directly at Ash's feet. Her intention early on *not* to fall in love had been the right idea if only she had held to it. But he'd been so irresistible and she'd had her guard down and had fallen in love. She decided that no physical wound or ailment she'd attended for another could have hurt any more than she hurt now from losing him—if she'd ever had him and she hadn't—not really. All she'd had to cling to was the promise they'd made his father.

Trying to forget her own troubles, she took special pains to be friendly with the other women at the laundry. For the most part they were good, hard-working women. Molly was a stoutly built, graying widow who was raising her five children alone. She had myriad worries—one child was deaf, another was wild and regularly into mischief—among other concerns. Still, Molly always had a friendly greeting and kind words for others. Another worker, Hannah, was a near-illiterate blowsy blonde who had a laugh like the bray of a donkey. She, too, was kindhearted. If her work was caught up and another woman was falling behind, she was the first to jump in and help. Although never married, she had two children. The trio lived with her mother on the edge of town in the same house where Hannah had been born. Sarah and Josephine, thin, harried-looking sisters, were the remaining two workers. They also had children. Josephine's husband had deserted his family a year ago, Sarah's husband was an alcoholic. The sisters were shy and quiet but kind.

Laila paid her fellow workers back for their kindness and

friendship by treating the burns they got from scalding water and hot flat irons. She gave practical advice whenever needed for one of their sick children.

In those first weeks, she also got to know most of the merchants she dealt with by their first names, and exchanged friendly conversation when there was time. She and Tansy took long walks on Laila's day off, and on one occasion took a picnic lunch to eat beside a nearby small creek.

Laila wrote Ash another letter: *Dear Ash . . . I demand to know why you have vanished to Portland without a word to tell me why! And what about your promise—our promise to your father? Why did you put me out of a job without the slightest warning? Don't you know . . . haven't you guessed that I love you more than words can say?* Swallowing myriad tears, wailing silently at the walls that life wasn't fair, Laila tore that letter also into tiny bits. A woman didn't chase after a man with letters like that.

She had never been one for self pity, but there seemed no way out of her doldrums although she continued to scold herself for being blue and unhappy. Maybe her feelings of depression were partially due to being a fish out of water in the new town, she decided. Other than the other workers and her boss at the laundry, Mrs. Averly, and the few merchants she dealt with, she knew no one else, no grownups, to socialize with. It would take time to get used to a place so different from the canyon, or St. Louis, or Kansas on the farm—no matter how pleasant it was on the surface.

As she was going about doing errands during her third week in La Grande, she was glad to spot Althea Estes crossing from the opposite side of the street.

"Althea! Miss Estes!" She smiled and waved.

Althea halted and stared in surprise and then hurried her way. "Miss Mitchell, isn't it? It's so nice to see you. Were you planning to come out to Lark Springs Farm?"

She shook her head. "I've been thinking of paying you a visit, but I hadn't made actual plans. Can you believe that I live here in La Grande now? I work at the Wisteria Laundry." At Althea's frown and look of surprise, she explained, "A real medical team has taken over the work I used to do in the canyon. I hated to leave, but there was no other work for me there. I had hoped for employment here as a doctor's helper, but—" she shrugged, "nothing."

"Oh, I'm sorry about that, truly. But welcome, dear. La Grande is much the better for you choosing us, our community. I was on my way to the general store. I come to town two days a week after school to teach piano to a child here. You've been here a week or two? I'm so glad our paths finally crossed."

"I'm glad, too." She thought for a moment, unwilling for their meeting to end so soon. She asked, "When you've finished with your errands would you like to meet me at the Palmer House for supper, Althea? I'd love a chance to—visit. I feel a bit of a stranger in town. It's been pretty lonely since I came."

"Of course, I'd love to. I was about to propose the same thing, myself."

Later that evening the two women relaxed over their after-supper coffee. Laila had asked Tansy to come along, but wasn't surprised that Tansy chose to have dinner, German fried potatoes and brown beans yet again, with the boisterous, happy Averlys at the boarding house.

Laila and Althea's conversation had touched casually on their meal, a delicious vegetable soufflé, the beauty of the Grande Ronde Valley, worrisome prices at the department stores. In the last few minutes, their talk had turned more personal.

"Your work at the laundry is only temporary, isn't it?"

Althea asked with kindly concern. She frowned over the rim of her cup and shook her head. "It's not right that your medical skills are going to waste."

"I hope my work there is only temporary." She told Althea about Tansy, that Laila had more than herself to support. "If a new doctor comes to replace Doctor Carter I will definitely ask for work with him." She said with a wry smile, "Of course it will be just my luck that he brings his own assistant with him, as happened in Venture." She toyed with her spoon, tracing a pattern on the tablecloth. "I've considered that I should look into taking classes in medicine, and better equip myself for the kind of work I enjoy. I understand that Blue Mountain University here in town closed its doors a few years ago for lack of financing?"

"Unfortunately, yes. And there is talk that it may never reopen, that the building will be razed."

"Well, if that turns out *not* to be true, and it reopens with classes in medicine, I will be first in line to sign up, if I have to beg my way in. I suppose I could take medical courses at a college in Salem, or Portland, but it would take a long time before I could save the funds to make such a move."

"To be honest, I'm surprised you're not married and rearing a *flock* of children. You are a very pretty young woman, Laila. A prize catch for some young man, I'd say."

"Thank you." She felt her face warm as she admitted, "I haven't had many opportunities in my past to meet someone." She hesitated, wondering how much she wanted to disclose. She continued, "More recently, I had the misfortune of falling deeply for someone who—who doesn't seem to share the feeling." She resisted the temptation to pour out her heart about Ash. To thwart a threat of tears she asked instead, "How about you, Althea? Do you have a special male friend?"

"As a matter of fact, I do." Her eyes sparkled, her face colored prettily, and she looked very feminine. "Mr. Reed is a retired county school superintendent. I've known him for years through our occupations. But more recently he has come to call on me as a—suitor. I believe he may have marriage in mind."

Laila laughed softly. "From your expression I would guess that your answer will be a definite yes."

"It will be. I care for him very much." Her expression was conspiratorial. "Actually, I've been secretly in love with him for years, that's one reason I've never married although others have asked. As you know, according to society's rules, a lady must be patient and wait for her gentleman to speak his heart. Until the big question has been popped, we can hardly say yes, can we?"

For a moment Laila didn't answer, considering her own state of limbo and then she answered, "No, we can't. And I pray your wait is soon over, Althea." She reached across the table to touch her hand, and smile.

"I believe that it will be." There was confidence in Althea's soft chuckle. She caught Laila's hand and squeezed it. "And I pray your gentleman love comes to his senses."

Following that evening—which the two women declared they had enjoyed tremendously—they often met to have supper together. Laila was thrilled to have a new friend, was glad they got along so well. Laila and Tansy began to attend church with Althea, and sometimes went out to Lark Springs Farm with Althea for Sunday dinner. Laila met Althea's Mr. Reed, a spry, warm-hearted older man who clearly was besotted with Althea. His eyes seldom left her face. He leaped to attend her at whatever small task she was occupied with, whether she needed his help or not. When he touched her by accident or otherwise, he looked like he might faint with joy. Althea was right to believe that he would soon propose marriage and Laila envied her.

She expressed her envy, and at last told Althea about Ash—named him as the one she cared for. "I'm embarrassed to say that I mumble to the walls at night, I tell them that I love him and can't help it; I plea for answers, for reasons why he did what he did, but there have been none." She laughed, but tears were close behind. She wondered how she could ever have thought she had no interest in Ash, those first months in the canyon. Her feelings now were that she could never survive the rest of her life without him—but she had to try and find a way.

Althea begged her, "Oh, my dear, don't give up on him. Something is holding your young fellow, maybe his own uncertainty, or maybe a problem with his business, but when he's able, he'll come and claim you. I feel it in my soul."

As much as Althea's words soothed and encouraged her, Laila's doubts remained. She was afraid of false hope. She had set herself up for enough pain by falling in love. A love she was forced to keep to herself, as Althea had done in her situation, for many years.

Laila and Tansy had been in La Grande four and a half weeks and there had been no word from Ash. If he had gone back to Conner Creek it would have been simple enough to learn her whereabouts, if he truly cared. But maybe he had no interest in hurrying his return to the canyon, now that his father was no longer there and he finally had the life he wanted in Portland.

One Sunday, Laila and Tansy were again having dinner at Lark Springs Farm. Althea seemed happier than usual and about to burst with news on the tip of her tongue, but that she was holding back. Maybe she was waiting for the right moment to tell it, Laila decided, amused. Later, as the two of them walked about the farm while Tansy fed corn to a pig through the barnyard fence, Althea confided to Laila that Mr. Reed had asked for her hand in marriage the evening before. "Of course I said yes."

"Althea, I am very, very happy for you." Chickens clucked around them as Laila hugged her. "You and Mr. Reed are perfect for one another! I know you'll have a wonderful life together."

"There is something else," Althea stood still, facing her, speaking quietly but with eyes aglow. "I will be going to Mr. Reed's house to live after we're married. He has a wonderful home in town, and it is what he wants to do. I do, too. We both have friends there, we'll be close to church, the stores. I love the farm here, but—" she grasped Laila's arms and shook her slightly, "it will now be up for sale. I want you to have it."

Sudden tears burned behind Laila's eyes. To own Lark Springs Farm would be the answer to her dreams. It was the ideal place to bring up Tansy. But buying it was impossible. She had a very small savings from sale of her cabin to the Stanfields, but not nearly enough to pay for Lark Springs Farm. Her salary at the laundry couldn't pay for garden seed, a shovel and hoe. "I–I can't—" she started to reply but Althea stopped her.

"Don't give me an answer, yet," she said softly, studying her face. "I'm aware of your situation, dear. But we may be able to work something out. I'm in no hurry to sell the farm, it won't be easy to turn loose of it, as it is. One of these days you may find other employment that will allow you to borrow from the bank, or have enough to give me monthly payments from your wages. I feel confident that this can be worked out, I truly do. Lark Springs Farm must go to you. I can only imagine how happy it would make your grandparents, if they could know it finally became yours."

Laila threw her arms around Althea and held her wordlessly. Finally, she found her voice. "Thank you, Althea. Thank you so very much." She saw no way to buy the farm, but Althea's thoughtfulness meant the world to her. And if there was any chance . . .

Chapter Twenty-Three

That same night, back at the Traveler's House, Laila wracked her brain for a solution, for some way to buy the farm. She considered moving, again, to yet another town, for other, more profitable work. But where, what kind of work? She'd been sure that La Grande was the right place, but it had not turned out to be so far.

Like a wooden-brained robot she got up each morning and, leaving Tansy in the care of Maybell, went to work at the laundry, facing one drudging, distasteful, backbreaking day after another. It might not have been so bad had Laila not been aware that a wonderful opportunity for her was on the horizon, but was as out of reach as the moon. If she had the farm, and the wonderful hot lake, she could turn it into a medical resort and help so many people. Help herself in turn, be able to provide well for Tansy. Laila would name the resort after her grandparents: *The Chapin Health Spa and Hotel.*

It was hard to fight the grip of unhappiness, hard to make herself see that the sun was actually shining, the sky was blue, that fragrant fall flowers bloomed, that Tansy was a happy child—possibly happier even than she'd been in Venture. For the first time in her life, Tansy had other children to play with from morning to night and she reveled in her new life. Laila, on the other hand—in a continuing state of numbness—made the trek to the laundry and back again to their room, each unpleasant twelve-hour day. Laila wanted to feel excited again, to be able to think, to form a plan that would make her dreams come true, but weariness, and lack of answers reigned, along with private longing for Ash.

Laila faked interest in lunchroom gossip at the laundry each day, she pretended enthusiasm for turning out mile-high stacks of shiny, pressed linens and thought that if the labor didn't kill her, the boredom would.

Where once she had been eager to make a life in the canyon any small way she might, here she wanted everything: she wanted Ash, she wanted Lark Springs Farm, she wanted every iota of happiness her hands and heart could hold. She was daily plagued with headaches and before long had wiped out her supply of headache powders and didn't feel she could afford to buy more. Normally a "good eater" she could barely eat and she put down her loss of appetite to sheer weariness.

One day at work, when she suffered particularly with a rocketing headache, she nearly jumped from her skin when blonde Hannah, at the next ironing table, squawked, "Gawd, who is that? He a god or some'pin'?"

Laila looked up and there was Ash in the doorway, dressed in a blue shirt and dark trousers, hair ruffled by the wind outside, his tie askew and his suit coat held slung over his shoulder. *He had come after all.* Her heart pumped with joy. Weariness, troubles of moments before became nothing and fell away. Whether his emergency in Portland was real, or not, didn't matter anymore. If he intentionally pushed her out of work by engaging the two Stanfields, so what? That didn't matter, either. She loved him heart and soul and he didn't have to explain a thing. He was here, and that was all that mattered.

She was set to run to him when she saw his face, saw that he glared at her and she halted, stunned. Bewilderment overtook her as she noted that he looked furious enough to tear a Douglas fir from the earth by its roots barehanded. Her heart constricted. Why was he angry at her? She watched him shrug into his coat and stride toward her, his shoulders huffed, face grim and furious. Her own ire began to rise. What did *he* have to be angry about? By rights, she should be tearing into him! She was the one who had been abandoned and thrown to the wolves!

All at once he was looming over her, so close she could smell his cologne and the fresh air he'd brought inside with him. His eyes blazed down on her and he looked disgusted. She frowned and asked, "Ash, what on earth is the matter, what are you doing?" She dodged out of his reach and put her hot iron back in its holder. Wiping her perspiring brow with the back of her arm, brushing damp tendrils of hair back from her face, she backed away and then tried to free herself as he grasped her hard by the elbow. "C'mon." He pulled her toward the door. The other women ceased work to stare.

"Ash, will you stop it! What are you doing? Wait—!" she cried as he swooped her into his arms and carried her toward the door. "Put me down!"

As she bobbed past them, Laila's work-mates smiled in wonderment. Hannah made ribald guesses as to the handsome gentleman's intentions which sent the other women into scandalized giggles.

"Ash, this is embarrassing. For heaven's sake put me down."

He answered by tightening his hold against her struggles. "I'm taking you out of here and there's not a force on earth that can stop me. What the hell are you doing in this place anyhow?"

At first she was too surprised to answer. Her throat was dry, her heart pounded in confusion, frustration, and anger. Her intention of moments ago to forget and forgive evaporated. "I was *working,*" she stormed, "and if you don't put me down and let me go back to my job, I'll be fired."

"Don't matter."

"Does matter."

They were almost to the door when the commotion brought her boss, Mr. Macaffee, charging out of his cubicle office in the back corner of the laundry. Past Ash's big shoulder she saw Macaffee sizing up the situation, his face turning red, his feet stomping as he came after them. "We got a big work-load here, why's everybody standing around gawking? Get back to work! Mitchell," he yelled at her, "walk out that door and you're fired!"

"But I'm not—he won't—" she sputtered, her face hot as fire.

Ash gave Macaffee a withering look over his shoulder. "You oughtta be able to see she's not walking out, I'm carrying her. She's got no business being here and don't expect her back."

With murmurs of disappointment at missing the rest of the show, Laila's fellow-workers went back to their tasks. Out on the sidewalk, Ash put her down but didn't loosen his hold on her. "You've got a lot of explaining to do," he growled at her.

"*I* do?" she was incredulous, "I have explaining to do? You're the one who went off without saying why—"

"I had to go."

"And I had to work here because you left me no other choice. Now it makes *twice* you've put me out of work. Don't tell me you have a defense for that?"

"You don't belong in a place like that. You had no business leaving the canyon."

"But it's your fault," she shouted furiously, standing toe to toe with him, "don't you understand?" She raised her fist to strike his chest but he caught her hand and held it.

"Simmer down. Sounds like we both have some explaining to do. Let's go somewhere where we can talk."

She realized suddenly that they weren't alone, that a circle of bystanders had gathered around them, watching, listening, grinning. "All right," she mumbled. "It appears that everyone from seven counties is eavesdropping."

Ash grinned crookedly at the crowd and explained to them, "I'm trying to tell her I love her but she won't listen."

"Better listen to him, Miss," a straw-hatted farmer nodded and grinned broadly, "he looks like a nice enough feller to me."

A grin tugged at Laila's mouth, her anger was beginning to fade although her head still swirled with confusion. She wondered if Ash really had said what she thought she heard. "Please, Ash, let's go, they're staring at us like we're a circus."

He took her elbow and led her a few paces down the street to a waiting buggy hitched to a sleek strawberry roan. "We'll go for a ride. Where to?"

"Anywhere. South out of town, west, east—I don't care as long as we get cleared up why you came charging into my work like that. But please take me to my boarding house first, I'd like to change my dress and tell Tansy we'll be gone for a while."

Laila's mind was so preoccupied as she and Ash drove out of town a short time later, she didn't at first realize they were headed east, in the direction of Lark Springs Farm. She turned to Ash on the seat, "Ash, why are you so angry with me? What have I done?"

Ash kept the horse at a walk. He looked down at Laila on the wagon seat beside him and explained, "I wasn't angry at you so much as I hated seeing you slaving in such a place. Before that I was afraid I'd lost you and it's nearly made me crazy. You were supposed to stay in the canyon and wait for me."

"I was supposed to *stay? Wait* for you? How was I to know that? You never said." She creased the fabric of her skirt between her nervous fingers.

"Sure you knew, we both did! We promised Pop we would start courting."

Her chuckle was strained as she reminded him, "We promised him we'd get to know one another better, yes. But it takes two on hand to court, you know. And how was I to stay in the canyon? It takes money to live and you put me out of work, or have you forgotten? I presume the Stanfields, *both* of them, are still there in my place. From every sign, you brought them in to be rid of me."

He looked shocked. He drew the horse to a halt in the road and wrapped the reins around the brake handle next to his knee. He turned and caught her shoulders. "Rid of you? I'd never do that."

"But you did. There was nothing for me in the canyon once the Stanfields took over my work. You're the one who engaged them to replace me."

"Hold on just a minute and listen to me!" His grip tightened, but his expression was deeply caring. "I wouldn't do that to you, I'd never do anything to hurt you. I didn't know, 'til Carl Stanfield arrived, that his wife was also his nurse. I didn't hire the two of them to replace you. And in the confusion of Pop being sick with pneumonia and all, there just didn't seem to be a chance to talk about it and let you know I didn't do that on purpose. Then, with Pop barely in the ground, I had to rush off to Portland."

She was silent a moment, enjoying the feel of hands caressing her arms, but still not sure of anything. "What happened there, Ash? Would you please tell me? You left so suddenly and I haven't known what to think."

"My hotel burned, a big part of it anyway."

She gasped, reached up to cup his cheek in her palm. "Oh, Ash, I'm so sorry. I had no idea." She felt sick that she'd believed that he'd had no real problem, but had just wanted to get away from her, away from the canyon. She owed him an enormous apology. "Ash, I'm sorry," she repeated.

He continued, "Hoodlums took advantage of the situation and tried to rob us. The Count, my hotel manager, went to stop them and they shot him. He nearly died."

Tears of remorse and sympathy stung her eyes as she looked up at him. "Is he all right?"

"He's on the mend now. Laila, I wanted to get word to you, to explain what had happened, but I've had to be in a dozen places at once, weeks on end. I was with the Count as much as possible at the hospital. I had to direct carpenters at the hotel. The police wanted my assistance to see that the criminals were identified and made to pay. I've had to hire and train new help to replace the Count."

"It had to be awful for you," she reflected, her heart in her voice, "to have so many horrible things happen at once."

"It's been hell," he agreed. "I can't remember the last time I had a full night's sleep, or got to finish a meal. But it was okay, I had things I had to do, and all the time I was there, the one good thing that kept me going was knowing that you were waiting for me back in the canyon."

She felt sick that she had let him down. It really was true, then, that he wanted her to wait, he wasn't getting rid of her. She warmed with happiness knowing how much she meant to him in his crisis, but there were still things she didn't understand. She told him, "Even if I hadn't had to leave to make my living, tell me this: How was I to know what you expected, what you wanted? How was I to know that you even cared—for me? Your behavior toward me has been the reverse for a long time, you know. I could have been an ugly witch you couldn't stand, the way you acted."

"You've never been an ugly witch to me, you're beautiful and I've loved you from about the first moment I saw you. I did my damned-est not to care," he admitted, apology written across his handsome face. "You scared me—you were different from any other woman I'd ever met. So independent, you didn't seem to need me, need anyone." His hand slid down her arm to circle her waist while she held his other hand. He pulled her closer. "But I got to like that independent streak, and once we both promised Pop that we would get married, I knew that's exactly what I wanted, and you agreed."

His face came down close to hers but she drew back and smiled. He was about to kiss her and end the conversation when they were nowhere near finished. "Ash! We promised no such thing—to get married."

"We did." He seemed to sincerely believe it as his eyes studied her face.

"No, we agreed with him that we would get to know one another better, that's all. There was no talk of marriage."

"That's what he meant!"

"Maybe he did, and maybe he didn't. The way things happened, I thought you probably didn't care for me as much as I cared for you. I had blessed little evidence of your feelings—any affection. You seemed angry at me, even then."

He groaned, "I'm sorry I wasn't able to talk everything over with you after Pop's funeral, sorry I had to leave without telling you good-bye. But you have to believe me, I *never* wanted to be rid of you—just the opposite in fact. When Pop asked us to get to really know one another and you agreed, I was the happiest man in the world—about that, though I was sorry our promise was over his deathbed. With both the doctor and his wife to take over, it seemed perfect—you were free to be my wife. I shouldn't have taken for granted that you'd just wait for me in the canyon, but I did."

She swallowed. "No, you shouldn't have. And I apologize for assuming all the wrong things." There was a singing in her heart, yet everything still seemed unreal. "Let's keep driving," she said, "there's something up ahead I want to show you."

"What?"

"A hot lake."

"A *hot* lake?"

"You'll see."

He tapped the reins over the roan's back and clicked his tongue but he didn't take his arm from where it circled her waist. It was cozy beside him in the buggy, and with just a tilt of her head she could easily snuggle into the curve of his shoulder. The trouble was, there was still so much between them that needed to be cleared up. She resisted the snuggling urge, sat straight, and looked ahead.

Chapter Twenty-Four

For Ash to express his feelings for her openly was new and different and—as much as it thrilled Laila—it was taking some getting used to. She was confident in her love for him, but she wanted him to be sure, and not make a mistake. He really didn't know her, although he might think that he did. He had talked rashly from the moment he charged into the laundry, and then on the drive he carried on as though everything was settled and they would be man and wife. She wanted that more than anything in the world but she must tell him who and what she was before any final decision about their future was made.

She edged a notch closer to him on the buggy-seat as the horse drew them along at a trot and a soft wind blew her hair. She never wanted her and Ash to be separated again, not like these last terrible weeks. At the same time her heart beat contentedly just to be near him, worry etched her mind knowing she must tell him the truth about herself before their relationship went further. About her life growing up, the way she'd had to live. She couldn't allow him to think he was marrying a fine lady, a person with a cultured past like his mother or Claudine, when the truth was so far at the other end of the scale. She had to tell him *everything*. That's really what Old Tom wanted. There was so much Ash didn't know.

She wasn't sure she could survive if after hearing her story he changed his mind about wanting to marry her, but she had to take the chance. She wanted nothing hidden between them.

He held her hand on the buggy-seat next to his thigh as they drove along. Every few minutes she sneaked a peek at him, often catching him looking at her in an intimate way that set her heart to racing. Still, she had to keep her senses.

She said in a while, "Ash, I have to apologize again. I thought your sudden trip to Portland might not be a serious matter, that it was likely just a ruse on your part to get away from the canyon. I'm not proud of myself for believing what I did. I should have known better, should have trusted you."

He shrugged after a brief silence, and said, "It's all right. I'd made it plain enough in the past how I felt about the canyon. I'm sorry for leaving you in such a predicament, without work or funds, to get by on your own by any means you could. I didn't mean to, and it won't be that way when we're married." He called, "Whoa," drew back on the reins, stopping in the middle of the road. "I can't go another mile without kissing you, holding you—" She smiled up at him, her eyes misty, and went willingly into his arms. He drew her close to his heart and his mouth smothered hers, setting off a tingle that raced through her blood, threatening a firestorm.

She said breathlessly after several moments, "Why do you want to marry me, Ash? I'm assuming your carrying on the way you have this afternoon is—is a proposal. I want us to be very sure about this."

He looked at her for a long moment, then told her huskily, "I want to marry you, my darling, because I'm so in love with you I can't bear not to have you by my side, in my bed, in my life! There hasn't been a day I haven't had you on my mind, from the time I first saw you climbing so prim and proper and beautiful off that boat at my dock. And insisting you were going on downriver to *live,* my God—" He threw back his head and laughed. "What an impression you made on me!"

"I wasn't, and I'm not, prim and proper, Ash." It took almost more will than she possessed but she drew back out of his arms. "You really don't know me. I know you're deluded and always have been, about who and what I am."

"I know how strong you are, Laila, and sweet. Lord, but haven't I seen it for myself, watching you make your own way in the canyon, helping folks, taking care of Pop and even shedding tears over the old rascal?" He leaned forward to place a lingering kiss on her lips, a kiss that reached the depths of her being and left her wanting more. He continued, "Not to leave out that you're the prettiest woman I ever saw, in the canyon or in Portland or anywhere else. I love you so much, Laila. I've never felt this way about anyone else. I know all I need to know about you."

"You sound so sure, Ash." A frown creased her brow.

"Hell, yes, I'm sure." He tried to kiss her again, his mouth trailing across her cheek, but she resisted.

"You might not be so sure, when I tell you about myself: Who I really am, where I came from, and why I came here."

"I've always wanted to know everything about you, not that it would change anything. But you've avoided talk about your past."

Because, she realized now, she had been afraid he would turn away from her if he knew what she really was. That she wouldn't have even his friendship, let alone his love. But now that he had made it clear that he intended to marry her, he had to know the truth, all of it.

Reading the solemn concern in her face, he quipped with a wide, loving grin, "What did you do, Laila, commit a murder?"

She shuddered slightly at the comment, then told him, "In a way, I think you can say that I did. I didn't mean to, but I'm responsible for my father's death."

The grin left his face. "Honey, you're joking aren't you? You're surely mistaken." His hands stroked her shoulders, then down her arms. He tried to pull her against him once more but she pulled back.

"Let me tell you, Ash, about when I was a little girl."

He nodded, took her hand in his and waited. His brow was so smooth, his expression calm, confident. She hated to think of changing that look on his face.

"I was about Tansy's age when this incident began. I lived with my parents on a Kansas farm. I'm sure my parents had worries, but for me it was an idyllic time. Then one day, we heard about a medicine show that was coming to Emporia, the town nearest our farm. The posters made it look so exciting, there were going to be clown acts, a performing bear, and I begged to go. Papa didn't really want to. There was a lot of work to do on the farm, and he didn't think he should take the time. He wasn't feeling well, either. He'd suffered for years with chronic stomach pain from an old war wound."

Ash nodded for her to continue.

"I begged and begged to go to the medicine show and my father finally gave in. I was disappointed in the show. The clown wasn't very good, and the bear was a tattered old thing who just wanted to sleep. But the showman's spiel about the cure-all tonic he was peddling was very convincing to both Papa and me. Papa shelled out a dollar for the 'medicine' and he drank the whole bottle that afternoon before we left the show. It made him feel better and he bought another few bottles to take back to the farm with us."

"So what happened, was the tonic poison? What happened to your father, and why do you take the blame?"

"You might say the tonic was poison. It was Hostetter's Bitters, ninety-proof alcohol with some flavoring added. *Cheap whiskey* presented as medicine."

"It killed him?"

Tears filled her eyes and it was a moment before she could go on, "Not right away. But once Papa felt the tonic heat his stomach, numb his mind to the pain, he couldn't give it up. I remember how shocked I was when I was about ten and I found a small mountain of brown bitters bottles in a hidden corner of the barn." She shook her head. "We knew Papa took a lot of medicine for his sickness, but not so much as that. Even after I discovered so many empty bottles, we didn't quite realize that he had become truly addicted, that Hostetter's Celebrated Stomach Bitters was making him a helpless, hopeless drunk. The stuff was strongly endorsed by the clergy in newspaper and magazine advertisements. How, with such fine souls advocating it, could his medicine be the problem?"

"They probably weren't aware of the alcohol content."

"No. How could they be when the tonic wasn't honestly labeled? And another irony—Papa was a decent, God-fearing man, had always been a teetotaler strongly against commonly known drink. Mama and I tried to help him, make him see a doctor about his stomach troubles, but by then he couldn't, wouldn't be helped. He wanted nothing so much as the oblivion he found in his 'medicine'. Eventually, he lost the farm. He lost a variety of other jobs he tried to hold throughout Kansas, and finally, in St. Louis. He died when I was thirteen years old. According to the doctor we got for him, too late, he had died of alcohol poisoning, liver failure." She wiped her eyes.

"I'm so sorry, but it wasn't your fault."

She nodded, swallowed against the thickness in her throat. "My mother and I did our best to make a living on our own for two years after my father's passing." She looked up at Ash, "There isn't a lot of work for an unskilled woman and a girl. Then my mother fell ill, of pneumonia. At the time we were living in squalor in a tent village for the homeless by the Mississippi River in St. Louis. I was fifteen, had to see her buried in Potter's Field because I had nothing."

"Darling, I'm so sorry! How on earth did you manage to

get by, then?" His hands held her tightly, his eyes were shadowed by the pain he shared with her.

She explained how she had walked the streets, knocked on doors, begging for work. How she had finally been hired by Ben Saugrain as his nurse after saving him from attack by a vicious dog. "He was a very unpleasant old man, but I needed a place to live, and food. I think now that I agreed to work for him, most of all because I felt guilty about Papa, and I wanted to help somebody, save somebody's life in return for ruining my own father's."

"Oh, Laila, darling, what happened to your father, to both your parents, was not your doing." He kissed the tears from her cheeks, then held her close. He said against her hair, "You were a small child. Your father was a man, an adult. He could have said no to the tonic, fought harder to be free of its grip."

"I've tried to tell myself that often enough. But the day I insisted that my father take me to the medicine show changed our lives drastically. It's hard not to feel at fault, even though I was a little girl at the time and the whole thing began in such innocence. It gave me a lot of satisfaction to bring my practical nursing skills to Oregon, to the canyon." She finished quietly, "It doesn't help my father, but it somehow makes it up to his memory, and to my mother's, when I'm able to help somebody else."

"And I took that away from you."

"You didn't mean to, Ash, I know that now. And you couldn't have known my chief reasons for wanting to help, to be a nurse, because I've never let anyone know my actual motives. My story was one I could hardly face myself, let alone tell others."

He began to kiss her fervently, on her mouth, her brow, her throat, and back to her mouth over and over as though he wanted to kiss away her pain, her feelings of guilt. When they caught their breath, he told her huskily, "I love you so much, my darling Laila. Now that you've told me this, I love you more than ever."

"But I am not what you believed, I am not a fine cultured person like your mother was, or your other—women-friends and that's why I told you everything. I want you to be sure about me, Ash, very sure."

"I am so sure I love you, I could shout it to the mountains. My very bones, know it. My flesh knows it, my heart and soul know it. I admit your independence scared me at first, and I was sure I didn't like that in a woman. Lately, I've come to realize that very few men are ever lucky enough to find a woman like you, one with the ability to adapt to anything, anytime, anywhere, and make a go of it, like you have. What scares me now, is that I'm not good enough for you."

She was taken aback and insisted, "Now, that's nonsense. You're perfect, Ash."

He laughed with pleasure. "I see that I have you fooled. I'll work hard to keep you that way."

With his arm about her shoulder, he snapped the reins in his other hand. "We were supposed to go see a lake, weren't we? A hot lake?"

"And something else," she told him with a small pleased smile. "I'm going to show you about the only positive thing I can show you, about my family, my people."

He looked down at her, mystified, but she patted his arm and motioned for him to hurry on.

"That's Lark Springs Farm," she told him when the homestead came into view. In evening's lavender shadow, the homey farm buildings, the fields where a few cows and horses grazed, the lake with steam rising above it—looked like a painting against the darker outline of the mountains. "That's the homestead my grandparents established."

He whistled under his breath. "It's beautiful. Do your grandparents live there? I want to meet them."

"They are no longer living. One of the main reasons I came to Oregon was to try and find them. But they've been dead for years. The farm belongs to someone else, the daughter of an attorney who cared for my grandparents in their last years." She pointed out landmarks to him, the buttes behind the lake, the main traveled road that passed the farm, the small white hotel near the edge of the lake. A flock of wild ducks lifted from the marshy lands by the lake as they watched. Laila sighed in contentment. "My Grandpa Chapin made sure the lake was part of the claim he filed on. He and my grandmother must have loved this valley; I think they had a good life here, they lived to be quite old, I understand."

"I have heard of this lake, now that I think of it," Ash told her, "but I had no idea it was this incredible. It's beautiful country in every direction." His brow creased thoughtfully and his eyes took on a gleam. "Why don't you buy this place, Laila? I can see how much it means to you."

"Well, if it were mine, I would turn it into a medical resort. I'd charge reasonable fees so anyone with sickness could come here for the soothing baths. But—" she told him ruefully, "I am the proverbial poor church mouse. As you can likely guess, I don't have the money to buy it."

"You could buy it tomorrow, if you want, and if the lady is willing to sell. I'll help."

"If you're suggesting you'd help pay for it, I couldn't accept that. You must have debts of your own, rebuilding your hotel and all. I've heard you mention that you want to build another hotel in Seattle, one in Idaho . . ."

He shook his head in strong protest, "You can't let a fine opportunity like this go by, and a blind man can see how much you love the place, how much you want it. If you'll let me, I'll buy it for you for your wedding present and I can afford it, too. If you don't like that plan, then buy it yourself. Whatever you do, don't let it go. Buy it, darling."

He was so insistent—where he'd got the idea that she might have money like that she had no idea. She said a bit resentfully, half-afraid he was making a joke at her expense, "Have you lost your mind, or this some kind of horrible joke? I have very little savings. I make a dollar a day at the laundry and they probably won't take me back after today. I hardly have enough to pay for a room, and certainly not enough to buy Lark Springs Farm!" Her face was hot and she drew away from him.

"I don't mean to get you upset," he told her sincerely, catching her in his arms again. "I came here to get you and bring you back where you belong, to the canyon, and to get you to marry me. But I also came to give you some news about Pop's will."

"Excuse me? I don't understand?"

"Pop left you the whole of Ruby Gold Ranch, and quite a bit of his own money besides that."

For a moment she was stunned, and then she protested, "He couldn't have. You're his son. He would leave his property to you, not to me."

"Pop thought a lot more of you, Laila, than he was ever able to let on. He thought you were the finest thing ever to come along to our part of the country, and I agree." He took a moment to kiss her mouth and still her confused protests. "If you won't believe me, there is a high-priced lawyer in Baker City who will confirm that I am telling you the truth about the will. Pop also provided for Kate. He knew how much you loved the canyon, that you appreciated the place so much more than I did. He left it to the right person."

"But that's no reason to leave you out—"

"He didn't leave me out. He left me two very valuable hotel properties in Indiana that came to him when my mother died. She had earlier inherited them from her family. I'm not poor, and I don't need the peach ranch, God knows how hard it was for me to stay on there for as long as I did. I stayed for Pop's sake, but," he added grudgingly, "I did it because I wanted to, too. It mattered a lot to me to make him happy. After you came, that gave me all the more reason to be there."

Laila's feelings began to leap inside her like a wild happy bird. It was hard to breathe as the import of what he saying began to sink in. And then, fighting for calm, resisting, she whispered past an ache in her throat, "I think the canyon is the most beautiful place on earth, and this place, Lark Springs Farm, is right there second. But Ash, the peach ranch and your father's money are rightfully yours. You were very good to him, you sacrificed for him for a long time out of your love for him. All of his property should go to you, and that's final. We will see the lawyer and get the papers legally changed."

"No, my darling, you won't turn down Pop's gift," he was adamant. He cupped her face in his hands and although his mouth had tightened, he looked at her with nothing but blinding adoration. "Damn it, my darling, from the first you have refused anything you thought might be charity. This time you can keep your precious pride, *and* say yes, too. Ruby Gold Ranch is a rightful, legal gift from my father to you, whether you take me in the bargain or not, and you'd be very ungracious to refuse—either the inheritance, or me."

She began to cry and laugh all at the same time. "All right, all right. I accept what your father has willed to me, I accept you. I love you with all of my heart and soul, Ash. But—there's one more thing. I don't come to you alone, Tansy is my child now."

"And I can't wait to be her father! You know I love Tansy." His chest seemed to swell and he looked so proud, "It's settled then." He lifted the reins to go, then dropped them as he changed his mind. He pulled her close and kissed her, tenderly at first, then deeper and deeper. "Time to go home," he said huskily, nuzzling her throat, "before we disgrace ourselves in public."

"But Ash—?" she lifted his face away from her throat so she could meet his eyes in the shadowy twilight, "where is home?"

He chuckled, "Your choice, since we have several and are on the verge of having yet another." He said expansively, "Portland at the Grand, in the çanyon at Conner Creek, here on Lark Springs Farm fairly soon . . ."

"The canyon to start with! I want to tell Kate we're going to be married, tell my other friends, too. But Ash, I want to see your hotel in Portland, too. I want to visit the city, see all of it with you soon."

"Have our honeymoon there?"

"That would be perfect."

He chuckled as his chin rested on top of her head, "We can spend time in Portland, live part of the time in the canyon if that's what you want, part of the time here on your Grandpa's farm. I don't think either of us, or Tansy, want to live back East so let's disregard Indiana." He caught Laila's chin in his big hand, and looked into her eyes. "It's up to you where home is, my love."

He was offering her the world as well as his love, and in a voice thickened with emotion she told him, "Home is where you are, Ash. Home is where we are together, wherever on the planet it might be." The shadows lengthened around them, and they made love while their driving horse stamped his feet and then dozed. Darkness fell, and the stars came out. They were home.

About the Author

Irene Bennett Brown has lived most of her life in Oregon, but she enjoys using Kansas, where she was born, as the background for many of her books. The significant role women and children played in developing the west, against incredible hardship, has long been neglected and it is their story she particularly wants to tell. Her recent works include a Kansas-based series of historical novels from Five Star Publishing, *The Women Of Paragon Springs*, about a group of women who build their own town as a means to survive the raw frontier: *Long Road Turning* (2000) *Blue Horizons* (2001) *No Other Place* (June, 2002) and *Reap The South Wind* (December, 2002). Her 1994 novel, *The Plainswoman*, (Ballantine) was a Western Writers of America Spur Award finalist. Previous to writing for adults, she authored several award-winning young adult novels, including *Before The Lark*, winner of a Spur Award and a nomination for the Mark Twain Award. She is a recipient of the Oregon Library Association Evelyn Sibley Lampman Award for significant contribution to the field of literature. Brown is a member of Authors' Guild, Western Writers of America, and is a founding member of Women Writing The West. She lives in Jefferson, Oregon with her husband, Bob, a retired research chemist. Her favorite leisure pursuits are reading, and exploring historic places—beginning with antique stores!